Quarterbacks Don't Fall For Invisible Girls

Emma Dalton

Cover Design by Wynter Designs

Quarterbacks Don't Fall For Invisible Girls

Chapter One

Brayden Barrington has got to be the most gorgeous quarterback in the history of Edenbury High.

And I'm not just saying that because I have a major crush on him.

Sitting on the bleachers on this beautiful mid-September day, I can't blink away as he and his teammates sprint around the football field. It's like there's a spotlight on him, illuminating everything that is Brayden Barrington. Star quarterback with a killer smile. The sexiest guy in the whole school—no, the universe. Even under all that gear, I can see his muscles bulging out...and my mouth drops open as I imagine touching that hard chest. Sliding my hand up that huge bicep, giving it a gentle squeeze. Heat rushes to my cheeks as my thoughts drift to Brayden sweeping me into those strong arms and whispering sweet words in my ear...

A whistle tosses my thoughts away. Peering around, I spot Coach Papas shouting directions at the team. They swallow up his words, each wanting to improve so they can be on their A game Friday night. I haven't missed a single game since Brayden became the quarterback last year. My friends would call me obsessed—if I had friends, that is.

As the coach continues to bark at the team, I flip through the papers on my lap. There must be at least ten club signup sheets, and yet I can't seem to find one for me. Chess? Not skilled enough. Science? Not smart enough. Orchestra? Not talented enough.

Do you see a pattern here?

Dad told me I need to look interesting on college applications, which is why I'm hoping to join an after school activity. But the truth? I just want friends, or at least for people to acknowledge that I exist. I'm a junior and have been invisible at this school since the first day of freshman year.

Sighing, I continue flipping through the pages, then return my gaze to the beautiful quarterback at the center of the field. He's waving his hands around as he calls out to his teammates. And they drink up his words like Gatorade. One thing Coach Papas loves about Brayden is his sportsmanship. He loves the team like they're his brothers. He'd take a bullet for them.

Practice is over and the guys rush toward the school building to shower. I gather my papers and make my way down the bleachers. As I step off the field and head for the doors, a brick wall slams into me and I fall splat on my butt.

"Oof!" The wind is knocked out of me and the papers fly out of my hands.

"Sorry, you okay? I didn't see you there," a deep voice says from above me amid fluttering papers. Glancing up, I stare into gorgeous sky-blue eyes. Eyes that belong to Brayden Barrington.

Someone giggles loudly a few feet away. "And Invisible Girl strikes again." Head cheerleader Teagyn Myers barks out in laughter. She and the other pom-pom twirlers are practicing here, too, under Teagyn's mom's supervision, Coach Myers. As a former cheerleader herself, she knows a thing or two about the subject. Coach Myers was also my mom's best friend, but that doesn't seem to make a difference at all. Her daughter has pretty much treated me like crap since we were in diapers.

Oh, and that whole Invisible Girl thing? Story of my life.

"Did I hurt you? Can you stand?"

I glance up at Brayden holding out his hand to me. I have no idea how long he's been standing there, and like I've lost my brain, I just stare into those beautiful eyes.

"Do you need to go to the hospital?" he presses.

I shake my head quickly and shoot to my feet like a canon. "I'm okay." My cheeks heat up even more as it dawns on me that I fell on my butt. Right in front of *the* Brayden Barrington. Someone kill me now.

He bends to collect the papers, hands them to me, then advances toward the school building. And I stare after him, taking in each and every part of him, etching him into my memory. Because this is the most I'll ever see or interact with the star quarterback.

Invisible girls are meant to be invisible after all.

***

"Dad, you home?" I call as I chuck my backpack on the

hallway floor and pop into the kitchen. He's at the stove wearing one of his "Dad" aprons. Today it's "There's No Chef like Papa." Mom would give him one every year on his birthday, and he would sweep her up in his arms and lay a big one on her, telling her over and over how much he loves her. I would watch them with my cheeks burning due to the humongous smile etched into my face. I would imagine what it would be like to have that one day with someone special.

But there haven't been any new "Dad" aprons or passionate kisses in the last three years. Because my mom's dead.

Trying not to sigh or let the pain prick my insides, I throw on a smile and walk up to Dad, who is so caught up in the soup he's mixing that he doesn't hear me approach. I give him a peck on the cheek before wrapping my arms around him. "Hey, Dad."

"Pumpkin!" He drops the wooden spoon and returns the hug. "How was school?"

It takes everything I have not to groan out of sheer embarrassment. How was school? I basically lie to him every day so he won't suspect just how miserable I am—I can't bear him worrying about me—and after my epic flop in front of Brayden, I want to pretend today hadn't happened. No, I want to pretend my *life* hasn't happened.

"Kara?" he asks, eyes narrowing in concern. "Is everything okay?"

I paste on a smile. "Of course!" I say too cheerily. "School was great, as always. How was work?"

"Great. Got a new recruit for Astor University," he says as he turns back to mixing the pot. "He comes from a broken home. I've never met anyone so resilient."

Dad's a college football recruiter for Astor University. The school is about an hour away from our small town of Edenbury, Georgia. He loves his job because he meets so many kids from different backgrounds and makes their dreams come true. He's very dedicated, maybe because poring himself into his job helps him forget the pain of losing Mom. It's been three years, but when you have that kind of love? I don't think the pain could ever disappear.

I swallow hard as a lump the size of Jupiter attacks my throat. Mom was my…everything. My best friend. My confidant. The one person in the world who understood me. And now she's gone and I have to navigate life all by myself. I mean, I have Dad, but he's so clueless sometimes. And I'm so scared of hurting him. I just want him to be happy.

He announces that the soup's ready and we settle down at the table. Dad's not the greatest cook—that was Mom's department—but the food's pretty decent. I can't complain, I can't cook worth crap.

"Any luck finding more extracurriculars?" he asks.

The image of me splatting on my butt in front of Brayden flashes before my eyes. "Ugh!" I groan.

Dad's eyes widen. "What's wrong?"

"Nothing," I quickly say. "I just feel so awkward sometimes."

He nods slowly like he's a little confused. "Isn't that normal

5

at your age?"

"Not for people like Teagyn and all the other cheerleaders," I grumble.

"What was that?" he asks as he takes a spoonful of soup.

I paste on another smile, this one probably showing too much teeth. "It's okay, Dad. You don't have to try to understand the teenage girl brain. I'll survive." *I hope.*

A serious expression crawls on Dad's face as he lays his spoon in his bowl. "Honey, I hope you know you can talk to me whenever you need to. I know it was always your mother's department…" He shifts in his chair. "But I'm fully capable of…er…helping you navigate these confusing and nervous years?"

I burst into giggles. "Dad, you look like you'd rather jump into a lion's den."

"I'm trying to be serious here, Kara."

"I know. I'm sorry. I didn't mean to laugh at you. But you have nothing to worry about. I'm fine. And I've got…friends to help." Ugh, I hate lying to him.

He nods slowly, relief clouding his features. "Yes, I suppose that's true. You have your girlfriends to help. Because they're going through the same things as you."

Yeah, if only the sky would open and a group of girlfriends would rain down on me.

Sick of lying and this conversation, I steer the conversation to something my dad loves—football. All his worries about me fly out the window. As for my worries? Unfortunately, they're still stuck to me like glue.

Quarterbacks Don't Fall For Invisible Girls

I offer to do the dishes, but he shoos me away to my room to get started on homework. I plop down on my bed with a heavy sigh, my body sagging into the soft mattress. Putting up the façade that I'm happy and everything is perfect is so *exhausting*. Why can't I have at least one friend? Someone who actually sees me. Then maybe Dad would stop worrying that he's doing a bad job at this single parenting thing.

Reaching for my phone, I open up the Spill It! social media app. It's all the rage these days. It was created a few years ago by multi-gazillionaire Easton Knight. His son, Easton Jr., is a new student at our school this year. He's already fitting in so well with the popular kids—and look at me. I've been with these kids since ninth grade, some of them in elementary school, and they *still* don't know I exist. It's not because I'm ugly, right? No, if I was ugly I'd still be noticed. I guess I'm just plain and boring.

My fingers bring me to Brayden's page. He's posted and tagged pictures with the football team and cheerleaders. They're at Mikey's Diner and are having the grandest time. They're not stuck at home with no friends like this pathetic loser.

I zoom in the picture to his face. He's such a hottie. Strong features, a chiseled jaw, the whitest of teeth. Zooming out, I catch the person he's smiling at—Teagyn Myers. The gorgeous blonde who's all legs and enough body to command the attention of every guy in the room. The way she grins at Brayden, it's like she's got him in the bag. That might as well be true—girls like her always get their way.

But my mom was a cheerleader, too. Her team won

nationals when she was a junior. She wasn't a witch like Teagyn. She raised me to believe that you can achieve anything you want—as long as you're kind to everyone around you.

I zoom back in to our star quarterback, scrutinizing that perfect face. As if someone like Brayden would ever notice someone like me.

Chapter Two

The last period bell rings and I gather my books and leave the classroom along with the other students. They pile into the hallway like ants, each toppling over one another to reach their lockers and be done with this place for the day. I'm pushed and shoved from side to side as I make my way to my locker. An elbow gets me in the eye, another in the stomach. One guy manages to shove me into a locker as he jogs over to his friend.

I'm left with my lips practically fused to the cold, disgusting metal locker. Congrats to Kara Gander—she just had her first kiss.

Sighing, I yank myself off and go to my locker, grabbing my things and then heading down the hall to the newsroom. The others haven't arrived yet, not that it surprises me. With no social life, I'm always first. But that's okay, I guess. Punctuality is a great quality.

Slowly, slowly, everyone else settles down and we all brainstorm next month's issue. Being part of the school paper is a great extracurricular activity and would look awesome for college, but Dad insists I need more. My grades are good, but that alone isn't enough anymore. Hence the reason I'm stressing out over those clubs. I still haven't found any I can join.

"Kara? Where is she?" Our editor, Martina, surveys the room.

Seriously? I'm, like, ten feet away from her. How does she not see me?

"Kara?" she says again. "Does anyone know where she is?" My hand shoots in the air. "I'm *right here.*"

Her brown eyes squint at me. "Oh, I didn't see you." She smiles. "Any ideas? Your piece on school lunch was fascinating."

She's sweet, but fascinating would be the last thing I'd call my article. It's not that it sucked, but this topic has been done over and over again.

As if she can read my mind, Martina stands and paces the room. "We know we don't reach many students here and that's okay. Or at least it was." She stops by Jason, our graphics guy. "It's my senior year and I want to go out with a bang. I want this year's paper to explode. I want it in every student's hands. Who knows? Maybe we'll be so popular we'll publish weekly instead of monthly."

The others exchange glances with each other, none of us sure what to make of her words. The paper exploding? Going viral? At Edenbury High? I don't think so.

But I appreciate and love her enthusiasm. If we change someone's life, then it'll all be worth it. And it wouldn't kill us to finally gain some recognition for our hard work.

"We'll need good stories," Martina goes on. "Better stories. Stories that will spin the Edenbury High Times on its axis." She lightly knocks her knuckles on Jason's desk. "So hit me with ideas."

Alexi's eyes light up like a light bulb went off in his head. "How smoking damages teen lungs?" he suggests.

Martina twists her nose. Gabby and Izzy roll their eyes. "That's so tired," Izzy says. "You're right, Marti. We need something that'll hook readers."

Martina plops down at her desk, tapping her fingers on the table. "Something that'll make them hungry for more. Come on, guys! What do kids at this school care about?"

"Football," I mutter as I scroll through my phone.

She leaps to her feet. "Not just football—star quarterback Brayden Barrington. He's the most popular kid at school and everyone loves him. He's *amazing*. Kara, you're a genius!"

"I am?"

She bobs on her feet like a little kid who's about to open her birthday present. "Of course! Let's get an exclusive interview with Brayden, dig deep, get to know him as more than just the quarterback. People will eat up our newspaper like candy."

The others smile and nod. I guess she has a point. Even I'm curious about him, want to learn every single detail about him. Like what's his favorite food and drink? Does he have dreams other than football? What are his fears and insecurities?

"Great, so it's settled. And Kara, we'll need it done by the end of the week so it can be ready for next month's issue."

My lungs freeze up, and it feels as if I've swallowed cotton.

"What? Me?"

"It was your idea. We know you won't disappoint. Okay, guys, what else?"

As they brainstorm, I just sit there, not believing what just happened. She expects me to walk over to the hottest guy at school and request an interview? Me, Invisible Girl? The person who went splat on her butt right in front of him?

She's got to be out of her mind.

It's on the tip of my tongue to beg her to give the job to someone else, but I press my lips shut. I've been with the paper since freshman year, but if I start causing problems, she might give me the boot. And I really need this job. Not just for college applications but because I enjoy being on the paper. I like being part of something, even if we barely get readers. And even though the rest of the team feels more like colleagues than friends. Still, it gives me a sense of purpose. Responsibility. I'm not sure I want a career as a reporter, but at least it's something.

Once our editor is satisfied, she dismisses us for the day.

"Kara." She stops me at the door. I turn around. "I'm really looking forward to that article."

I only manage to nod because I can't move my lips. It's like they're frozen shut with fear and anxiety. I'm not normally an anxious person, only when sexy quarterbacks with hair like satin are around.

She smiles brightly. "See you later."

I nod again and leave the room. My legs take me to the nearby bathroom and I bend over a sink, my breathing heavy.

"Okay, okay, Kara," I tell myself. "Breathe. You can do this." Lifting my head, I gaze at my reflection. "You're a strong, confident young woman." I snort. Me? Strong and confident? If I was so confident, I wouldn't blend into the walls like paint.

No. I'll march right up to Brayden and request the interview like a pro.

Ugh, no. I'm plummeting into a sinkhole and there's no one there to pull me out.

Letting out a heavy breath, I collect myself and exit the bathroom. The halls are pretty deserted, except for a few wayward students who are finishing up with clubs or practice.

"I just have to get my book from my locker," a voice says from down the hallway. A familiar voice. A voice I've been dreaming about since middle school. It sends a tingle down my spine every time I hear it.

Brayden and his football buddies march to his locker like royals. In this school, they pretty much are. I'm not complaining or anything, but these boys can get away with anything. And I mean, *anything.*

"Man, you totally killed it out there!" one of the guys says to Brayden. The rest of the team toss compliments his way, but he waves them off with that girl-melting smile of his.

I hide behind the corner, but keep my eyes on him. He's at the center of the group, telling them he's nothing without the rest of the team.

Not only is this Adonis sexy, he's modest, too. And

friendly, approachable—at least to people who aren't invisible. He's just...perfection.

The guys chat and laugh some more before Brayden fetches his book and they walk out the door. I pop out from my hiding spot and stare at his retreating form before the doors shut after them.

I feel sick to my stomach, like the food from this afternoon will find its way back into the world. How the heck am I going to do this? Just the thought of being within twenty feet of him...I might literally throw up now.

I slam my head into a locker. "Ugh."

Chapter Three
Brayden

"How was practice?" Dad asks the moment I step foot into the house. He and Mom are in the kitchen working on dinner. She stands before the stove and he's behind her, arms wrapped around her waist. It's an odd sight for sure, since the two of them haven't been getting along since my older brother Brock died two years ago. I guess that marriage counselor's finally paying off, though I know things could change in an instant with those two. Sometimes they're best friends, other times they hardly speak to each other. But I'll count my blessings now and hope this streak continues.

"Was fine," I tell them. "Coach is determined to beat Barefield High this Friday and we've been working really hard."

"That's great, honey," Mom says with a grin. "We're very proud of you."

Dad turns to face me. "Will there be recruiters at the game?"

I shake my head. "Not this time. I guess I'm not...good

enough."

Mom covers the pot she was mixing and walks over to me, placing her hands on either side of my face. Staring into my eyes, she says, "Don't say that about yourself, Brayden Anthony Barrington. You *are* good enough, and recruiters would be insane not to grab you."

I nod, pulling my face from her grip. "I know, Mom. Thanks. I guess I'm just nervous for the game."

Dad waves his hand. "You'll do great, son. We're all rooting for you." His smile is there, but there's no mistaking the pain in his eyes. I know what they're telling me—that Brock would be rooting for me, too.

I slide onto a stool at the counter and reach for a cookie from the jar. Everyone knows the only reason I got the QB position was because of my brother.

But I don't want to feel sorry for myself, especially now when it seems my parents are in a good mood. I know I'm a good quarterback, but there's always room for improvement.

"Mommy, I'm hungry. When's dinner?" My five-year-old sister Bailey creeps into the room, glancing around. "And Sally is, too. Is she here?"

Sally is Bailey's imaginary friend. Last week it was Benjamin from Canada. Now it's Sally from New York. I have a feeling this one will stick around longer, since the two of them have a lot in common. Like sports and tea parties. Benjamin never liked getting his hands dirty.

Mom smiles at her. "Dinner will be ready soon and I haven't seen Sally."

Bailey's eyes widen. "Maybe she ran away again?"

I reach for her and drag her onto my lap, messing up her sandy brown hair. It's the same color as my hair. And Brock's, too. We all have the same features, inherited from Mom. "Hey, kid. I'm sure Sally will come back soon. Did you have fun at school?"

"Yeah." She spends twenty minutes relaying every detail of her day. Who spilled juice on whom and who had an accident in the bathroom. I can listen to her for hours and never get bored. She's so adorable—and I'm not just saying that because she's my little sister.

"Did the tickle monster visit you at school?" I ask her.

Her blue eyes widen again. "No...!" She ducks away, trying to free herself from my grip. She knows very well what's coming for her.

Laughing, I gently dig my fingers into her stomach. "He's here now!"

She giggles and wiggles and screeches as I continue tickling her. "Not fair," she manages to say through her laughter. "You're bigger and stronger than me."

I drop my hands. "Okay, then tickle me."

She rolls her eyes. "You're not ticklish."

I grin. "Maybe I am today. But you need to catch me first!" After gently dropping her to her feet, I take off toward the living room. Bailey chases me up the stairs, past the hallway, and down the stairs in the back.

"Careful!" mom calls after us. She's gotten a little overprotective ever since Brock died in that car accident. Dad

17

worries a lot, too, but not as much as Mom.

"Bray!" Bailey shouts after me, huffing and puffing. She chases me back into the living room now. "I'll never catch up to you."

Chuckling, I stop in place and she smacks right into me and falls to the floor. I whirl around and bend down to her. "Are you okay?"

She giggles as she leaps onto me, throwing me to the floor. Well, it's more like I let her throw me down. She buries her fingers in my stomach. Because she's so small, I barely feel anything, but I wiggle around like she did a few minutes ago.

"Okay, okay you win," I tell her.

"Yay!" She beams. "And what's my prize?"

I bend my head forward. "Whatever you want, my queen."

"Princess!"

"Forgive me, my princess."

She laughs again as she taps her chin, as if solving an algebra equation. "Piggyback ride."

"Piggyback ride it is."

And she hops onto my back.

Chapter Four

The popular table is so stuffed with chairs and kids on those chairs, I don't know how they have enough air to breathe. And right in the center of all that is my assignment.

The bell will ring in another few minutes. I have to do this, even if the thought of actually talking to Brayden sends a swarm of butterflies into my stomach.

After sucking in a deep breath and letting it seep out of my nose, I get up and march over to his table. No heads turn in my direction as I edge closer to the holy popular table. I might as well dance around the entire cafeteria stark naked—no one would even notice.

Coming to a stop right across from him, my breath hitches. My chest feels like it's clogged with cement. He's there—*right there*. But he doesn't even notice me.

I try not to sigh.

He laughs at something a wide receiver says. Oomf, that laugh can cure cancer. Seriously. I can stand here all day and just listen to him laugh.

OMG, I really need to pull myself together.

I can do this. Can totally do this. Yep, no biggie. Just grab the attention of the most popular guy at school, who also happens to be the sexiest guy at school. I can so picture him being picked for the sexiest man on the planet when he's older. When he's on a pro team and the whole world knows his name. Everyone will love him. All the women will love him…

My fantasy just turned sour. Because I know I'll be just as invisible as an adult as I am now. They tell us things will be different once we're out of high school but is that *really* true? Doubt it.

I shake my head. I have to stop stalling. The bell will ring soon. Before I lose my nerve, I step closer to the table and say, "Brayden?" But what leaves my mouth could barely count as a squeak. Brayden continues chatting and laughing with his friends.

I clear my throat and try again. "Brayden?"

This time, I nearly shout it. And this time, every single person at the table whips their head in my direction.

Talk about feeling naked in front of everyone. Scratch my comment about dancing in the nude.

"Uh, yeah?" he asks. His sandy brown hair falls into his eyes *perfectly*. I wonder what it would feel like to tangle my hands in those beautiful strands. Would his hair feel soft?

Blinking, I realize everyone at the table still stares at me. My cheeks flaming, I stammer, "C-can I talk to you, Brayden?"

"Sure. Be back in a sec, guys."

He slips out of his chair and follows me to the side. I catch someone mumble, "Who is that?" and try not to roll my eyes. And I also try not to hyperventilate. Because this is the closest I've ever been to Brayden. He's so much taller than me, I might as well be gazing up a mountain.

"You wanted to talk to me?" he asks. Once again, his hair falls into his eyes *perfectly*. His chest is so buff it's nearly straining against his fitted white T-shirt.

"Yes," I say. Then the words tumble out. "Can I interview you for the school paper? Our editor wants to do a piece on our amazing QB. We want to showcase you as more than just an amazing quarterback, you know? We want the school to know the guy behind the uniform. So will you agree to do it?"

His lips gently lift, mesmerizing blue eyes dancing. "Amazing QB?"

Oh, gosh. Even when he's half-smiling I feel like I'm going to die.

"It's not like I think you're amazing or anything," I babble. "I'm just quoting Martina. Our editor."

OMG, what the heck is coming out of my mouth?

"So Martina the editor thinks I'm an amazing quarterback," he says.

"Well yes. Duh. Of course she does. Why wouldn't she? It's not like she's alone. Well, not me. Like I said."

I need to shut up ASAP. Seriously, Kara, just shut the heck up.

I clear my throat. "So will you do it? The interview? I promised her I'd have it done by the end of the week."

He shrugs. "That's fine."

"Cool. I also have to shadow you a bit. Watch you do your thing. But you'll barely notice I'm there."

Because I'm the Invisible Girl.

"Hey, are you okay by the way?" he suddenly asks.

"What?"

"I knocked into you pretty hard on Monday. Looks like you had quite the fall."

Can the floor open up and swallow me?

Please?

Like now?

Right now?

Before I drop dead from embarrassment?

He steps a little closer, and I stumble back, my heart zooming through my body. "Are you okay, Kara?" he asks softly.

I get lost in those spellbinding blue eyes. I've never seen a more beautiful shade. Like the sky on a gorgeous day.

Brayden Barrington actually knows my name.

"You're not saying anything," he continues.

"What? Oh. Yeah, I'm fine. Thanks for asking."

"You sure? Some of the guys complain I hurt them on the field."

"Yeah, because you're like a freakin' brick wall."

His eyes widen. "Is that what it felt like? I'm so sorry. I should really pay attention to where I'm going."

"No! That's totally fine! You can knock into me whenever you want."

His eyes grow a little small as a small chuckle escapes his

lips. "I'd rather not, but thanks." He nods. "Let me know when you want to get together for that interview." He returns to his table.

I turn to the wall and gently knock my head into it. Once, twice, three times. Maybe there's a reason why I'm so invisible—because I'm a freak of nature. Who says that to a person? And to the most popular guy at school. Ugh! Why can't I have a do-over?

When I glance back at his table, I find him once again talking and laughing with his friends. He doesn't look back at me once.

With another sigh, I return to my table to finish my lunch.

***

I sit on the bleachers with my notepad and pen ready. I've watched Brayden at practice and at games many times, but I never had to describe the experience on paper. Hopefully I'll be able to write a decent article on his skills and talent, and not gush how dreamy and sexy he is.

And kind. I can't forget kind. He actually asked me if I was okay. I thought he didn't remember even bumping into me. And he knows my name!

Enough. Seriously. None of it means anything.

But Brayden Barrington is kind as well as hot. It's so hard to find that. Can my crush on him get any bigger? I think my heart will explode.

But where is he? The rest of the team is already on the field. Once they start practice, it dawns on me that he's not coming.

I'll admit watching the rest of the team without Brayden

23

isn't as exciting. And since I'm writing an article on the quarterback and not the team, I don't have a reason to stick around. Time to head back home alone and do homework alone and spend the rest of my night alone.

I'm about to start my trek to my house when I remember I left my math textbook in my locker. And I have a murderous test on Friday. So not looking forward to that. I do okay with math, but it frustrates me so bad I want to tear my hair out half the time. This is another reason I wish I had at least one friend. So we could suffer together.

Once I grab my book, I stop by the bulletin board to see if there are any posters for clubs I missed. If I can't find anything good, I'll just choose science or orchestra. I'm not a brainiac, but I'm sure the science geeks won't kick me out for my lack of intelligence. And it's never too late to learn an instrument, right?

No new posters. Guess I'll sign up to both and try my luck. Just as I turn around, I catch something from the corner of my eye. The words "Book Club." Quickly spinning around, I scan the small poster squished to the side, practically buried beneath all the other posters and announcements.

"Love to read? Love to gush about books? Then join the Edenbury High Book Club! We're a small group, but a fun one. We eat, drink, breathe books. And the best part? There are no skills involved! So what are you waiting for? Join today. We meet in room 1B every Monday and Wednesday. Remember to bring your favorite book and a smile!"

Holy heck, Edenbury High has a book club??? Since when? Without a second thought, I hurry over to room 1B and throw the door open.

Three heads snap up and stare at me.

"Oh, sorry," I stammer. "I thought this was the book club?"

"It is." A girl with red hair lifts a book. *Mansfield Park*, by Jane Austen.

They all stare at me like they have no idea why I'm here.

"Are you accepting new people? I saw your poster on the bulletin board."

A pretty girl with dark hair and bright hazel eyes says, "Wait, you want to join?"

"Uh…yeah. Is that a problem or something?"

"Of course not!" she says with a laugh. "We just never expected anyone would actually join."

"Why not?" I ask.

"Because it's been just the three of us since last year," the redhead explains. "We were starting to wonder if anyone at this school can even read."

The three of them laugh, though the last girl, the one with curly dirty-blonde hair and brown eyes, laughs silently. When her eyes catch mine, she quickly looks away and focuses back on her book, the tips of her ears growing pink.

"Ladies of the Edenbury High Book Club, it looks like we have a new member!" Dark Hair says. "Come in, come in." She motions for me to enter. "My name is Danielle Wood. Dani for short. I'm the president."

"And I'm Charlie Raine," the redhead says. "Well, my real name is Charlotte, but that's so not me." She gives me a sweet smile. "Welcome to the club." She holds out her hand.

I shake it. "Thanks. I'm Kara Gander."

"And this is Ally Bensen." Dani nods to the dirty-blonde who looks like she wants to hide away in her book.

"Hi," I say.

She nods and focuses back on her book.

"Ally's a little shy," Charlie explains.

"Welcome," she says in a barely audible voice, a shy smile tugging her lips.

"Thanks so much," I say as I sit down near Charlie. "I can't believe this. You're telling me there's been a book club here since last year and I didn't even know about it? I *love* to read."

"Yeah." Charlie chuckles. "We all do. Where have you been?"

I look from one girl to the other and shrug. "Invisible. Where have you guys been?"

They all exchange a glance. "Invisible," they say.

"I thought I was the only invisible girl here!" I say, getting way too excited. Then my neck heats up. "I mean, it sucks you guys are invisible, too, but now I don't feel so alone anymore."

Charlie shrugs. "We don't mind it."

"*You* don't mind it," Dani corrects. She focuses her attention on me. "But you don't have to be invisible with us anymore. We see you, Kara."

I smile. "And I see you."

And just like that, I've found my place. And my people.

Chapter Five

I wring my fingers in my lap as my gaze flicks to the clock on the wall. It's five to six. Brayden should be here any minute. I wonder if he cares enough about the interview to be on time. I mean, I know for a fact he doesn't read the Edenbury High Times, so it's probably the last thing on his mind.

I've been home alone since school ended, not that it's a surprise. Sometimes Dad doesn't come home until later. Normally, it upsets me, but considering that the hottest guy at school will be gracing this house with his presence, I'm glad Dad's not here.

I fidget in my spot on the couch, staring at the clock some more. A minute to six. Then six o'clock. He's still not here. Maybe he forgot? We confirmed the time before he left for practice. I would have stayed to watch like I usually do, but I rushed home to tidy the place up. And I won't lie and say I didn't bake cookies. Currently, they're sitting on the kitchen table, waiting to be scarfed down. I'm not the greatest baker by any means, but this is Mom's recipe, pretty much the only thing

I made with her.

Would Brayden like them?

Nah. I'm sure many girls have baked treats and pastries for him.

I can't take this stress of waiting anymore and am about to turn on Netflix, when the bell reverberates throughout the house, nearly knocking me to the ceiling.

He's here. He's *here*. Brayden Barrington, at my house.

The bell rings again, shoving my thoughts away. Taking a deep breath and wiping my sweaty palms on my jeans, I slowly get to my feet and amble to the door. It feels like I'm walking through an endless tunnel until I finally reach the door.

"Yes?" I call.

"It's Brayden Barrington? I'm here to see Kara Gander?"

A breath I didn't know I was holding releases from my lungs. It's not a dream. He actually came.

Sure, he probably cares more about his image and reputation than he does about the paper, but as long as he's here, that's all that matters.

"Hello?" he calls.

Right. Focus, Kara.

Clearing my throat and counting to five to try to regulate my breathing and my nerves, I open the door a crack and peek out.

Brayden stands there casually, hands in his pockets, beautiful sandy brown hair swept over his eyes in a messy way that's oh so sexy. He just has this cool and calm aura around him. Like, he's chill and laid back and not afraid of anything.

He smiles at me. "Kara, hi. I wasn't sure I was at the right place."

I laugh lightly. "Yeah, sorry about that. I was uh…cleaning up. I baked cookies for…" My eyes widen. "I mean, cookies for my dad and me. He really likes cookies."

He grins again. "Who doesn't? Cookies are my favorite snack in the world. No one beats my mom's, though. I could eat hers every day of my life and die a happy man."

I widen the door and he steps inside. "I feel the same way about my mom's cookies."

He narrows his eyes, as if studying me. "Chocolate chip?"

I shut the door behind him. "Chocolate chip."

"Cool. I can't wait to meet her." He scans around. "Are your parents home?"

"No, it's just me." I gesture toward the couch. "Have a seat and we'll begin. Do you want a drink?"

He smiles again, his entire face lighting up. Seriously, that smile is doing crazy things to my body right now. Would it be nuts to turn up the air conditioner? Because I'm sure this room will melt any second now that he's here.

"Sure, a drink would be great. And maybe some of those cookies?"

It's like he can read my mind, and that sends a jolt through my stomach. "What would you like? Water? Coke?"

"Coke is fine, thanks."

"Okay, just make yourself comfortable and I'll be back in a second."

He drops down on the couch and glances around the living

room. I watch him, still unable to believe that this guy is in my house. *My* house. Invisible Girl.

His head turns and our eyes meet. "You okay, Kara?"

The way he says my name? It sends a new swarm of butterflies into my stomach, this one more intense than the last. "Yeah, I'm fine. I'll be back with the drinks."

"And cookies," he reminds me with a chuckle.

I nod and slip into the kitchen, taking a few seconds to collect myself. Then I peek back into the living room and find him texting. A girl probably. A guy like him definitely has the female population at school lined up.

After grabbing two cans of Coke from the fridge and the plate of cookies from the table, I enter the living room. He's put his phone down and is inspecting the room again.

"Thanks," he says as I hand him his Coke and place the cookies before him. "These look great." He doesn't hesitate to chomp a huge chunk off. "Wow, crunchy and chocolatey. Yum."

I laugh, my cheeks heating up so strongly it's like I fell into a furnace. "I'm glad you like them."

He reaches for another. "I do. They're amazing. You have to thank your mom for me."

I tuck some hair behind my ear and shift on the couch. I don't want to tell him Mom died, and I don't know why. Am I worried he'll feel sorry for me?

"Is that your dad?" He pulls me out of my thoughts. Glancing up, I catch him staring at one of the pictures on the wall, of me, Dad, and Mom with our arms wrapped around each other and smiling at the camera. That was taken three years ago when we went to Miami. And two months after that, she died of cancer.

"Yeah."

"Nigel Gander? Recruiter for Astor University?" he continues.

"Yeah, that's the one."

He smiles. "That's really cool. Are you guys close?"

Honestly, I'm a little uncomfortable with his questions. No one has ever asked that before because no one has ever noticed me. The fact that this sexy, popular guy wants to know about my family, it sends me for a whirlwind and I have no clue how to handle it.

He shakes his head. "Sorry, that's personal. You're here to interview me, not the other way around. I'm ready to begin." He holds up his hand. "After one more cookie, if that's okay?"

I motion with my hand. "Go ahead."

"Thanks." He takes a bite. "I'm ready when you are."

I grab my tablet where I've put together some questions and Martina added hers as well. "Okay, as you know we're writing an article about you for the Edenbury High Times. We want to get to know the school's pride and joy—our quarterback Brayden Barrington. I'll ask you questions and you can choose whether or not you want to answer them. If you want to skip a question, just say pass. And if you're uncomfortable with anything I say, please tell me. If you'd like something to remain off the record, I'll respect your wishes."

He nods slowly. "I'm a little nervous, to be honest."

I lift a brow. "No one has ever interviewed you before?"

He shakes his head. "But I'm also excited. Does the newspaper reach anyone outside of school?"

"Um…not really. We're very small and hardly anyone reads us."

"Oh, that sucks. You guys probably work so hard and you don't get recognized for it."

I just stare at him with my jaw practically sweeping the floor. That's what I've been complaining about since I joined the paper two years ago. We *do* work hard. We put our minds, bodies, and souls into the paper, but it just ends up on the floor, stepped on, kicked around, a place for kids to stick their gum on.

"Well, I mean, yeah. But you work hard, too. I know it's not easy being the quarterback." I clear my throat. "Anyway, let's start." I press the record button on my phone. "Hi, Brayden, thanks for joining me. Why don't you tell us how you got interested in football?"

He leans back on the couch. "Sure. My dad loved football ever since he was a little kid. His dream was to play ball in high school, college, and then join a pro team. But he couldn't follow his dreams. His dad got into an accident when he was twelve and was paralyzed from the neck down. His mom took care of his dad while maintaining a full-time job. Money was tight, so my dad gave up football to get a job and help support his parents and younger siblings. Once he graduated high school, he got a full-time job while studying for college in the evenings. He was never able to fulfill his dream to play pro football." He pauses for a second, a smile tugging his lips. "When my older brother Brock and I were little, Dad shared his love of football with us. My brother eventually joined his middle school football team and I followed suit. Our family is obsessed with football and Brock wanted to fulfill my dad's dream for him." His smile drops and his eyes flash with pain. "But he never could. He died two years ago."

I nod, my throat tight. I know exactly how he feels, since I lost my mom, too. "I…" I clear my scratchy throat. "I'm really sorry about your brother. He sounds like he was the perfect brother."

"He was," he says, so low I can barely hear him. "I'm trying to match up to him, but I don't know." He glances down at the phone between us. "Wow, I completely forgot we're on record."

"Do you want me to edit any of that out?"

He shakes his head. "Please don't. I'd like my brother to be remembered for the amazing person he was."

"He definitely will be."

He looks at me, so deeply and intensely it's almost as if he's looking inside me, reading all my raw emotions. I shift in my seat and his gaze breaks. "Thanks," he says.

I peer at the tablet for my next set of questions. "How does it feel to be quarterback?"

"Humbling. It's an amazing opportunity and I'm grateful for every second of it. But I can't take all the credit for our team's performance. I wouldn't be where I am without them."

"You're being modest."

He shakes his head. "No, I'm serious. We're a team and every member is just as important as the quarterback. We lift each other up. Strengthen one another. It's a brotherhood that runs deeper than blood."

"That's really great." I look at my notes. "What are your interests outside of football?"

He lifts a brow. "You mean when I'm not working out?" He chuckles. "Just kidding."

My eyes zero in on that broad, strong chest, the muscles flexing every time he breathes. The room has gotten even hotter than it was fifteen minutes ago.

"I like to hang out with friends," he tells me. "Spend time with my family. We watch football together. I play tea party with my little sister, Bailey."

"Tea party?" The image of this huge boy bent over a tiny tea table with his little sister flickers in my mind. And a warm feeling rushes through me. I never imagined he'd be into that, but I don't know anything about him.

He holds up his finger. "But Bailey is adamant that people know she likes to get down and dirty, too. She'd make a killer quarterback one day."

I smile. "You sound like a wonderful big brother."

"Thanks. I want to be a good role model for her."

I blink at him, not believing a word he just said. I assumed he was a stuck-up jock, like all the others. I *did* have a feeling there was more to him, but I thought I was just convincing myself, painting a picture of a guy who didn't exist. Now I learn he does exist and man, my massive crush on him has increased tenfold. "That's so…that's so sweet." I glance at the tablet. "Uh…who inspires you?"

"My older brother Brock. Not a day passes where I don't think about him."

I give him a sympathetic and understanding smile. It's on the tip of my tongue to tell him he's not alone, but I press my lips shut. This isn't about me. He's in the spotlight right now.

"And he's your hero as well?" I ask.

"Definitely."

I look up at him. "If this gets too much to bear, just tell me and I'll shift to another topic."

"I'm all right. Talking about my brother helps, you know?"

I nod, though I don't really know what he's referring to. Other than to Dad, I've never talked to anyone about my mom. I never had friends.

I think back to the girls I met yesterday at the book club and how excited I am to be part of something. But then I remember I'm in the middle of an interview and I need to focus and be professional.

Brayden spends some time talking more about Brock. I'm not sure I can fit all of this in my article, but I can listen to him talk for hours. It's like I'm lost in those beautiful eyes.

"Off the record?" he says.

Nodding, I stop recording and give him my full attention. "Everyone expects me to be this confident person, right? Big man on campus and all that. But sometimes, I'm just as scared and worried as any other kid my age. I worry about disappointing my parents, my coach, my teammates, my little sister. And Brock. I worry I'm not living up to him." He shakes his head, his fingers plowing through his hair. "Sorry about all that. Do you have more questions?"

"A few. Ready to go back on record?"

"Shoot."

I press record and look at the next question. "If you wouldn't be doing football, what would you do?"

He rubs his chin. "Honestly? I have no idea. I grew up with football. I eat, sleep, breathe football. It's not just something I do. It *is* me. Ingrained in me. I'm pretty sure if I would be reincarnated a hundred times, each time I'd play football."

I grin shyly. "And you'd be amazing at it every time. Um…next question…when you're a hundred years old and are on your deathbed, what would you have liked to have accomplished in your life?"

His eyes seem far away as he ponders this. The only sound in the room is from the ticking clock. Sometimes it bothers me, seems so loud for some reason, but now with Brayden next to me, it's soothing.

"I would like to think I had a good, happy, satisfying life. I would like to have been a good football player, inspired many little kids to go after what they want. If I were to get married and have kids, I would have wanted to be a good husband and great dad. I would have liked to die a happy man knowing I did good in the world, that I changed people's lives."

The more he talks, the more I find myself falling deeper and deeper. He's so…different from what I imagined. So deep, his emotions so raw. He's not afraid to speak his mind and say how he feels.

I wish I could kiss him right now…

Blinking that thought away, I say, "Amazing, thank you. One last question." I glance at the one Martina added last minute. "The girls of Edenbury High are dying to know if the star quarterback is single." As soon as the words are out, I cringe. Why would she put that question there? And force me to ask it? Why????

He smiles so warmly and sexy that I'm literally seconds away from turning into a puddle on the floor. "Yes, I am currently single."

I read the follow-up question out loud, only because I know Martina will have my head if I don't. "And how would you describe your perfect woman?"

He glances at the coffee table, eyebrows furrowed. "Someone kind and sweet. Someone I can be myself around, have fun with, chill with. Someone who's brave enough to be herself and not follow a crowd." His head lifts and he stares into my eyes. "Someone who will be special to me, someone I can pour my heart out to."

"And…you haven't found her yet?" I breathe, unable to control my thumping heart.

"No," he whispers, eyes still boring into mine. "But she's out there." His voice is so soft it sends tingles all over me. And his words? So darn romantic that I can't take it anymore. That puddle I'm turning into? Yeah, it just transformed into a lake.

My eyes drop to his lips. They're so close…look so warm and inviting…

I leap to my feet. "Thanks so much for doing this interview with me." I hold out my hand.

He glances down at it, then at me. Slowly, he brings his hand closer to mine. But before he has a chance to shake it, I withdraw mine and tuck some hair behind my ears.

He drops his hand. "Thank you for having me."

I nod a few times because I don't know what else to do with myself. Then I escort him to the door, where he gives me a large smile.

"I'll see you tomorrow, Kara. Thanks again. You're a very good interviewer. I was nervous, but you calmed me down and made me feel so comfortable."

My throat is too clogged to talk, so I just nod and croak. He narrows his eyes at me like he's not sure why I'm being so weird, but he smiles politely and saunters off, hands in his pockets.

I stare after him until he climbs into his car and speeds off. Shutting the door, I lean against it and shut my eyes. My chest heaves as I try to catch my breath.

What's wrong with me?

The knob twists and I yelp as the door opens, nearly sending me crashing into the wall across.

"Kara?" Dad places his hand on my shoulder. "Why are you so jumpy? Did something happen?"

"What? No, of course not. I'm totally fine." I force a smile. "How was work?"

"Good. You hungry? How about we order takeout tonight? I'm too tired to cook."

"Sure."

We settle on Mexican and dig in fifteen minutes later when the food arrives. Dad talks about something football related, but my mind wanders. I replay the interview with Brayden over and over in my head. And each time, my heart skips a beat.

Chapter Six

As soon as I walk into the cafeteria on Friday, my eyes zero in on the jock table. At Brayden. Just like every day. But it's different now. Because he and I shared an afternoon together.

I know, I know. It was all business. I bet he won't even remember the encounter next week—maybe not even tomorrow. But I sure as heck will. I'll remember it for the rest of my life. Because that's the most time I'll ever spend with a guy like him.

The lunch lady smiles as she hands me lunch, asking me how my day is going so far. She's so sweet for asking. I tell her it's going well, then pay for my lunch and walk away with my tray.

"Hey, Kara!" someone calls.

I scan around, but don't see anyone. Maybe I was imagining it? I bet there's another girl here with the name Kara. A popular girl. Shrugging, I head to my usual table at the side of the room.

"Kara Gander!"

Okay, I was definitely not imagining that.

Quarterbacks Don't Fall For Invisible Girls

I survey the room another time, and then I see them—barely. Three girls crowded around a small table at the back of the room. I can hardly see it because all the other tables and chairs, and the people sitting on them, block. Charlie's waving frantically at me.

My cheeks lift in a ginormous smile. I almost forgot I have friends. I'm so used to sulking into the cafeteria alone. But I don't have to do that anymore.

I hurry over with my tray and that ginormous smile still on my face. "Hey, guys!" I say as I slide into the seat next to Charlie. "We've seriously got to do something about this invisibility thing."

"It's the curse," Dani says.

"Curse?" I ask as I cut into my grilled chicken.

Charlie rolls her eyes. "Dani thinks we've been hit with an invisibility curse on the day we were born."

"How else would you explain why the kids here don't see us? Even my teachers forget about me sometimes. It's so annoying."

"Who cares what they think?" Charlie mutters. She focuses on typing on the laptop in front of her.

"I don't know about a curse," I say as I bite into my chicken, "and I don't know about you guys, but the reason I'm so invisible here is because I'm boring."

"Plain and boring," Dani says with a sigh as she tosses some of her dark hair over her shoulder. "You can be my twin."

"I don't think you're boring," a low voice says. "Either of

41

you."

I glance at Ally, who's playing around with the peas on her plate.

"Thanks," I say.

She gives me a shy smile.

"And you guys will never be boring in my book," I continue. "You are officially my favorite people in the world."

"Yay." Dani claps enthusiastically. "I love making new friends!"

I laugh.

Her cheeks turn bright red. "Sorry. Ugh, I sounded like I'm five years old again. Awkward things are always coming out of me. You'll have to excuse my stupid mouth."

"From one awkward girl to another, I get you."

She shakes her head. "No, you don't get it. No one comes close to my awkwardness."

"I'm the reigning champion," I tell her.

"If you'd look up awkward in the dictionary, you'd find Danielle Wood there."

I laugh again. "Are we seriously fighting over who's more awkward?"

She thinks about it for a second and then laughs. "We are so weird."

"Embrace the weird," Charlie says as she continues to type.

I'm about to ask her what she's so busy with, when there's a commotion by the jock table. Two football players are balancing spoons on their noses. It seems there's a competition whose will last longer.

My gaze immediately sprints to Brayden. He's not watching them, he's busy scrolling through his phone, brows deep in concentration. I wonder what he's so serious about.

"You think there's anything in their heads other than air?" Charlie says.

My head snaps in her direction. "You think all jocks are dumb?"

She nods in their direction. "They did the same thing in middle school."

"Some are smart, though," I say. "Like Brayden."

She shrugs.

"I had an interview with him yesterday," I inform her and my new friends. "He's deeper than you'd think."

Dani raises a brow. "You had an interview with Brayden? For what?"

"The school paper."

"You're on the paper?" Ally asks.

I roll my eyes. "Not again."

Dani's light up. "Of course! You're Kara Gander. I always love reading your articles."

Warmth enters my bloodstream. "You read my articles?"

"Yep. They're so much deeper than some of the other articles. You can definitely write."

It feels like my heart might burst out of my chest. "Thanks. That means a lot."

"Why did you interview him, though?" Dani asks.

"Martina, our editor, wanted to get more kids interested in the paper, so she assigned me with digging under Brayden's uniform to find the guy underneath."

"And what did you find?" Ally asks.

My heart hammers in my chest as his handsome face and jaw-dropping blue eyes flash before my eyes. Trying to keep my voice steady, I say, "He's sweet. Smart. Determined. And he's such a good older brother. You'll see in the next issue. It should come out in a couple of weeks." A happy sigh escapes my lips as I replay the interview in my mind. Then I turn my head in his direction and find him chatting with his teammates. "He's a total babe." My eyes snap wide open. "I mean..."

"Oh my gosh, you like him!" Dani practically yells.

I motion with my hands. "Keep your voice down!"

Her hazel eyes light up like fire. "Of course you like him. He's such a hottie."

"I don't like him," I say. "I have a major, *massive* crush on him." I groan and bury my face in my arms. "You don't know how hard it was to interview him," my muffled voice says. "I kept staring at him like some psycho, imagining what it would be like to kiss him..."

Dani whistles. "You've got it bad."

"I know." I lift my head and look from one girl to the other. "I'm so pathetic."

"Why do you say that?" Ally's soft words say.

"Because he's a popular jock and I'm the Invisible Girl. He's way out of my league."

"That's true," Dani muses.

"It doesn't have to be like that," Ally argues. "Anything can happen."

"I hate to break it to you, Ally, but this isn't one of your romance books," Dani tells her. "This is real life. And in real life, jocks go with cheerleaders and people like us end up with...not them."

"The best we can do is salivate over them from afar," I add.

Ally looks down at her plate and continues playing with her peas.

I glance back at the jock table. "It's like they live in another world."

"It's fine," Dani says with a sweet smile. "You've got us and the book club. We're starting *Wuthering Heights* on Wednesday, okay?"

"Cool."

I dig back into my grilled chicken. As far as school lunch goes, Edenbury High's is pretty good. Not gourmet or anything, but the kids, thankfully, aren't running off to the bathroom every day.

"Oh my gosh, do you hear that?" Dani grumbles. She glares at something, or someone, in the distance before narrowing her eyes back on her plate and stabbing her chicken. "My ears are bleeding."

Ally smiles to herself while Charlie rolls her eyes and mutters, "Not again."

"I'm not going to forget it that easily, you know," Dani goes on. "Sue me if I hold grudges."

"What are you talking about?" I ask.

"You don't hear it?" Dani asks.

"Hear what?"

"The guy who's laughing like an elephant?"

"*What?*"

She glares at one of the tables in the distance. "*Him.*"

I stare at all the other kids, but I don't see anything. "I have no idea what you're talking about."

"Easton Knight," Charlie explains.

"I had to give him a tour of the school on the first day," Dani tells me. "He was a new student and the vice principal asked me to. He was *such* a jerk. Arrogant and cocky and so *rude.* I was sacrificing my time to welcome him to the school and make sure his transition was easy, and that was how he repaid me? Ugh, every time I think about it, I start to boil."

Ally tries to hide a laugh.

Dani throws her a friendly glare. "It's not funny."

"It kind of is."

"You're getting worked up over nothing," Charlie says. "He probably doesn't even remember you."

I look over to where he's sitting at another popular table. Not with the jocks, but right next to it. They all are pretty friendly with one another, though.

"So not fair he's a new kid and managed to fit in with the popular kids while we're invisible," I say.

"What do you expect when you're a frickin' billionaire?" Dani mutters.

"You're saying he bought his friends?" I ask.

"No. I'm saying money gives you status."

I sigh as I fall back against my chair. "And that's why we live in another world."

"Why do the three of you constantly talk about them?" Charlie asks as she continues typing on her laptop. "Who wants to be popular anyway?"

"You're telling me you're fine being invisible and not cool?" I ask.

She lifts her shoulders. "I don't care what other people think."

"I wish I were like that," I say.

She shrugs as she continues to type.

"What are you typing so frantically anyway?" I ask.

"English paper. I have to get it done before lunch is over."

"You forgot to do your homework? Sucks. Need help? English is my favorite subject."

"It's not for me," she mumbles as her fingers fly over the keys. "It's for Macy."

Macy? As in one of the cheerleaders? I glance at their table and find her and Teagyn checking their makeup in their compact mirrors.

Turning back to Charlie, I say, "Those jerks are bullying you into doing their homework?"

Her hands pause over the keys as she pastes her eyes on me. "No one forces me to do anything. It's not my fault the teachers here don't give enough work." And she continues to type.

Huh? I look between Dani and Ally. "Wait, did she just say she's doing extra homework for fun?"

With a grin, Dani throws her arm around Charlie. "That's Charlie. Our resident nerd."

"A crown I wear proudly, thank you very much."

"Wow," I breathe. "That's amazing. You must be a genius."

"I don't do labels."

"You can be like a rocket scientist."

"I do plan to work for NASA," she informs me.

My mouth falls open.

We resume eating, talking about our classes, when heels tap on the floor. Glancing up, I find Teagyn passing our table. She stops and grins at us, wide and fake. "Oh look," she says, mockery in her tone. "It's the invisible loser table."

Dani's mouth opens and gibberish starts flowing out. It's as if she's desperately trying to form a coherent sentence but is failing miserably.

Teagyn bursts out in laughter.

Charlie's eyes sprint from her laptop to the head cheerleader. "Well, we can't be *that* invisible if you see us, can we?"

Teagyn snorts before whirling around and marching to the popular table, heels clacking on the floor.

"Darn it," Dani grumbles as she tears her fingers in her hair. "I hate how weird and awkward I get with people like her. People I'm not comfortable with. I just freeze up and can't defend myself."

I give her an understanding smile. "I know exactly how you feel."

"Good thing we have Charlie, huh? She's not afraid to speak her mind."

"Yep, someone had to put her in her place. Good, I finally

finished the paper." She closes the laptop and stands. "Going to the library to print it. See you guys later."

I stare after her with my jaw practically sweeping the floor. Then I turn back to the others. "How much is Macy paying her?"

"Nothing," Dani says. "Charlie claims getting paid for it defeats the purpose. I don't really get what she means by that."

"She wants to do it for fun," Ally explains. "If she gets paid, it's no longer fun. It's work."

"A rare breed, indeed," Dani says with a laugh. "But we love her."

"Maybe hanging around her might rub off on me," I say. "I can do with caring less what people think of me."

Dani waves her hand. "Been there, done that. Her nonchalance has not rubbed off on me, and we've been friends since last year."

"Oh. Bummer."

"It's okay to want to be seen, you know," Dani says. "It's okay to care what other people think."

"But it's silly to think I could ever be popular," I say.

She twists her nose. "Probably. I mean, we're juniors. We've been invisible since the first day of ninth grade. What could change that? Other than a meteor strike."

"No meteor strikes in the foreseeable future," Ally says.

"That's okay," I say with a smile. "I have you guys now. And that's better than any guy, or popularity."

Both of them return the smile.

As we continue to eat and chat, my eyes trek to the jock

49

table again. I know, I just said I don't need a guy when I have these awesome girls, but I lose all control when Brayden is concerned. Or maybe my silly heart thinks he and I established some sort of connection because of the interview. I mean, he divulged something slightly personal to me. But it's ridiculous to think that means anything.

I catch sight of Charlie walking back into the cafeteria with what looks like the printed paper. She steps up to the popular table and hands it to Macy. She barely looks at Charlie as she grabs it and tucks it into her bag. Then a few other cheerleaders and jocks pass forward other assignments to Charlie.

When she returns to our table, she's beaming like she just struck gold. "I have so much work for tonight!" she gushes.

"A rare breed, indeed," I say with a laugh. I'm starting to love her and the others already.

The bell rings. We get up with our trays and start making our way to the garbage area. Just as I'm about to deposit my tray along with the others, I hear a "Woops!" and then someone bangs into me, knocking me into the small table that holds the discarded trays.

"Sorry!" Dani says. "That was me tripping over my feet. I'm such a klutz."

"Are you okay?" I ask her.

"Yep. It's just a typical day in the life of Danielle Wood. It happens so often it doesn't even faze me anymore." She shrugs. "I am what I am."

"Don't worry about it," I assure her.

She offers me a thankful smile.

"Let's walk together to our lockers," she suggests.

As we do, Ally asks me, "Are you going to the game tonight?"

"Brayden's QB. So that would be a heck yes."

She laughs softly.

"What about you guys?" I ask.

"We've attended games in the past, but it's not really our thing. We usually get together at one of our houses."

"Oh." I kind of feel like I'm being left out. I just became friends with them and already I feel rejected.

"We can go to the game and then hang out after," Dani suggests. "No, that'll be too late and my mom will kill me. Tomorrow, then?"

"Really?" I ask. Then I realize how desperate I sound and mentally kick myself.

"Sure," she says with a smile. "You're part of the group now."

"Thanks, guys. You have no idea how much this means to me."

"Actually, we do," Charlie says. "We were exactly like you before we formed the book club."

"Whose idea was it?" I ask.

"Mine," Dani says. "I didn't really have any friends and figured there had to be at least one person I could be friends with. And you know the best way to make friends is to find common ground."

The bell rings.

"Darn," I groan. "I wish we had more classes together."

"Same," Ally says.

"We'll meet at the game?" Dani asks.

"That's cool with me," Charlie says.

Ally nods and I give them a thumbs up.

As I head to my next class, I want to skip like a little kid. Because finally since my mom's death, things are starting to look up.

Chapter Seven
Brayden

Nerves. They're kind of a funny thing. Butterflies in your stomach or ants crawling all over your body or knees knocking into one another...whatever it is, they can seriously drive a guy insane. The fact that I have nerves makes me even more nervous. But my mom always says having nerves before an important event is a good thing because it means you care. If you didn't care, you wouldn't be nervous. That's why I know football is the right path for me. The only path.

The interview with Kara Gander yesterday has me thinking all day. I never really gave thought to what my life would be like if I didn't have football. Would I still be...me? I'm not that naïve or cocky to assume I'd have the same friends. That people would like me. Sometimes I wonder if my friends are my real friends or if we're just tight because we're on the football team. Then I tell myself to stop philosophizing. I'm a high school kid trying to keep his crap together. I don't have time to ponder whether or not my friends are true or not.

"Captain!" Jerry slaps my back as the team and I get ready in the locker room. "Ready to smoke Barefield?"

"You bet," I say.

"Can't wait to see the look on their faces when we wipe the ground with them," DeAngelo says. He slams a fist into his other palm. "I've been wanting to slap that smile off their faces since they beat us last year."

That was an epic disappointment. A memory I would rather not revisit.

"Don't worry, guys," I say. "We got this in the bag."

All the guys start to cheer and whoop.

Coach Papas gives us a pep talk, and then we run into the field. I stare out into the stands and locate my family immediately. Mom and Dad wave at me and Bailey jumps up and down when she sees me, waving her foam finger. She yells so loud, I swear you can hear her on the moon. How that little girl can let out such loud sounds is beyond me. But that just makes me love her more than I already do.

Even though I know no recruiters are coming, I survey each and every person on the bleachers. And then I internally sigh.

"Head in the game, head in the game!" Coach calls.

I'm about to focus on the game, when I catch familiar straight brown hair. I narrow my eyes, trying to make the person out. That's definitely Kara sitting with her friends. Did she come…to watch me? Then it hits me—of course she came to watch me, she's probably still working on the article. And for some weird reason, that thought…hurts a little.

I shake my head. I'm being ridiculous. Must be feeling all these crazy emotions that I can't make sense of. I just need to take a deep breath and let it out. Focus. Get my head in the game, like Coach said. Because we need to beat Barefield High. I need to smoke their QB. Because if we lose to them again, we'll never live it down.

Once the game starts, I get in the zone. It's what Brock and I always called it—total concentration. It's just me, the team, the opponent, and the ball. No spectators, no cheerleaders, nothing.

And like the blink of an eye, it's over. We won.

The stands go wild. I laugh when I hear Bailey cheer at the top of her lungs. There's no doubt about it—the kid is my number one fan.

"Good game, man." I hold my hand out to Barefield's quarterback, Tanner Murphy. He throws his helmet to the ground and stomps away.

Okay, I'm not going to lie and say that didn't feel good.

The team and I hug and slap each other, cheering and exchanging congratulations. A few guys clap my shoulders, telling me they couldn't have done it without me. I know they look up to me, but the truth is I could have done better. We won by only a few points. Was my performance good enough to attract recruiters?

It's not long before all the cheerleaders crowd around us, shrieking in glee and jumping, waving their blue and gold pom-poms around. Many of them fling their arms around me or kiss my cheek.

"We're celebrating at Mikey's!" DeAngelo announces.

Everyone continues to whoop and cheer.

"Bray!"

I turn around and find Bailey bounding toward me, Mom and Dad right behind her. She throws herself into my arms. "You won! You won!"

"We did," I laugh.

"You were on fire!" she squeals. "The best quarterback in the world. My big brother. I wanna be like you one day!"

"You'll be an amazing quarterback."

"I know! Because I have your jereens!"

"You mean genes?"

"Yeah, that!"

Chuckling, I lower her to the ground. Mom wraps her arms around me and kisses my cheek. "You were fabulous."

Dad rubs my shoulder. "Proud of you, son."

"Thanks."

"We'll let you celebrate with your friends," Mom says. "See you at home."

"Where are you going?" Bailey jumps up and down. "Can I come?"

"He's hanging out with his friends, sweetie." Mom takes her hand. "You'll play with him at home."

She frowns. "Okay. See you later, Bray the Bulldozer!"

"See ya, squirt."

She pushes out her chest and stands on her tippy toes. "I've grown a few inches since this morning. See?"

I ruffle her hair. "Wow, you really did."

"Bring me back a chocolate shake, okay? Bye!"

She and my parents leave the field. I head into the locker room with my teammates. The place is abuzz with talk about the game, all of us on a high we won't come down from until after the weekend.

I'm excited, for sure. Happy as heck. But I've got this niggling in the back of my neck. I did the best I could, but is that enough? Will a recruiter come check me out?

"Saw the loser's face?" Jerry says with a slap on my chest. "Wish I could have framed it."

"Hmm?" I blink at him.

"Tanner Murphy, man!"

"Oh. Yeah. Sure."

"You good?"

"Fine."

DeAngelo sits on the bench and looks at me. "Don't seem fine. What's up?"

I sigh as I lower myself next to him. "No recruiters."

"They'll come," Jerry assures me. "If you continue playing like this all season, schools will fight over you." He slaps my chest again.

"I don't know," I say. "You know how stressed I get. I'm scared I'll choke like I did last year." I cost us too many games, which is why we never made it to the playoffs. That's the thing about me—when I'm in the zone, *I'm in the zone*. When I'm not...I'm not.

DeAngelo and Jerry exchange a look.

"You need confidence, man," DeAngelo says as he

playfully punches my shoulder. "We don't have time for stress."

I sigh as I rub my hands down my face.

"Too bad you don't know a guy who knows a guy who knows a recruiter," Jerry says. "Someone to put in a good word for you."

"Yeah," I say with a snort. Then I straighten up. "Wait a second. Kara's dad is a recruiter for Astor University."

"Who?" Jerry asks.

"Kara Gander? She writes for the school paper."

Jerry and DeAngelo share blank looks. "Our school has a paper?" Jerry wonders.

"Anyway, I was at her house yesterday doing an interview for the paper. Her dad is Nigel Gander."

DeAngelo's eyes widen. "I've heard of him. Pretty tough guy to impress."

"Yeah." I blow out some air.

DeAngelo snaps his fingers. "That's it! That's your in. Tell the daughter to put in a good word for you."

"I barely know her. I can't just ask her—"

Jerry springs up and starts pacing. "Asking her to put in a good word for you isn't good enough. Who knows if she even likes football enough to care? And Nigel likes to get to know the players before he recruits them."

"So what do I do?"

With a smile, he drops down near me. "This is what you do."

Chapter Eight

"Your house is adorable!" Dani gushes as I invite her inside. She gazes around the place like she can't get enough of it. She's the first to arrive out of all three girls. We decided to gather at my place because Dad's not home and we can have some girl time. "So homey. And the furniture is cute. Did your mom design it?"

A log lodges in my throat as I nod. "Yeah, before I was born. She put so much of herself into it."

She smiles, but it drops when she sees the solemn expression on my face. "What's wrong?"

I shake my head, forcing a smile. "She died three years ago. Cancer."

Her eyes register pain and sympathy as she places her hand on my shoulder. "I'm so sorry, I shouldn't have—"

"No, it's fine. I love that we have this house to keep her memory alive. Like when I look at that recliner?" I nod to it. "I can see my mom staying up late getting sucked in a good book."

She smiles. "Is that where you got your love for reading from?"

"Yeah. She would have loved the club and you girls."

"Thanks. It means a lot to hear you say that. It's not every day people tell me they like me, except for my parents."

We sit down on the couch, where I've prepared snacks and a stack of movies. They range from action to romance to horror. I'm not that close with the girls yet and have no idea what their preferences are.

"Yeah, I know what you mean," I tell her. "Invisible and all that. You think we'll go our whole lives being invisible?"

"I hope not. I'm going to be a famous Broadway dancer and all eyes will be on me." She lifts her head high, then chuckles. "And you...you're going to write for a famous newspaper and everyone will read your articles."

I laugh, her words touching my heart. "Honestly, I'm not sure I want to follow that path. I don't really know what I want to do. But Broadway? That's so cool."

Her cheeks redden slightly. "But I'm nowhere as good. I was just exaggerating. Sometimes I don't watch what comes out of my mouth. No, all the time. But dance is my life. I mean, I'm not part of a team or anything like that. I just take lessons a few times a week at a dance studio. My instructors think I'm good, but for someone as uncoordinated as me? It's going to take a lot of hard work."

"Uncoordinated?"

She playfully rolls her eyes. "Did you forget that I tripped over my feet yesterday in the cafeteria? When I was little, I was so uncoordinated my mom put me in dance class to help. I'm a little better now, but like I said, nowhere as good as the other dancers. But I need to dream big or else what's the point, you know?"

I nod slowly. "Yeah, you're lucky you have big dreams. Me? I just want my crush to know I exist."

She smiles crookedly. "How did the sexy quarterback look last night? Sorry I couldn't make it to the game. I had to work."

My cheeks redden. "He performed exceptionally and brought the team to victory."

"No, how did he *look*?"

I throw my hands up. "I don't know! He wore a helmet."

"Uh huh." She giggles.

I'm about to say something, but the doorbell rings and I invite Charlie and Ally inside. They, too, compliment the house and I tell them it was all Mom. When they find out she's no longer with us, they're as sympathetic as Dani. Their kind words make me want to cry. I haven't had anyone other than Dad to talk to about her. Now I have three girls who I know will always be there for me. It's like we have a silent understanding between us, something intangible, but completely present.

"Are you okay?" Ally asks with wide eyes.

I didn't realize the tears rushing down my cheeks. I quickly wipe them with my sleeve. "I'm just glad you're all here," I say.

Charlie smiles warmly. "Us, too."

"The Four Musketeers!" Dani pumps her fist over her head and we all laugh.

"I really like the sound of that," I tell her.

Charlie waves her hands around excitedly. "The Four Musketeers who use books instead of swords to defeat their enemies."

"Speaking of books," Ally says. "Did you guys bring *Wuthering Heights*?"

I gesture to the pile of DVDs on the coffee table. "I thought we could leave the reading for the club and watch a movie. If you guys want."

Dani places her hand on my shoulder. "You're part of us now, Kara. Don't be scared to speak your mind and don't ask us permission for anything. A movie sounds awesome."

"But we need food first," Charlie warns. "I can't do anything on an empty stomach."

Dani's eyes catch sight of the backpack sitting at Charlie's feet. "Don't tell me you brought homework here."

Charlie shrugs. "I thought we might get some done."

Ally and I exchange a glance and chuckle.

As they argue back and forth about doing homework on a Saturday afternoon, Ally and I flip through the DVDs, each of us making a pile of the ones we're interested in.

"Romance?" I ask as I check out her stack.

She nods, cheeks flushed. "My favorite genre."

Then she starts adding horror to her stack. I raise my eyebrow for an explanation, and she laughs gently and softly. "You're going to think I'm weird."

"You and the others can never be weird in my books."

She gives me a shy but thankful smile. Then she bends

close. "It's not a secret, since the others already know this, but my dream? It's to watch a horror movie with a guy. Maybe we're lying on his couch or his bed, and I get so scared he wraps his arms around me and comforts me." She covers her face. "I'm pathetic, aren't I?"

My thoughts drift to Brayden and me snuggled on his bed, his strong, protective arms around me as I bury my face in his massive chest because I'm terrified of the movie.

"No," I say, unable to hide the dreamy tone from my voice. "It's not pathetic at all."

She smiles a little more confidently.

"Are there any guys…?" I ask.

"What are you guys talking about?" Dani asks. It seems she and Charlie are done arguing.

"No," Ally quickly says. "There are no guys. No one would ever fall for the shiest girl at school."

Charlie wraps her arm around Ally's shoulder. "Our girl here is a hopeless romantic," she informs me. "She's obsessed with the men in her novels and has this perfect guy envisioned. I don't want to hurt your feelings, Ally, but such a person doesn't exist."

"At least Ally *has* dreams of her perfect guy. Not everyone here hates romance like you do, Charlie," Dani says, sticking out her tongue playfully.

Charlie returns the action. "Of course Ally can dream about a guy sweeping her off her feet. I just don't want her to get hurt."

Dani is about to argue, but Ally lifts her hands. "I know

there's no such thing as a perfect guy. That's why I'll never find him. So I'm okay with falling in love with the men in my books." Her cheeks are so red, I wonder if maybe there *is* someone she's set her eyes on at school. I mean, she wouldn't blush so fiercely about a character, would she? I doubt it. But I don't call her out on it because it seems she wants to keep that to herself, and I'll respect my new friend's wishes.

Dani focuses on the movies. "So…what have we decided?"

"Pizza," Charlie says.

"I meant the movies."

"I know. I'm just letting you know I want pizza. Do you want me to order it, Kara?" She slips her phone from her pocket and clicks on the app. "Tell me what you want, guys."

We each give her our order, then try to agree on a movie. Ally wants romance, Charlie's interested in a documentary about microorganisms—the girl loves science—Dani wants a musical with more dancing than singing. And me? I'd like anything with a storyline that'll suck me in. Okay, and it wouldn't hurt to have romance in it. Then it'll give me a chance to picture Brayden and me doing all the things the man and woman do on the screen. Like hold hands, kiss, declare themselves to each other forever…

Dani snaps her fingers in my face. "I think we lost you for a second."

"Sorry. Have we decided?"

Charlie frowns. "Two votes for romance, so it looks like majority wins."

I get to my feet. "I'll grab some plates from the kitchen

while we wait for the food to arrive. Start the movie and I'll be back in a few."

The bell rings the second I turn toward the kitchen.

"Food's here!" Charlie cheers. "Do you need help, Kara?"

"No, that's okay, thanks."

I make my way to the door and throw it open, expecting to see the delivery guy. But my jaw crashes to the floor when I spot a tall guy with a massive chest and silky sandy brown hair standing there. The sun reflects off his mesmerizing blue eyes, making them look like gems.

I just stare at Brayden. "You're not the pizza guy."

His eyebrows furrow. "Pizza guy?"

I laugh lightly, pushing my fingers through my hair. "I mean, hi. How can I help you? Is this about the article? I haven't written it yet."

He shakes his head, giving me a bright smile that's oh so Brayden and oh so sexy. I'm going to die. "No, I'm not here about the article."

I nod and wait for him to go on.

"Can we talk?" he asks, voice a little hesitant. Man, even when he's hesitant he sounds so sure of himself. It's like a natural talent or something.

"What's taking so long!" Charlie shouts from inside.

Brayden's eyes flit to the slightly open door. "Oh, you have company. I can stop by later."

"That's okay. We can talk out here."

I shut the door behind us and gesture for him to take a seat on the porch steps. Then I cringe. You don't ask the most popular and sexiest guy at school to sit on your dirty porch steps!

But he drops down like it's no big deal, sweeping that silky hair out of his eyes, making it perfect-messy that makes me want to touch it. But I curl my fingers in my lap.

"Kara."

I love when he says my name. It's so smooth and gentle and makes me tingle all over.

He lifts a brow, and I quickly shake that thought away before he thinks I've lost my brain. "Yeah? That's me, Kara." Then I cringe. Maybe I really *have* lost my brain.

He smiles warmly. "Saw you at the game. Do you have enough material for your article?"

I just nod because I can't seem to do anything else. He noticed me at the game? Out of all the people crowded on the bleachers, he saw *me*?

He leans back on the steps, shooting that sizzling smile my way. Doesn't this guy know that every time he's near me I'm at risk of melting into a puddle?

I have no clue why he's here or what's taking him so long to say whatever it is he needs to tell me. But that's okay because this gives me a chance to stare at perfection as long as I want.

I don't know how much time passes before he finally says, "I have a proposition. No, not a proposition, but more like a favor."

I just stare at him. The star quarterback needs a favor from me, Invisible Girl?

"My friends and I were talking about, you know, getting

recruited into a school with a good football program. And since your dad is a recruiter for Astor University…" He searches my face. "My friends suggested I get close to him, let him get to know me. Then he'll be so impressed by me and my performance as QB that he'll recruit me in a heartbeat. My friends' words, by the way, not mine." He laughs lightly, though his sounds cool and confident, like music to my ears.

"They figured the only way to get close to him is through you," he continues, unsure eyes meeting mine. "If we'd grow…friendly. Maybe even more than that." He brushes his fingers through his hair, a nervous tick, but on him it once again looks so calm and collected. "They suggested we grow close so I'll get to know your dad well and…"

"You mean like fake date?" I ask.

His eyes meet mine. "Yeah. That's exactly what I mean. But only if you're okay with it. Honestly, when my buddies brought it up, I shot it down. It didn't feel right. But my future is on the line here. Football means everything to me, and you have no idea how competitive it is out there, how hard it is to catch the attention of recruiters."

I'm not completely familiar with that world. Dad talks about his work here and there, but I don't know what it's like to be in Brayden's shoes.

But holy heck, he wants us to fake date? Me, fake date *him*?

"I know it's crazy," he continues. "But I need to do this for my dad, for my brother. I've worked my whole life for this and if I don't follow my dreams, then what am I? What has my life amounted to?"

I just gape at him. He's so raw and real right now. Another guy might brush his emotions aside, or mask them with cockiness. But not him. He wears his emotions on his sleeve and isn't embarrassed for others to take a peek at them.

He pushes some more fingers through his hair, managing to keep it fresh and shiny and not oily from all that touching. "It's so selfish of me because I know you wouldn't get anything in return…"

"No!" I say before I can stop myself. "I mean, I don't have to gain anything. I'll do it."

He narrows his eyes in confusion. "You'd really do this for me?"

I smile. "You're a great QB and an even greater person. I want my dad to see that. I know he can be a tough cookie sometimes. I want you to get into the school of your dreams and have all the good things thrown at you."

"Thanks. But I'm only doing this if you're totally one hundred percent on board with this. I don't want you to feel pressured or anything."

I shake my head. "No pressure whatsoever. Honest."

He gets to his feet, grinning deeply, warmly, and appreciatively. "Thank you, Kara." His eyes focus on something in the distance. "I think your pizza is here. Enjoy and I'll see you on Monday."

I watch his retreating form, trying not to explode into a million tiny pieces. What just happened? What in the world have I just agreed on?

The pizza guy stands before me, annoyed. He places the

two boxes in my hands, accepts his tip, then climbs into his car and drives off.

I'm left standing with the warm pizza slowly cooling off, my thoughts a jumbled mess. Brayden and I…boyfriend and girlfriend?

Shaking that off, I enter the house and find my friends nearly dying of hunger.

"Finally!" Charlie zooms to the boxes, placing them on the dining room table. The others gather around her.

"You could have grabbed something from the fridge, you know," I tell them with a chuckle.

Dani turns to me, pizza on a plate. "What happened? Where were you? Flirting with the pizza guy?"

"Haha, you wish," I tell her, heading over to the box and plucking out a slice. After placing it on a plate, I lower myself between her and Ally. Charlie seats herself at Dad's spot at the head of the table.

"Brayden came over," I tell them, then lower my face to the table and squeal as low as I can, but it's pretty much impossible. I don't even have an appetite, but my stomach is crying for food.

"Wait, wait, wait," Dani says. "What do you mean he came over?"

Lifting my head, I smile so widely it might slice my face in half. "He came over to *my* house. To talk to me."

"What did he want?" Charlie asks. Ally bends close, like she's dying of curiosity.

I peer down at my pizza, then slowly take a bite. Usually, I love pizza, but because I'm tingling all over, it's hard to feel anything. "He asked me to pretend to be his girlfriend."

They blink at me.

"It's so my dad can get to know him and recruit him for Astor University," I quickly explain, defensive for some reason. And I don't know why. These girls wouldn't judge me.

Charlie holds up her hand. "One second. He's using you to get to your dad? That's wrong on so many levels. You shouldn't have agreed."

"No, it's not like that. He's not using me at all. He was so kind and sweet when he asked. Like, he made sure I was totally okay with it. He's not using me if I know I'm being used, Charlie."

She frowns, but doesn't say anything. Dani looks deep in thought, as if she's trying to wrap her head around the whole thing.

"Football means the world to him," I go on. "He lost his brother two years ago and he wants to go pro and make his family—especially his brother—proud of him. And I don't mind helping out. It's not like I'll get hurt or anything."

Ally rests her hand on my arm. "Won't you, though? You have a massive crush on Brayden. Won't it hurt you to be so close to him, knowing it's all fake and he doesn't feel the same way about you?"

I give her a strained smile. "Brayden and I live in two different worlds. There's no chance in heck we'd ever date for real. So if this is my only chance to get close to him and spend time with him, then I'll do it. And yes, it's going to be hard, but hanging out with him is better than nothing at all. At least this way, I can live out my fantasies, for a little while, anyway."

Ally squeezes my arm. "Are you absolutely sure you want to do this?"

"I am. Even if it'll be fake, my memories will be real." I give them all a wide smile. "I'm a big girl and I'll be okay. All that matters to me is being near him."

"If that's what you want, we'll support you," Dani tells me. "And you're a good person for helping him accomplish something that means so much to him."

I shrug. "I don't just have a huge crush on him, I'm kind of invested in him, you know? I think it's because of the interview. I got to know a side of him I didn't know he had. Like how much football is ingrained in his life and his family's. It ties them all together. And ever since Brock died...I just understand him."

Dani grins crookedly. "Or maybe it *is* your massive crush and you'd do anything for the guy."

Rolling my eyes, I grab a napkin and chuck it at her.

Chapter Nine

I've had the most amazing dream. Brayden Barrington came to my house on Saturday and asked the Invisible Girl to be his girlfriend.

I smile at the ceiling as sleep starts to leave my body. Too bad it was just a dream. Because just pretending to be his girlfriend would last me a lifetime. Yeah, I wouldn't need a boyfriend for another twenty years because I would have my fix just being that close to Brayden.

With a sigh of pleasure, I roll onto my side and continue to imagine what life would be like fake dating him. My gaze lands on my vanity, and I notice a strange object sitting there. I squint to try to make it out, but I have no idea what it is. It looks like a makeup bag. Why would there be...?

My body jolts up in bed as I gape at the bag. Wait a second...holy heck, it wasn't a dream! I borrowed my mom's makeup and placed it on the vanity so I would remember to put some on. Because I need to play the part of Brayden Barrington's girlfriend. And his girlfriend would wear makeup.

Quarterbacks Don't Fall For Invisible Girls

After going to the bathroom and getting dressed, I plant myself at the vanity and open the bag. A whole lot of foreign stares back at me. I have no idea what any of this is.

I tentatively reach inside and pull out a brush, examining it from side to side. I knew I should have watched some YouTube tutorials on how to apply makeup. But I thought I could just wing it. I mean, most women put on makeup every day—how hard can it be? But that was before I saw the alien contents in this bag.

I asked Mom a few weeks before she died if she could teach me, and she told me she would. But then she died and I had no one else to ask. And honestly, I wasn't really interested. Trying to have a boyfriend was the least of my concerns after my mom died. And then I just assumed I was too invisible to ever snag a guy. But things are different now.

I fall back against my chair with a defeated sigh. No, things are not different. Brayden isn't my real boyfriend. He's just *pretending*. So breaking my head trying to figure out this makeup isn't even worth it.

But will people buy us being together if I look like a toad?

I grab my phone and send a group text to my friends.

Kara: Anyone have time to give me a quick tutorial on makeup? Just the basics.

Dani: The last time I tried to put on makeup, my dad thought I was abducted by aliens.

Ally: I don't own makeup.

Charlie: I don't do makeup.

I try not to groan.

Ally: I can ask my older sister for help. She's the makeup guru.

Now I just feel pathetic. I'm nearly seventeen years old and don't know how to put on makeup. Even twelve year olds know how to do this.

Kara: It's fine. I'll figure it out. Thanks, guys.

I don't have that much time before school starts, so I quickly search for a five minute tutorial on the basics of makeup application. It seems simple enough.

But five minutes later, I realize there's nothing remotely simple about makeup. My lipstick smears my teeth, I nearly blind myself applying mascara, the eyelash curler looks like some sort of medieval torture device, and my smoky eye looks like a smoky mess. I grab makeup remover wipes and scratch the entire thing. Maybe people won't notice us together and I'll have time to learn this stuff later.

I finish getting ready and fly out the door, wishing Dad a good day. Good thing the school is a ten-minute walk from my house. Mostly everyone has already arrived—the student parking lot is almost full and there are throngs of students marching to the doors.

I stop dead in my tracks and swallow hard. Once I walk through those doors, I'll no longer be Kara Gander. I'll be Kara Gander, girlfriend of star quarterback Brayden Barrington.

Fake girlfriend, Kara. How many times do I need to remind myself? Maybe until my heart will stop doing somersaults—which will be never.

Taking a deep breath, I throw my head up and march into

the building. It's not long before my head starts to droop and my knees knock into one another. I rush to my locker and get my stuff, my heart thumping wildly in my chest. Can someone my age have a heart attack? I hope not. Because if I survive it and they ask me what caused it, I'd have to tell them it's because I have a massive crush on my pretend boyfriend.

Breathe, Kara. Breathe.

"Kara, hey." Someone throws an arm around me and yanks me to his chest. "There's my girl."

I shove away from the person, only to realize it's Brayden. He stares at me in utter confusion.

"Oh, Brayden!" I say. "B-bo-boy…"

"Boyfriend?" he says.

"Yes, boyfriend!" I grab his arm and stretch it around me. Except, we're standing too far apart and I end up jerking him toward me. His jaw knocks into my temple and we both cry out in pain.

"Sorry!" I say.

"I didn't know trying to wrap my arm around my girlfriend would be physically painful," he jokes.

I start laughing uncontrollably. Like a freakin' hyena. What can I say? I laugh when I'm nervous.

"Sorry, it's my fault," he says. "I sprung up on you out of nowhere. Attempt number two?"

My throat so tight I can't speak, I nod vehemently.

"Okay." With a smile, he steps closer and stretches his arm over me, gathering me close to his chest. "Attempt number two is a success."

And I start giggling like a loser. And then I feel him. Oh my gosh, I feel him. His strong arm around my shoulders, the hard muscles of his chest. The warmth of his body. My eyes flutter shut as I sink into him. Pure bliss.

"You sure you want to do this?" he whispers.

My eyes fly open. "What?"

His eyes search mine. "Are you sure you're okay with this? Because there's still time for you to back out."

Is he insane? Does he really think I'd give *this* up? I'm in Brayden's arms. My body is pressed against his. The way his arm is wrapped around my shoulder, so gentle but firm. So perfect. It's exactly how I imagined it would be.

"Kara?" he asks.

"I'm fine," I assure him. "Totally okay."

His chest heaves in relief. "Okay. Thanks again."

"You don't have to thank me. I'm happy to help."

"Thanks, Kara. You're awesome."

I smile like a dope. Brayden Barrington just called me awesome.

"Can I walk you to class?" he asks.

I light up like I got struck by the sun. "Sure!"

He's about to lead me away, when I remember I didn't have a chance to grab my books. So the result is half of me being pulled by him while the other remains planted in my spot. "Ouch! Sorry, I just need to get my books."

"Right." He waits while I gather my things, then gently slips them out of my arms and tucks them under his free arm. "I've got that for you."

Oh, wow, he's such a gentleman.

As he leads me down the hallway to chemistry, heads start to turn in our direction. And they all stare. I feel like a queen being escorted by her handsome king. Some of them gape at us like they're not sure they're seeing correctly, others whisper to each other. Several point.

I look up at Brayden, worried he won't like the stares or pointing fingers or whispers and call the whole thing off. Which I know would be the right thing for my sake, but I don't want to call it off.

But he just smiles pleasantly to everyone like it's no big deal he's got his arm wrapped around a nobody.

"Who is that?" someone whispers as we pass her. "Is she new?"

"What is she wearing?" someone else whispers. "That's so decades ago."

"Retro," her friend says. "I kind of like it."

I once again look up at Brayden, but he doesn't seem bothered by their comments or stares.

He must sense me watching him because his gaze falls to mine. He tucks me closer to his chest like he wants to protect me—or comfort me?—and asks, "You good?"

"I'm great," I murmur as I get lost in those gorgeous eyes. Then I shake my head to snap out of it. "I mean, yeah, I'm good. I didn't think they'd stare like this."

He shrugs. "Sorry. That kind of comes with the territory of being who I am."

"Sorry I'm not wearing any makeup."

He looks at me. "What?"

"I tried putting some on this morning, but I'm telling you, it's worse than my trig homework. And the YouTube tutorials didn't help. Either I'm a complete moron or…a complete moron."

His chest rumbles as a soft chuckle escapes his lips. "You're not a moron. You're one of the smartest people I know. And don't sweat it about the makeup. You look great."

I freeze as his words find a home in my brain. Did he just call me smart? And he said I look great?

But then I start wondering if he's just saying these things because he's supposed to. As my boyfriend, he should compliment me, right? Or maybe he's trying to make me feel more at ease about this arrangement. Or perhaps he's buttering me up to get close to my dad.

He stops walking and looks back at me. "What's wrong?"

I swallow the huge lump in my throat. I can't be like this. I have no idea how long he and I will pretend to date, but if I don't keep my heart in check, I'll end up hurt. So pasting on a smile, I say, "Nothing," and I wrap my arm around his waist like I've been doing it all my life. "Thanks for the compliments, b-boy…" I shut my eyes for a second. "Boyfriend. You're not so bad yourself."

"I'm an amazing quarterback, right?" he reminds me. "According to Martina, editor of the Edenbury High Times. Though it seems all of her staff doesn't share her feelings."

I stop walking and gape at him. "Oh my gosh, you remember that conversation?"

"Of course I remember it."

"Ugh." I slam the heel of my palm against my forehead. "I'm sorry I said that. I was just so nervous to ask you to do the interview and—"

"It's okay," he assures me with a laugh. "I'm just teasing you."

I gape at him, dumbfounded. "Oh…you're just joking?"

He laughs again. "Of course. I admit, it was kind of cute how nervous you were," he says as he continues to lead me to chemistry. Were the hallways always this long? Feels like it's never-ending. Or maybe we're walking too slowly?

"Cute?" I ask. Has the room gotten super hot?

"Yeah. It's cute how much you care. How dedicated you are to the paper."

"When no one at school even cares," I finish for him.

His eyebrows come together. "I'm sure lots of people care."

"Not you," I point out.

"I'm grabbing a copy of every issue. Promise. And I'll tell my buddies to grab one, too."

"You don't have to do that," I quickly say. "I was just kidding too. We have more readers than we think."

"Well, I'm glad to hear that," he says as he stops before my chem classroom. "But I'll still grab a copy, hot off the press."

"Thanks. And thanks for walking me to chem."

"I'll be waiting outside for you after class is over."

My jaw nearly hits the floor. "You'll what?"

"I'll wait for you after class to walk you to your next one.

Even though my classroom is at the other end of the hallway."

"You really don't have to do that! I can find the classroom myself. I have been going here for over two years," I say with a laugh.

"It would be my pleasure. It's what a good boyfriend would do for his girlfriend." He winks with a charismatic grin.

Once again, I'm melting into a puddle at his feet. But...is he putting more effort into trying to be the perfect boyfriend just to score some points with my dad? Or is this the way he'd be if he really did have a girlfriend?

"So I'll see you soon, girlfriend." He steps closer to me with his arms raised.

I stumble back and hit the wall. His eyebrows dip.

"Oh, sorry! I forgot for a sec." I move up to him and close my arms around his middle, pressing my cheek into his hard chest. Feels like I'm fused to him. Yeah, I can totally live like this.

For a second, it feels like Brayden rubs his hand down my back. But the sensation is gone so fast I'm sure I imagined it. I step out of the hug and say, "See ya, boyfriend." I wave and enter the classroom.

All heads turn in my direction. Like when Brayden and I walked through the hallway, some people stare, some point, some whisper, and some turn up their noses. Looks like some even want to say something to me, but don't know what. For the first time since I entered Edenbury High, I no longer feel invisible.

Chapter Ten

Today has been wonderful so far.

Brayden is my (fake) boyfriend, the kids at Edenbury High know who I am (even if they might not know my actual name yet), I aced my English paper, and there's lasagna for lunch.

Okay, maybe I'm packed with adrenaline. But I can't help it. Even though we're pretending, I feel like my life is changing. I feel...confident. No longer ashamed of being myself. Hopefully this feeling will carry on once Brayden and I part ways. That thought makes my chest ache. That's why I push it away whenever it surfaces in my mind. I don't want to face it yet.

The lunch lady smiles as she hands me lunch, once again asking how my day is going so far. With a huge grin, I tell her it's going great, so thankful that someone at this school actually sees me. Then I pay for my food and make my way to our table in the back. The others are already seated there, Dani and Ally chatting over plates piled with lasagna while Charlie pores over what looks like calculus. She cuts a slice of lasagna every few minutes, keeping her gaze fastened on her papers.

"Calculus, huh?" I say as I slide in next to her. "You're playing in the big leagues now."

"Calculus two," she corrects. "For two students. Need to have them ready before sixth period."

I gape at the others, but they just laugh.

"So what's the news around school?" I ask as I bite into my lasagna. Yum.

"Word around school is that Brayden Barrington has a girlfriend," Dani says.

I widen my eyes as far as they can go. "Really? Who is she? Must be super cool."

Dani grins. "The coolest. Too cool to be sitting at this table, that's for sure."

Giggling like I've never giggled before, I gush in a whisper, "It's so much fun, you have no idea! Brayden's so sweet and charming. He's acting like the perfect boyfriend. He actually waited for me between periods to walk me to my classes. And all the other kids have noticed me!"

"But he's pretending," Charlie reminds me.

"I know," I assure her. "Believe me, I know. But I'm totally cool with it." I sigh happily. "His chest is so strong. And warm. And it smells so good. If I die right now, I'll die a happy woman."

Dani laughs as she guzzles down her drink, which results in her squirting some water out of her nose. "Ugh," she says as she wipes her face. "Awkward girl is at it again."

"Are you really sure you're okay with this?" Ally asks me.

"Because it looks like you're in deep."

"Of course she's in deep," Charlie says as she continues working on the math. "She's in love with him."

"That's my point," Ally says. "Like I said on Saturday, she'll get hurt."

"I won't get hurt," I promise. "I have the situation under control."

"I've read this stuff many times in books," she says. "When one of the partners secretly has a crush on the other and he or she doesn't share the same feelings—"

"Thanks for being concerned, Ally, but this isn't a book. It's real life. And yeah, he doesn't know I have a massive crush on him, but I'm gaining so much from this fake relationship. It's the only way I can be close to him."

"You can tell him how you really feel."

"Yeah," I say sarcastically. "Like that would end well. He'd run for the hills. Guys like him don't end up with girls like us, Ally. My life isn't a romance novel."

"I know, but...never mind." She looks down and plays with her lasagna.

"I'm sorry," I say. "I don't mean to shoot you down. I like hearing what you have to say. You don't have to be shy around me. I mean...I know I'm new to the group, but...should I shut up? I'm talking way too much."

"Nah, no way," Dani says.

"We're okay," Ally says with a smile. "I just don't want you to get hurt."

"Thanks. I know to keep my feelings in check. This is like

the coolest thing to have ever happened to me."

She smiles. "I'm happy for you. If you're happy."

I sigh as I fall back in my seat. "I am."

A shadow looms above me. I look up to find Brayden smiling down at me. "There's my girlfriend."

I grin. "There's my boyfriend."

"Sit with me?" he asks.

The way the sun seeping in through the windows shines down on him? Makes his sandy brown hair look golden.

"Oh, um, I'm eating with my friends."

He nods. "No prob. I'll meet you outside to walk you to your next class."

"Okay," I say with a goofy smile as he returns to the popular table. "Boyfriend."

"Have you lost your mind?" Dani hisses. "Go sit with him!"

I look between all three of them. "You sure?"

Ally nods and Charlie waves her hand.

"But I want to sit with you guys. My friends."

"But we meet up for the club and at each other's houses all the time," Dani says. "It's not every day you can sit with your fake boyfriend at the popular table."

"Shh!" I motion with my hands.

"Yeah, you're not exactly faking anything if you sit at the loser table," Charlie says.

"This isn't the loser table," I tell them. "It's the winner table." I wrinkle my nose. "That sounded lame."

They laugh. "A little," Dani says. "But we know what you

mean. Still, everyone's staring at you."

"They are?" I crane my neck in different directions, taking in all the heads facing me. Dani's right—everyone's looking. Probably wondering why Brayden's girlfriend is sitting in a spot they didn't even know had a table.

"I guess if we want to be taken seriously, I should sit with him," I muse. "At the popular table."

"You'll be fine," Dani assures me.

"Um, okay. I guess I'll see you guys later."

"Good luck," Ally says. "And be careful."

"Thanks. I will be."

Lifting my tray, I turn toward the table at the center of the room. This is a dream come true for me—how many times did I lie in bed and imagine this very moment? Being Brayden's girlfriend and sitting at the popular table, dressed in designer clothes, looking pretty, acting confident? Except, my clothes aren't fancy. I'm not wearing makeup. And I sure as heck don't feel confident.

Brayden notices me and waves me over, a sweet, inviting smile on his face. My knees go weak just by his smile. Some of the kids at his table turn to look at me. I can do this. I *can* do this.

When I'm only a few feet away, Brayden stands and puts his arm around me. "I'll introduce you to everyone. Don't worry, they're cool."

"Okay," I say, my voice slightly trembling.

With another sweet smile, he tucks me closer to his body. I think he miscalculated the difference in our weights because he tugged just a little too strongly and his cheek brushes against mine. A spark zaps through me, causing every hair on my body to stand on edge. But it doesn't look like our contact had any effect on him. He just continues leading me to his table.

"Hey, guys," he greets as he gently pushes me forward. "I'd like you to meet my girlfriend, Kara."

Every single head lifts and stares at me. I've always dreamed for this to happen, but I never imagined it'd make me feel so naked.

I raise my hand in a small, lame wave. "Hi," I croak.

"Barrington's girlfriend," one of the wide receivers says, getting to his feet and clapping me on the back. It's such a strong blow that I stumble forward and cough. "Whoops, sorry. You're a tiny thing."

"It's okay," I manage to say between coughs.

Brayden brings over an unoccupied chair from the nearby table and motions for me to take a seat. "Thanks," I tell him as I lower myself. All pairs of eyes fixate on me, causing sweat to gather on my palms. I wipe my hands on my knees.

Brayden starts to introduce everyone, as if I don't know them all by name. I might be invisible, but not a single person at this table is. The jocks all say hi and give me genuine smiles, but the cheerleaders are all fake. Teagyn doesn't even smile.

"How long have you been together?" her friend Clarrie asks.

"We just got together yesterday."

"Cute," she says, though from the tone in her voice, she doesn't find it even remotely cute. I know some cheerleaders can be snobs, but maybe they'll like me once they get to know me? And maybe we'll still be friends once Brayden and I "break up."

"You know," Teagyn says as she tilts her head to the side and studies me like I'm an animal at the zoo. "I've never seen you here before. Are you new?"

She can't be serious. Of course she knows who I am. She made fun of me last week when Brayden knocked into me and I fell flat on my butt.

"She's not new," Brayden says. "Don't you read her articles in the Edenbury High Times?"

"The what?"

"The school newspaper," I tell her. "We publish every month."

Her eyebrows shoot to her forehead. "I wasn't aware our school had a newspaper. How *adorable*. I should really check it out."

"Our next issue is next week," I tell her with a smile.

From the look on her face, I'm positive she won't read a single issue.

The table grows painfully quiet. Not knowing what to do, I pick up my fork and dig into my lasagna.

Every single girl at the table turns up her nose. "Ugh, how can you eat that?" Clarrie says. "There's like a thousand calories in that."

I shrug. "It's delicious. So worth the calories."

"I guess someone like you would feel that way," Teagyn says as she stabs her fork into her lettuce and brings it to her lips.

Did she just call me fat?

"What does that mean?" Brayden asks.

When I glance at him, I realize he genuinely doesn't understand her side comment. Boys can be so clueless sometimes.

"Oh nothing." She gives him an overly sweet smile. "Your new girlfriend is adorable."

Brayden beams at me. "She is, isn't she?"

My cheeks and neck heat up. Does he really mean that?

I'm about to tell him thanks and that he's cute, too, when Teagyn and the other girls talk about cheerleading. They're working very hard to qualify for the regional championships. The team hasn't been doing well the last few years.

"Maybe you guys need something to motivate you," the wide receiver suggests.

"Or maybe some of us just don't have the talent," Teagyn says. "I can't wait until I cheer for a college team."

They all shift uncomfortably in their seats. Wow, did she just diss her teammates?

Thankfully, one of the football guys starts talking about a funny thing that happened during class, and the atmosphere shifts to a more pleasant feeling.

"So Kayley," Teagyn says. "What do you like to do for fun?"

"It's Kara," I say, trying not to roll my eyes. She totally did that on purpose.

I'm about to answer, when a chime echoes in the room.

Saved by the bell! I bet she'd make a face or side comment at whatever I say.

"Let me get that for you." Brayden sweeps all my garbage on my tray and piles it on top of his.

"Oh, you don't have to do that," I try to say, but he's already making his way to the garbage.

"Come, girls." Teagyn tosses her glossy blonde hair over her shoulder and stalks out of the room, leaving her tray on the table. Some of the less popular cheerleaders scramble to clean up.

Brayden returns to the table and slings his arm around me. "Ready to head to your next class?"

"You don't have to walk me," I protest.

"I don't mind."

I look back at my friends' table and see them all watching me. Dani looks excited, Ally a little worried but curious, and Charlie waves with a smile. I missed hanging out with them at lunch. I mean, I loved sitting next to Brayden, but I thought the popular table would be more fun. Maybe I need to give it some time. After all, a foreign person is sitting at their table now, someone who most people didn't even know existed. Hopefully things will look better tomorrow.

"Thanks," I say when Brayden and I stop before history. "Good luck on your test."

"How do you know I have a test?" he asks.

I go still. I may know he has a test because he complained about it on social media last night.

"I'm not stalking you or anything," I stammer. "I looked

you up last night on Spill It!. I thought about sending you a friend request, but…"

"Oh yeah, that's a good idea. And maybe we should change our statuses to 'in a relationship'. I'll add you after class."

"You sure that's a good idea?" I ask. "I mean…when we end things…"

"Yeah?"

"Won't you look like…I don't know…"

He steps a little closer. "What are you trying to tell me, Kara? If you're uncomfortable about this arrangement…"

"No, no! It's nothing like that. I just don't want you to be embarrassed when we end things."

It's not like I'll have anything to be embarrassed about. No one follows me on social media.

"That's very thoughtful," he says with a smile. "But I'll be okay." He nods toward the classroom. "I'll see you soon."

"Okay. Bye, boyfriend."

He winks and walks away.

I stare after him, my heart galloping in my chest. Then I sigh happily and settle down at my desk.

Chapter Eleven

What a day. From being so close to Brayden, to sitting at the popular table, it's enough to make my head spin. I did things today I haven't done in my sixteen years on this planet.

I face-plant on the couch, my mouth fused with the cushion, and yell. I don't know at what or why, I just need to let all this out. Me and Brayden. Brayden and me. I sigh happily, feeling myself sink through the cushion like it's a cloud.

Keys jingle from outside before the door opens and Dad walks in. As soon as he finds me sprawled on the couch, he rushes over, face tortured with worry.

"Are you okay, Kara? Are you hurt?" His eyes scan me from top to bottom, searching for damage.

I roll onto my stomach. "No, I'm not hurt. Not at all." I face him, a bright smile on my face. "Today was the happiest day of my life."

Dad's face eases up. "I'm so glad to hear that. Do you want to talk about it as I prepare dinner?"

"Sure." I sit up. "Need help?"

"I'd love that."

We gather the ingredients and start. Dad's responsible for the main course and I work on the side dishes. We've never done anything like this before, which is a shame because I love our bonding time. I didn't realize how distant we've grown since Mom died. I don't think we did it on purpose, it's just one of those things that happened.

Maybe because I've always been sulking in my room.

Well, I'm not sulking anymore.

Dad grins at me. "So tell me about your day."

"It was amazing, Dad. Brayden Barrington asked me to be his girlfriend."

Dad's eyebrows knit. "Barrington. The name sounds familiar."

"He's quarterback at my school," I tell him. "So awesome and amazing." I stop myself from gushing because I don't want to ruin this for my fake boyfriend. He has a plan to win my dad over and I'm not going to screw it up with my babbling and being overly exuberant.

"He asked you to be his girlfriend?" Dad asks. "That's wonderful, honey." He smiles unsurely, as if he's not exactly sure what this means or what he's supposed to do with the information. I've never had a boyfriend before, so this is new for both of us. "Do you like him?"

I laugh. "Yeah, I really do. Like a lot."

"That's great. Tell me about him."

I freeze for a second. Even though I interviewed him, I

realize I don't know him so well. Like, what's his favorite color? Food?

"He's so kind and sweet," I tell him. "And nice."

"What about his grades? Is he a good student? I wouldn't want a boyfriend to distract you from focusing on your studies."

I stop chopping some carrots. "Dad," I groan. "I'm really excited right now and you're kind of ruining this for me."

"Sorry, pumpkin." He heads over and wraps an arm around me. "I just worry. Doing this single parenting thing without your mom…" His voice trails off.

I lean up to kiss his cheek. "You're great. Just ease up on the boyfriend thing. You trust me, don't you?"

He laughs. "Of course I do. It's him I don't trust."

My heart sinks. That's not good. If my dad already distrusts Brayden, then how is he going to eventually recruit him?

"Brayden's not like other guys," I quickly say. "He's different. Responsible. Thoughtful."

"I'd like to meet him one day."

I nod, my head not here. Why am I freaking out that my dad wants to meet my fake boyfriend? This isn't about me, it's about him. He needs to make a good impression for himself, not for my benefit.

"Cool," I say with a wide smile. "Of course."

Dad returns it and we continue working on dinner. When we're done, we settle down at the table to eat. My thoughts are on Brayden throughout the entire meal. I wonder what he's doing right now.

Slipping my phone out of my pocket, I scroll through his social media. A few friends have tagged him in pictures they uploaded a few minutes ago. It seems like he's hanging out with the football team, cheerleaders, and a few others at Mikey's Diner. In one picture, Teagyn is so close to him she's seconds away from brushing her lips against his. I zoom in on the picture to get a better view of his face, trying to determine how he feels about her. He told me during the interview that he's single, searching for someone special. Is she her? But if that were true, what's taking him so long to ask her out? I'd know if they dated before, since I've had a crush on him since middle school and I know exactly who he dated. Stalkerish, I know, but I can't help being obsessed with him. Mom would tell me I'm being unhealthy, that I should find someone who would appreciate me. But I want him. For real.

But I'll take what I can get. For all I know, this might be my first and only boyfriend.

"Pumpkin, please put your phone away," Dad says before I have a chance to study the picture.

I quickly exit the app before he can see who I'm spying on. "Oh, sorry, Dad."

He smiles. "That's okay. Why don't you tell me about your day?"

I shrug. "Nothing special happened."

He lifts a brow. "What about the boyfriend?"

My cheeks heat up. "Oh, right. Yeah, he asked me to be his girlfriend and I said yes."

He takes a spoonful of rice and swallows it down before

asking, "Were you texting him just now?"

I glance down at my phone. I wish. Brayden wouldn't text his fake girlfriend. What for if Dad or no one else can see?

"Yeah," I lie, forcing a smile.

He shakes his head. "Kids these days. When I was your age we actually had conversations with our friends."

I try not to roll my eyes at how many times he says this. "I know, I know." I get to my feet. "I'm going to do homework."

I go up to my room and plop down on my bed with my phone. Now that I'm alone, I study the picture. It was taken at an angle that doesn't let me see his face so well, only that he's smiling. At her? I've got no clue. But it doesn't matter anyway. Cheerleaders go with quarterbacks. This dates back to the beginning of time. People like me remain on the last rung of the social ladder.

I'm not feeling sorry for myself, just staying it like it is.

I spy on him for another ten minutes before starting my homework. When I get stuck on math, I text Charlie for help. She's more than happy to lend her assistance.

A text from Charlie comes when I'm working on chemistry and don't have a chance to check on it. But when my phone dings two more times, I'm too curious to ignore it. Maybe she's telling me about the homework she's got piled up from other kids. I still can't believe she does this for fun, but she loves school and I'm in awe of her genius brain.

Looking at my phone, my heart catapults to the ceiling when I notice who those three texts are from.

Brayden: Hey, Kara. What's up?

Brayden: I just got home from Mikey's. Sorry I didn't invite you, but it was last minute and I wasn't sure if it's your scene.

Brayden: You there?

Brayden texted me? Why? What for? Dad can't see this.

My fingers stumble as I tap out a text.

Kara: Hi, Brayden. It's okay, I don't mind. We're not really dating, so you don't have to be forced to invite me everywhere.

His response comes a few minutes later.

Brayden: I wouldn't call it being forced. I just thought you might want to hang out.

Kara: Oh, right. Yeah, I'm cool with Mikey's.

Brayden: And my friends? Do you like them?

I have no idea why this is important to him. Once he's recruited into his dream college, none of this will matter. But I'm not going to try to psychoanalyze this guy.

Kara: I don't know them well yet. They seem cool, though.

Brayden: They are. What are you doing right now?

Kara: The dreaded thing we call homework.

Brayden: Ha, I feel you.

Quiet.

His next text comes a little while later.

Brayden: See you tomorrow, girlfriend.

Kara: Right back at ya, boyfriend.

Later that night, after my homework is done and I've showered, I lie in bed with my phone on my stomach. Silly me hopes he'll text again, but of course he doesn't. My friends do, which I'm really grateful for.

But it's not the same as my fake boyfriend.

Chapter Twelve

Like yesterday, everyone stares at Brayden and me as we make our way down the hallway, his arm wrapped around my shoulder and mine around his waist.

"I told my dad about you," I say as we stop by my locker so I can grab my books.

"Really? And?"

"He's happy for us and wants to meet you soon," I say.

He smiles. "That's great. I'm really looking forward to it. Meeting your dad will be such an honor for me."

Hugging my books to my chest, we head for chem. "We'll just have to pick a time when it feels right. Like, not too early and not too late."

He nods. "Right."

We reach my classroom and just stand there, looking at each other. He's about to say something, when some of his friends clap him on the back, trying to drag him off. But then they see me standing there and they salute. "Sorry, man. Didn't see you're with your girl," Jerry says. "What's up, Kara?"

"Not much."

Jerry and the others slap Brayden's hands before walking off. As I watch them go, a thought hits me and I face my fake boyfriend. "Brayden, can I ask you something?"

"Sure."

"Who knows about our arrangement?"

His eyebrows come together. "Just Jerry and DeAngelo. Why?"

I shrug. "Well, if we're trying to make this believable, no one can learn the truth. Because my dad might find out and then...well there goes your chance."

He smiles. "You're so nice for worrying about that, but no sweat—the guys won't tell anyone. They know how desperate I am to impress your dad and they won't do anything to screw that up."

"What about the cheerleaders? Teagyn?"

He shakes his head. "It's just Jerry and DeAngelo."

Jerry must be a very good friend because he treats me as though I really *am* Brayden's girlfriend. He could be rude to me or ignore me or treat me like the invisible person I am, but he doesn't. I'm glad Brayden has friends he can trust. Rely on.

Same way I've got my girls to rely on. I still can't believe I've met such wonderful girls who are just like me. Sometimes I need to pinch myself to make sure I'm not dreaming.

"Kara? The bell rang," Brayden interrupts my thoughts.

I snap in and glance at him. My eyes widen. "You'll be late to class. You should go!"

He chuckles softly. "That's okay. My teacher's pretty laid

back about attendance, especially toward certain students."

My eyebrows furrow. "Oh, you mean like athletes?"

He winks. "Perks of being the quarterback. But I really shouldn't take advantage of my teacher and get my butt to class. I'll see you later?"

I wink. "See ya, boyfriend."

He laughs again. "You know? I never get bored of you calling me that." And he walks off, leaving me standing there with no darn clue what the heck he meant.

I mean, the guy's had girlfriends before. So why would my calling him boyfriend mean anything?

"Miss Gander, please enter the classroom so I may begin my lesson," my teacher demands. Peeking into the room, I realize that class has already started.

My cheeks heating up faster than metal, I scurry inside, mumble an apology, and find my seat. A few kids snort at one another. Several others have their gazes fastened on me. I bet most think this thing with Brayden is just a fluke, like his brain short-circuited. They must be so shocked to see us still together. Not that I blame them. Invisible Girl and the star quarterback? It's a match made in fantasy land, nothing more.

***

"Hey," Brayden greets as I dump my books in my locker after last period. "Any plans after school?"

I shrug. "Not really. Why?"

He grins. "Want to watch me practice?"

I just stare at him, my insides poking with hopelessness. He doesn't know I've always watched him practice. For years. Yes, he has many things on his mind, like getting recruited to a top college, but it still hurts that he's never noticed me. He's never wondered why he crashed into me the other day? Why I was there?

And does he know I haven't missed any of his games since last year? Wow. Even though I shouldn't be surprised, this really hurts.

His eyes search mine. "Kara? Are you okay?"

I hike my backpack straps up my shoulders. "I'm fine."

"Cool. So will you come watch me practice? If you don't have other plans, that is."

"Why?"

His eyebrows knit. "Why what?"

I quickly shake my head. "Never mind. Yeah, sure I'll come. I *am* your girlfriend after all."

He laughs. "Thanks. I've got to get changed. See you on the bleachers?"

"I'll be there, boyfriend."

He chuckles. "Later, girlfriend." He walks off.

I still have no clue why he wants his fake girlfriend to watch him, but I'm not going to question it.

Outside, I make my way to the bleachers, where many other kids, mainly girls, are seated. Most are here to watch the football players practice, some to watch the cheerleaders at the other end of the field.

I feel heated eyes on me, and when I glance to the left, I catch Teagyn glaring at me. What the heck? What have I done to her?

But then I look at the football players and find Brayden waving both arms at me like he's flagging down a helicopter.

My heart skips a beat as I take in that wide smile and the glee in his eyes. Wow, he's a very good actor. If I didn't know any better, I'd think the man truly has feelings for me.

"That your girl?" one of the football players, a guy who doesn't eat lunch with the rest, asks him. Brayden grins and nods, sending me another smile.

"Good for you, man," another says. "I wish my girl would watch me practice. She'd rather go shopping at the mall with her friends instead. You're lucky, captain."

My heart sinks. Is that why he asked me to watch him practice? So he can show off to his teammates that he has a loyal, supportive girlfriend?

He's captain and the quarterback, so he has a reputation to uphold, but why does it have to be at my expense? But then again, I agreed to this. I have no right to complain.

Waving back at him, I shoot him a large smile. He returns it before following his coach's orders.

I keep my gaze on Brayden and Brayden alone as the team practices. No matter how many times I watch, it's always so interesting and new. Brayden has a talent for always keeping the games fresh and intriguing. And so intense and suspenseful. One time last year, he scored the winning touchdown with two seconds left to the game. He pretty much saved the day. I was so happy for him that all I wanted to do was float down the bleachers, into his arms, and tell him how amazing he was.

Footsteps *clink clank* on the bleachers before four girls drop down near me, one on either side and the others on the row before me. All are freshmen and all stare at me with wide eyes.

"Can I help you…?" I ask unsurely.

The girls glance at one another, as if not sure who should speak. I try to see over their heads to catch Brayden do his thing, but they're blocking me. So much for watching him practice.

"How did you do it?" one of the girls asks, her eyes wide. The other three play with their hair, as if not sure what to do with themselves.

"Do what?" I ask.

She giggles. "Snag the attention of Brayden Barrington."

"You're not exactly…uh…" another adds, glancing at my faded jeans and loose green T-shirt.

I follow her gaze. "What? Popular?"

She nods.

"Or pretty," another pipes up. Her friend shoots her a look, elbowing her in the ribs. "Or cool."

"Oh, um. Thanks," I mutter. They don't have to remind me of my flaws. I see them every time I look in the mirror.

Giggler bends close. "So? Tell us your secret, oh wise one."

"My secret?"

Now all four bend close. "How did you get Brayden's attention?" they urge.

The coach blows his whistle, and I once again try to see over their heads, but their hair is too poofy and curly. Is Brayden owning practice? Probably. He always does. And I love seeing every second of it. If these girls would move…

"Well?" one of the girls snaps. "Tell us everything!"

I want to laugh out loud. They want to know how to catch the attention of the most popular guy at school? For starters, have a dad he wants to get close to. Or write an article about him and be forced to interview him. Or even better! Have a fake relationship with him. Because all three of those things worked for me.

But of course I don't tell them that. I just roll my shoulders and tuck my hair behind my ears. "Just be yourself and everything will fall into place."

Their jaws drop. Then they exchange confused and bewildered expressions with one another.

"That's it?" Giggler asks. "You were just yourself and he chased after you?"

Oh, man. I'm in serious trouble right now. Who am I to give advice when I don't even know anything? I'm just Invisible Girl who'd never in a million years have a real boyfriend. And these girls are looking up to me for guidance?

I laugh awkwardly, pulling at some loose strands of hair that slipped out from behind my ear. "Well…yeah. I mean, you can't force a guy to like you. Or even notice you. They have to notice you on their own."

They exchange those same confused glances again.

"But," I continue, holding up my fingers, "Sometimes that's not enough. Sometimes you have to do a grand gesture to catch their attention. Then they'll get to know you and fall in love with you."

"Brayden's in love with you?!" the girl with the curliest hair, the one blocking my man, bursts out, eyes so wide they'll pop right off her face.

I laugh again. "Um…well, yeah, I guess."

They squeal.

"Oh my gosh, oh my gosh. I'm totally posting this."

She reaches for her phone, but I say, "No! Don't do that."

She freezes and looks at me in shock.

"It's just…private, you know? You can't announce it to the world."

She tilts her head from right to left, thinking over my words like she's never considered it. "But if he loves you, what's he trying to hide?"

"We just got together a few days ago and everything is still so new. So please don't post things about us."

"Fine, you're right. I'm sorry. I'm just so excited because there's hope for us. I mean, you're not cool or pretty or popular and you snagged him. And we're prettier than you."

They smile and get to their feet, hurrying back to their seats to continue watching the boys. I try not to let their words bother me, but of course they do. Honestly, I never thought I was pretty, but I always figured I was cute, cute enough for guys to notice me anyway. Now thanks to them, all I think about is what Brayden sees when he looks at me. A friend, someone to fake date. Never the real thing.

Coach blows his whistle, dismissing the guys for the day. Brayden's eyes zero in on me and he waves again. I wave back, my heart thumping in my chest. Even when we're pretending, that smile could shatter me into a million pieces and then paste me back together.

He motions toward the locker room, telling me he'll quickly get changed and take a shower. I nod, letting him know I'll see him soon. As he washes off, I start my homework. The cheerleaders are still practicing and I hear Teagyn yelling at her teammates to focus or they won't win their competition.

The girls dare not answer back lest they fear her wrath. I feel for them, I really do. No one deserves to be yelled at like that, like they're nothing more than ants on the ground.

They're lucky to be cheerleaders, though. If Mom were still here, would she be disappointed that I didn't follow her path?

"Hey," a voice says from above.

Glancing up, I find Brayden standing there, his hair wet. He sits down and glances around. "It's weird to see the field from this point of view," he tells me. "To watch the show instead of starring in it."

"But you go to pro games, don't you?"

"Not really. I did when I was younger, but I don't have time now. But yeah, I love going to games. There's nothing like being in the stands, cheering for your favorite team. Being part of something."

I smile. That's exactly how I feel when I watch him play.

"Sorry I didn't watch you much during practice," I tell him. "These freshmen girls were talking to me about you."

"Really? What did they say?"

My eyes widen. I can't tell him they were so shocked that a girl like me snagged the sexy quarterback. I'll look like an even bigger loser than I already am. "Oh, um. They just told me I'm lucky to be dating you, that's all."

He doesn't say anything as he stares off at the field. And I watch him, trying to read his expression. What's he thinking? Why did he suddenly grow so quiet? Is it something I said?

We must be sitting like this for a few minutes, him staring at the field and me at him, before he turns to me. "Kara, you *are* okay with this, right?"

I lean back, then quickly catch myself when I remember I'm not sitting on a chair but on bleachers. "You keep asking me that."

He nods, brushing his hand through his hair. "I know. I just want to make sure you don't have any regrets."

"Of course I don't have regrets. We're trying to get you into one of the top colleges in the country. Why wouldn't I want to help?"

His smile is so warm and sexy and appreciative that I feel like I'm floating to heaven. "Thanks, that's so nice of you."

"Yeah, that's me. Nice," I say.

He smiles again, then gets to his feet. "I'd better go home now."

I stand, too, wishing we could sit out here a little longer, but I know that's never going to happen.

My mind selfishly conjures up different excuses to try to persuade him to stay, but I glue my lips together.

Brayden gestures to the school and we head inside. We're quiet as we walk.

"What are you thinking?" he asks as we make our way to his locker to fetch a textbook he forgot.

"Nothing," I say. "School, life, the usual. Why do you ask?"

He shakes his head. "No reason. You're just quiet."

I laugh. "So are you."

"Guess I've got a lot on my mind, too. We'll be seniors next year."

"Yeah."

Quiet.

He grabs his book and we leave the building, parting for the day. He wishes for me to have a good day, tells me he'll see me tomorrow, and walks to his car. I stare after him, wondering if I'll ever have a chance to ride in that car with him. To be in an enclosed space with him, maybe listening to music.

As if he feels me watching him, he turns around before getting inside. My body goes still. Crap. He caught me ogling him. Now he's going to think I'm the biggest loser in the world.

But he smiles and waves, sending a calmness over me. Maybe he doesn't think I'm a loser after all. Maybe it's time I stop thinking of myself as one.

I wave back, maybe a bit too frantically, and then he climbs into the car. I sigh as I imagine the two of us riding into the sunset like I've seen in romance movies.

That's all this will ever be—as though I'm living a romance movie.

Chapter Thirteen

The lunch lady gives me an extra scoop of spaghetti and meatballs. I thank her before making my way to the popular table, where all the jocks are already seated. There doesn't seem to be a cheerleader in sight.

Brayden's face lights up when he sees me approach, a large smile conquering his lips. I return the smile, ordering my heart to stop beating wildly.

"Meatballs," DeAngelo says with a pleased smile. "You've got taste, man. All the other girls eat salad, salad, salad. Boring, boring, boring. I like a girl with an appetite."

Brayden smiles at me. "Me, too."

Calm down, heart.

All the guys at the table have a heaping pile of spaghetti and meatballs, too. I know they'll go for seconds, and maybe thirds. Don't athletes have to eat like ten thousand calories a day or something?

I twirl some spaghetti with my fork and bring it to my lips. "You only live once, right?"

DeAngelo winks at Brayden. "I like your girl."

He smiles at me before cutting into his meatball. I try not to let the disappointment wash over me that he didn't say something like "I like her, too." But what can I expect? The terms of our agreement were very clear. This is all an act. No one is supposed to have actual feelings for the other one.

"Where are the cheerleaders anyway?" I ask.

"They had an emergency meeting," Jerry tells me. "They'll probably be here soon."

I guess I should bask in this cheerleader-free meal, however long it'll be. It's not that I have anything against the cheerleaders here—my mom was one, too—I just wish they were a little nicer to people on a lower social tier than them.

We continue eating our spaghetti and meatballs—which is delicious, by the way—discussing music and TV, and of course football. About fifteen minutes later, the cheerleaders file into the cafeteria with looks of death. Seriously, it's like all of their grandmas died or something. Some of them go to buy food while others come straight to the table, including Teagyn. She's carrying the worst expression of all—it looks like she'll burst into tears any second.

"Hey, ladies," Jerry says. "Missed you."

They ignore him as they settle down at the table.

"Was the meeting okay?" Brayden asks, gaze moving from one cheerleader to the other.

"No!" Teagyn whines. "Everything is ruined!"

"What happened?" DeAngelo asks.

"Clarrie broke her leg during practice yesterday."

"Is she okay?" Brayden asks.

"She's fine," Teagyn cries, close to tears. "But now we're short a cheerleader."

"What are we going to do?" another asks as she roughly bites into her tomato. The thing squirts everywhere, causing some of the other girls to shriek.

"Mom wants to have tryouts," Teagyn tells the guys. "We had them the first week of school and could barely find anyone decent."

"Harsh, Myers," DeAngelo says.

"It's the truth!" she cries. "That's why we have no alternates."

"Maybe you'll find someone good this time around," Brayden suggests.

Teagyn rolls her eyes like he said the most idiotic thing in the world. "We don't want someone good. We want someone *amazing*. We need to go to nationals this year."

"You shouldn't put so much pressure on yourself."

My eyes widen to epic proportions when I realize those words escaped *my* lips.

Teagyn's head snaps up and she looks at me like she hadn't noticed me sitting here all this time. Narrowing her eyes at me, she says, "Who are you again?"

"Uh...Kara Gander. I'm with the Edenbury High Times."

"And my girlfriend," Brayden adds.

"No, I don't mean that," Teagyn says, still glaring at me. "I mean, *who the heck do you think you are?*"

"Uh..."

"You're not part of any team or any competitive sport. You don't know what it's like to have a dream, a goal. You don't know what it's like to have everything you worked for snatched away from you because of someone's stupid mistake."

"It was an accident, Teagyn," one of the girls says in a low voice, like she's worried the queen will slice off her head.

"She was careless," Teagyn snaps at her. "And because of that, we might not qualify for the competition."

"You should hold tryouts," Brayden says. "You never know what will happen."

"Whatever. I need air. Come." She grips the sleeve of the girl next to her and yanks her off her chair, not caring that she was about to take a bite of her salad. She drags her out of the cafeteria.

Jerry whistles. "Intense."

"You have no idea," one of the other cheerleaders mumbles.

"I know what she's going through," Brayden says with a thoughtful expression. "Her mom's the coach. She won nationals when she was a junior. It can't be easy to live up to that."

It feels like I just got buried under layers and layers of dirt. Does Brayden…like Teagyn?

"Let her cool off," DeAngelo suggests. "She'll be fine."

A short while later, Coach Myers's voice sounds over the loudspeaker. "Attention, please. Due to an unfortunate accident, one of the cheerleaders sustained an injury. She will not be able to perform during the games or participate in the upcoming competition. The cheerleaders are down a member and will be having tryouts tomorrow after school. If you think you have what it takes, please come to the gym after school."

I wish I had what it takes. Wish I had my mom's cheerleading genes. But I've never been coordinated enough. Or pretty enough. Or confident enough. For a few seconds, I imagine what it would be like if I followed in her footsteps. Dressed in the cute blue and gold outfit with matching pom-poms, waving my arms and shaking my body, cheering for my boyfriend Brayden as he scored the winning touchdown...

Okay, maybe the last bit is too much, but...would Brayden and I date for real if I was a cheerleader?

Before I have a chance to dwell on it, the bell rings and we all leave for our classes.

***

"I don't see him as a hero," Charlie says. "I see him as a villain. And honestly, I don't even know why some women love him. I don't find anything even remotely attractive about him."

My time with the girls during the book club is a moment I cherish and look forward to every Monday and Wednesday. But I can't concentrate on anything. All I think about is how proud my mom would be if I followed in her footsteps and became a cheerleader. We had a lot of things in common, but one thing I swore to her I'd never do was be a cheerleader. But that was before she died. Now it seems like I want to grasp onto anything related to her, just to keep her memory alive. Because one of my greatest fears is forgetting her. Forgetting how she looked like, how she smelled, the way her eyes sparkled when she smiled, or how intoxicating her laugh was. When she laughed, you had no other choice but to join her. It was so contagious. And it had the magical power to make me feel better, no matter how upset or sad I was.

"He does have some redeeming qualities," Ally says.

"Yeah? Name one."

Without meaning to, a massive sigh shoots out of my lips. Ally's mouth snaps shut as she and the other two turn to me.

"Yeah, I'm a little bored with this, too," Dani admits. "Let's talk about something else. *The Hunger Games*!"

"Again?" Charlie says with a groan. "We discussed that book to death. Any more and I'll turn into a zombie and eat your brains."

"But there's so much to talk about! And we can compare them to the movies."

"Didn't we decide we were going to focus on the classics for this semester?" Ally asks. "And if we're going to pick something more modern, can we please go with the *A Lady of True Honor* series?"

"Regency?" Charlie makes a face. "I hate regency romances!"

"You like Jane Austen," Ally reminds her.

"That's different."

"How is it different?"

"I don't know. It just is."

"Guys, quiet a second." Dani's eyes focus on me. "Something wrong, Kara?"

I shake my head. "I'm fine."

Now Charlie and Ally study me, too.

"Something is wrong," Charlie says. "You're never this quiet."

"Thanks," I mutter.

"I like when you talk," she says. "You always have something interesting and unique to say."

"I agree," Ally says. "If you want to talk about what's bothering you, we're right here. You can tell us anything."

I lower my head on my desk and turn it toward the window, where none of them can see my face. Because I'm scared I'll cry any minute. "I'm just...sad. I miss my mom. A lot."

They're quiet for a bit, and then Ally says, "I'm sorry you lost her. It must have been so hard. Sorry for saying sorry. I know some people hate that."

"I wish I knew what to say to make you feel better," Dani says in a sympathetic tone. "But I won't pretend and say I know what you're going through."

Charlie rubs my shoulder. "Just talk to us, Kara. Tell us how you feel."

"Most days I'm okay," I whisper, so low I'm not sure they can hear me. "Some days I hurt. Then there are days where I'm in so much pain, I don't know if I can move on. And today..." I blow out a breath. "I just wish she were here."

I hear all of them stand and then they wrap their arms around me. It causes more tears to pour out of my eyes. We haven't been friends for long, but they've become my best friends. Feels like I've known them my whole life.

I turn my head in their direction and give them a small smile. "Thanks. I'm glad I can talk to you guys about her. I don't have anyone else to talk to."

"What about your dad?" Dani asks.

"We talk about her sometimes, but I don't want to hurt him. He always gets sad—he loved her very much."

"Sorry." Ally rubs my arm.

I swallow and lift my head off my desk, wiping my eyes. "She was a cheerleader for Edenbury High. Her team won a trophy for the school her junior year. She's in the picture in the hallway."

Charlie's brows come together. "Wait, isn't that the same year Coach Myers won that trophy?"

I nod. "She and my mom were best friends."

Dani's eyes snap open wide. "No kidding."

"Yeah. But they grew apart after they graduated. Her mom cheered for a college team and my mom studied nursing. Then they both got married and lived separate lives. It's funny they both ended up here in Edenbury. But I don't think they were able to rekindle their friendship. Or maybe they didn't want to."

"Sucks that happens," Ally whispers. "I hope we'll stay friends forever."

"You kidding?" Dani exclaims. "We're going to marry quadruplets and raise our kids together."

"Quadruplets?" I say with a laugh.

"Well, it was triplets before," she admits. "But you're part of us now, Kara."

I smile. "Thanks, guys. I feel better already. I just wish…" I sigh as I push some hair away from my face. "I wish I could follow her legacy."

"You mean…be a cheerleader," Dani says.

I nod.

"Why can't you?" Ally asks.

"Um, have you looked at me?" I point to myself. "This is not a cheerleader's body. Or face."

"What are you talking about?" Charlie says. "You're beautiful."

"You can be the greatest cheerleader in the history of cheerleading," Dani says.

I shake my head. "I have no rhythm or coordination. Or stamina."

"Have you ever tried?" Charlie asks.

"No. In middle school, my mom asked me if I wanted to try out, and I told her a hard *no*. Me shaking pom-poms? Then she died and I couldn't even bear…" I swallow as tears prick my eyes. "And now…"

"Now you're ready," Ally says.

I shake my head firmly. "I'm not ready. I'll never be. Because it's not me. I can't try to keep my mom's memory alive by doing something that's not for me."

"I think you can do it," Ally says. "No, I *know* you can do it."

"But I'm the Invisible Girl."

"All the more reason to do it!" Charlie says. "Why can't girls like us be cheerleaders? Why can't we have fun?"

117

We all exchange looks.

"Yeah," Dani says, pumping her fist in the air. "Power to the nobodies!"

"That might work if said nobody can actually cheer."

"Who said you can't?" Dani asks.

"*I* know I can't. Whatever, it was just a silly thought. There are other ways for me to feel connected to my mom. And um…" I laugh lightly. "I thought that maybe if I become a cheerleader, Brayden and I could date for real. Ugh, another silly thought. I don't want to change. I want to be me."

"But popular," Dani teases with a smile.

I roll my eyes. "Like that could ever happen." I pick up *Wuthering Heights*. "Let's continue dissecting Heathcliff."

"You sure you're okay?" Ally asks.

I wave my hand. "Yeah, totally. I mean, come on. Me a cheerleader? I want to hang out with you guys at our awesome club."

"You can do both, you know," Ally says.

"Actually, it would be a little difficult," Charlie says. "Cheer practice is always at the same time as the book club."

"So we'd change our schedule around," Dani says. "Just like we do for Ally's choir practice."

"Yeah, we can do that."

"Guys! I told you I don't want to be a cheerleader. Just forget it."

"You can at least try," Dani says. "Maybe you inherited your mom's genes."

"You heard what happened to Clarrie. Not only would I

break all my limbs, I'd break everyone else's, too. And then the whole school would hate me for breaking the poor cheerleaders."

"At least you would have been a cheerleader for five minutes," Dani jokes.

I throw my eraser at her.

As we continue discussing the book, every part of me fills with warmth. Calm, comfort. The complete opposite of how I felt only ten minutes ago. All because I have friends. Friends who understand me and care about me. I don't know if Dani's wish will come true and we'll marry quadruplets and raise our kids together (that is a heck of a reach), but I do know that we'll be friends forever.

That brings me more comfort than anything else possibly can.

Chapter Fourteen

Why is my locker crammed with so much junk when it's so early in the school year? I stick my head and shoulders as far as I can, searching for my history notes. I dumped them in here yesterday after Dani used them to study for a test, and they completely vanished. Or got devoured by all the useless junk in here.

"Oh no!" a deep voice says from behind me. "The locker's eating my girlfriend."

I yank my head out and turn around, coming face to face with Brayden.

He laughs like he's embarrassed. "That sounded better in my head. Sorry."

"No, it was funny. Cute. Hi, boyfriend."

"Hi, girlfriend. Did you lose something?"

"My history notes."

"Need help?"

"That's okay," I start to say, but his head is already buried in my locker. "Wow. You've got a lot of stuff."

Quarterbacks Don't Fall For Invisible Girls

"You mean junk," I say, my face heating up with embarrassment. "Sorry, you don't have to look through it."

"I'm very good at finding lost things. You have no idea how many times my sister loses her toys and I have to search through all her stuff...is this it?" He pulls his head out and hands me some papers.

My eyes widen when I realize it is indeed my history notes. "My hero," I say with a laugh.

He grins. "Anything for my girl."

How I wish he really means those words.

We both stand there awkwardly looking at one another.

"So," I say the same time he starts to say something. "You go ahead," I tell him.

"No, you go."

"Oh, um...I didn't really have anything to say." I laugh lightly. "We were just standing in this awkward silence..."

He chuckles. "Yeah."

"What were you going to say?" I ask.

He shrugs. "Nothing really."

"Oh."

And we're quiet again.

"It's a bad sign if the boyfriend and girlfriend run out of things to talk about," I joke.

He slides his hands into his pockets. "I guess we need to work on our communication," he says with another chuckle.

I wonder if we'd be this awkward if we were dating for real, or if we wouldn't shut up because we'd have so much to share with each other. Oh my gosh, what if it were the complete opposite and we didn't have a *single* thing to talk about? Would that mean we're not compatible?

I want to kick myself. Why am I even worrying about this when Brayden and I will never date for real?

One of the cheerleaders marches up to the bulletin board that's only a few feet away from my locker and pins a notice on the board. Cheerleading tryouts after school.

I stare at the words, lifting my fingers to trace the letters. If only I were good enough and could make Mom proud of me.

"Hey, you okay?" Brayden asks.

I drop my hand. "What? Oh no. I mean yeah. I'm fine. It's just that…never mind."

He glances from me, to the sign, back to me. "Does it have anything to do with cheerleading tryouts?"

I sigh. "I was thinking of trying out and my friends encouraged me, but I don't know."

"I think you'd be great at it."

I gape at him. "You really think I could be good at it?"

"For sure," he says with a full smile. "You're fun and very supportive of the football team. And you'd look really cute in the uniform."

I just stand there, frozen, his words playing over and over in my head. But not settling in my mind. Because there's no way he was talking about me. *No way.*

"Kara?" he asks, placing his hand on my elbow.

I blink and look at him. "No one has ever…I mean, I never thought…" I take a deep breath to regulate my racing heart. "The truth is, I've always wondered…but I never thought I could actually do it."

I want that connection to my mom so badly…

"What makes you think you can't do it? You never know what you're capable of until you try. The sky's the limit and all that. Just believe in yourself. Like I believe in you."

I gape at him again. "You do?"

"Of course. Girlfriend." He playfully punches my arm.

Right, he's supposed to believe in me, since he's supposedly my boyfriend. Are his words sincere or is he just telling me what he thinks he's supposed to say?

As if reading my mind, he leans closer so only I can hear his next words. "I'm not feeding you a pile of BS because I'm supposed to. I meant what I said."

I think I might have died and floated up to heaven.

My friends tried to talk me into giving cheerleading a shot yesterday at the club meeting, but I didn't have the confidence to actually go through with it. But it's different with Brayden. He makes me feel like I really *can* do this. That I can conquer the world. And not because he's supposed to say it—his words are genuine.

"I…I think I want to do this," I hear myself say.

His eyes light up. "Really?"

"You have me convinced," I say with a nervous laugh.

He laughs, too. "I think that's a first. You have no idea how many times I try to get Bailey to eat her vegetables when I'm babysitting her. Maybe I'm not a total loss in the convincing department."

"Just flash her that smile of yours and she's sold," I say.

Then my eyes widen. "I m-mean, no, that wouldn't work on your sister. That would be weird." Ugh!

He laughs again. "More like all she has to do is flash her toothy smile and I'm sold. Do you have any siblings?"

I shake my head. "No, just me. I asked my parents for a little sister for my eighth birthday, though. It was a definite no."

"I hear it's fun to be an only child, but it can be lonely, too."

"Yeah," I say. Especially now when it's just Dad and me. I clear my throat. "Anyway, um…"

"I'll walk you to class."

Once I'm settled in my seat, I shoot off a text to the girls, asking them to meet me in the gym during lunch. I need to have a killer routine if I'm to win the spot on the cheerleading squad. I can already feel my mom smiling down at me.

***

Coordination and I are not a good fit at all, but my friends don't give up on me. Luckily, Ally's older sister tried out for the cheerleading team during her sophomore year and taught Ally the routine. So we somehow manage to put together something that seems semi-good. Good enough to win that spot? No clue. But at least it's something. And my mom's talent must have been passed down to me, even if it's just a little. And maybe that will be enough to snag me the spot.

Somehow, I make it through the rest of school. When the final bell rings, my heart nearly catapults out of my chest. The time has arrived. Oh my gosh, I think I might faint.

Dani, Ally, and Charlie are waiting outside my classroom,

each of their cheeks flushed with excitement. Just having them here with me eases my nerves.

"Ready to be a cheerleader?" Charlie asks.

"As ready as I'll ever be."

We head to the gym. I don't know why I assumed no one would be here. At least thirty girls are waiting to try out. I swallow hard as I take in their perfect cheerleader bodies. There's no way I can do this.

"We're losing her." Dani puts her hands on my shoulders and looks into my eyes. "Forget everyone else. You've got this."

"I…I don't know." My breathing is irregular.

"Your mom is here with you," she whispers. "You can do this."

I *do* feel my mom. I know she's looking down at me and is super proud. Even if I don't get the spot, I know she's happy for me.

"We'll be in the stands," Ally says as she rubs my arm. "Good luck."

"You'll do great," Charlie adds.

"As we say in show business, break a leg," Dani says. Then she cringes. "Wow, that is so not a good thing to say to someone about to try out for cheerleading. Because if you break a leg, you're screwed."

I laugh, and some of the tension leaves my body. "No, it's perfect. Thanks, guys."

They wave and find a spot on the bleachers.

"Kara!"

I turn around and find Brayden racing toward me. "What are you doing here?" I ask. "Don't you have practice?"

"Told Coach I'm not feeling well. Can't miss your big day. Good luck!" He playfully slaps my shoulder before finding a spot on the bleachers.

I just stare at him. He's going to watch me try out for cheerleading? What if I make a total fool of myself?

No, he's here to support me. His presence should make me strive to do well. After all, he was the one who pushed me to do this. Because I was too afraid to push myself.

"I'm going to call out all the names I have here," Teagyn says from where she sits at a table with two other cheerleaders. "Just say here when I call your name."

She starts to list them off. But she doesn't mention my name.

"Okay, everyone on the list is here," she says. "Let's start."

I raise my hand. "You didn't call my name."

She squints at me, looking me over from top to bottom like she's never seen me before in her life. "What's your name again?"

It takes everything I have not to roll my eyes. She sure as heck knows my name. "Kara Gander," I say.

"Kara, Kara, Kara." She runs her pen down the list. "I don't have your name here. Sorry, you didn't sign up in time."

"What are you talking about?" I demand as I move a little closer. "I put my name on the sign-up sheet during lunch period."

She shrugs. "It's not here. Maybe try out next year? Okay,

let's start."

"You can't do that!" I nearly explode. "I *signed up*—"

"First up is Felicia Montgomery!" Macy calls out.

My lips snap shut. My eyes rove over my friends. How could this be happening?

"Excuse me." Charlie marches over and stands before the table with her hands resting furiously on her hips. "I saw Kara sign up. And I have two other girls who can verify the same."

Teagyn keeps her eyes on her for a few seconds before stating, "You all must be blind because her name isn't on any of the sign-up sheets."

"What a load of bull—"

"It must just be a misunderstanding," Brayden says as he comes to stand next to me. "I also saw Kara sign up."

Teagyn glances at him before narrowing her eyes at me.

"Come on, Teagyn," Brayden says. "She's just one person. I'm sure you can squeeze her in."

She presses her lips together so tightly they turn white. "Fine. Only as a favor to you, Brayden."

He grins. "Great." Then he touches my arm. "Good luck, Kara."

I fist my hands at my sides as I walk off to the side so Felicia can start her routine. Yeah, I admit it feels good to have a guy like Brayden stand up for me, but it also doesn't feel good for two reasons. One, I should be able to stand up for myself. And two, Brayden isn't even my real boyfriend. So would he have stood up for me had we not made his arrangement? Definitely not. I know, I agreed to this. But man, the more time passes, the more I realize how difficult this is. But I'm not backing out. I made a commitment, and I want Brayden to follow his dreams. Even if I may get hurt in the process.

Some of the other girls have amazing routines. I swallow as one by one they wow Teagyn and her crew. I need to tell myself to believe in myself. This may be my only shot at bridging this connection to my mom.

"Okay," Teagyn says with a scowl. "It's Gander's turn."

My heart starts ramming against my ribcage. This is it. This is my moment. After the next few minutes, I will either be a cheerleader or a cheerloser.

"Are you even here?" she asks, nothing but pure irritation in her tone.

I rush to the center of the gym. "I'm here."

She narrows her eyes. "Don't waste our time. What we do is serious. Not useless like your pathetic book club."

Ouch. Did she just diss our book club? I glance at the others and see that Charlie looks like she wants to bound off the bleachers and slap her hard across the face. Dani looks livid and Ally hurt.

I'm about to try to stand up for myself and tell her she has no right to talk about the club that way, but I'm not exactly in a position to yell at the head cheerleader, am I? I *do* want to get on the team after all. So without a word, I start my routine.

I admit, the nerves get the better of me. I forget a few steps and stumble a few times. I don't have to look out at the audience and see the expressions on my friends and on Brayden to know this is a train wreck. Even if I did a flawless routine, it

128

would still be a disaster. Because Mom's cheerleading genes have passed over me. Not just passed over—they took one look at me and said, "Nope."

When it's over, I can barely look at Teagyn and the other girls' faces. I don't need to see their mockery. But I have no choice. Macy's covering her mouth, obviously trying to hide giggles, and Teagyn has such a satisfied smirk on her face that I want to get sucked into the ground.

She glances back at the papers in her hands. "Looks like that was everyone," she announces. "Give us a few minutes to deliberate."

I walk to the side and fold my arms over my chest, facing my back to the bleachers. I don't want to look at my friends and see the sympathetic looks in their eyes. Because it'll make me cry. And I definitely don't want to see Brayden's face. I wish he hadn't come to watch me.

"Okay!" Teagyn says as she claps her hands. I reluctantly turn around to face her, my heart fluttering in my chest. "The girls and I discussed it and…Felicia Montgomery, welcome to the Edenbury High cheer team!"

With a squeal, she barrels over to them, hugging them. "Thank you so much!"

"You were great," Teagyn says, with what looks like an actual genuine smile. "Can't wait to have you on the team."

I knew I didn't make it. Even if I did have a good routine, Felicia was amazing. And she's got the perfect cheerleader look.

"Gander?" Teagyn calls.

I look at her.

"Can you come here for a sec? We want to talk to you about something."

My heart starts racing in my chest again. Could it be…? Maybe they want to offer me a spot, too? Maybe I hadn't performed so terribly after all? With shaky knees, I make my way over to them.

"Cute routine," Macy says. "Where did you learn it?"

"A friend taught it to me."

"Would that be a friend from your little club?" Teagyn asks as she studies her nails.

"Yeah," I say, not sure where she's going with this.

Her eyes snap to mine. "And you thought you and your loser friends could put together some routine and you'll magically land on the team?"

"What?" I stammer. "I don't—"

"And you thought someone like *you* could actually be a cheerleader?" She chortles. "Don't you know your place, freak? We?" She motions to herself and the other cheerleaders. "Are up here." She hovers her hand over her head. "And you?" She stretches her hand as low as it can go. "Are down here. Don't think for one second that you could ever play with the big girls. Because you are a loser and you will always be a loser. Okay, sweetie? So next time try not to embarrass yourself and *don't* waste our time."

Tears prick my eyes as I keep them on her. She and the other two cheerleaders start giggling—about me or someone else? Who knows. But I just stand there glaring at her like there's no tomorrow.

She turns her head back to me and raises her eyebrows. "Is there something you want? Isn't there a Star Trek convention that's calling your name?"

"Why do you have to be like that?" I demand with a shaky tone, trying my hardest not to bawl my eyes out. "Just because you're a cheerleader and popular, you don't have to be a jerk."

Her eyebrows lift even higher. "Excuse me?"

"You could be nicer," I say, the tears starting to slide down my cheeks. "I know I didn't do a good job, but it was important to me. You could have been kinder."

She stares at me for a moment before bursting out laughing, causing the others to follow suit. "What are we in— kindergarten? You want us all to be friends? Newsflash, loser, this is the real world. And in the real world, you don't always get what you want. You have to be talented and you need the drive. And sorry, sweetie, but you have neither. So run off and do what you do best—stay invisible."

I turn on my heels and march out of the gym, the tears rolling freely down my face.

"Kara!" I hear my friends call.

"Kara, wait up!" Brayden says.

Oh, gosh. He's the last person I want to see right now. I cried in front of everyone. How mortifying.

"Kara, stop." Ally wraps her hand around my arm, forcing me to stop. "Kara."

All three of them stand before me with worried and sympathetic eyes.

"I'm done," I mutter as I wipe my eyes. "Teagyn's a jerk."

"Mega jerk," Dani says.

"Kara?" Brayden's voice says. I crane my neck to look past Ally's head and see him making his way over.

"No, I don't want him to see me," I moan.

"Come." Charlie grabs my arm and yanks me into the girls' locker room. A man-free zone. Ally and Dani quickly follow and shut the door.

"Thanks," I tell her.

She winks. "I've got you."

With a heavy sigh, I drop down on one of the benches and bury my face in my hands. "I knew this was a bad idea. Why did I let him convince me I could do this? I made a total idiot of myself in front of all those people. And *him*."

"You did a good job," Dani says as she lowers herself next to me and rubs my back. "I know your mom would be proud of you."

I yank my hands from my face. "Proud of me? I totally bombed it. She would have been ashamed to have me for a daughter."

"The important thing is that you tried," Ally says. "You put your heart and soul into it. That's what your mother would have been proud of."

"It doesn't matter," I say as I yank off my gym clothes and dress into my T-shirt and jeans. "I'm never doing anything like this again. Teagyn's right—girls like me need to know their place. I should do what I do best: stay invisible."

"Don't let her get to you," Charlie says. "She's just a mean cheerleader. I'm proud that you told her off."

"Why does she have to be like that, though?" I ask as I sit back down. "Just because she's head cheerleader and the most popular girl at school, she has to be a jerk?"

"I overheard her arguing with her mom the other day," Ally tells us. "Her mom was putting so much pressure on her to win regionals so they could go to nationals. Coach Myers wants her daughter to follow in her footsteps. You should have seen Teagyn's face—I've never seen her look so small."

"So all this is her mom's fault." Charlie shakes her head. "What's with parents putting so much pressure on their kids?"

"Pressure or not, that's still no way to treat people," I say. "Whatever, let's just forget about the whole thing."

"Are you okay, though?" Ally asks.

"I will be once I pretend this never happened."

She slides her hand into mine and gives it a gentle squeeze. "You have us, remember? The Four Musketeers."

I smile. "I don't know what I would do without you guys. Seriously, you have no idea how much your friendship means to me."

Dani squeals as she throws her arms around me. "Yes, we do! We were all in your shoes once. And honestly, I always felt like our group wasn't complete. Three never seemed like a good enough number. Four is so much better."

"Agreed," Charlie says while Ally nods with a smile.

"Thanks, guys." I hug all three of them.

"I think this calls for ice cream," Dani says.

I laugh. "You don't have to ask me twice."

Chapter Fifteen
Brayden

I don't blame Kara for not wanting to join me and my friends at Mikey's tonight. She's still pretty upset about what happened at cheerleading tryouts today. I hope she'll be okay tomorrow. I don't like seeing people hurt or upset. And I certainly don't like seeing the girl who's doing something so kind for me upset. Kara doesn't gain anything from fake dating me, yet she's so willing? I've never met anyone as kind as her. The girl has a heart of gold.

I wonder why she doesn't have a boyfriend. Well, whoever he'll be, he'll be lucky to have her in his life.

"Brayden!" Jerry slugs my shoulder. "Where you at?"

I take in the huge table with most of the football players and cheerleaders occupying the chairs. Martha, the owner, knows to attach pretty much all the tables together to make room for us all. I guess our football team has quite a reputation here and the servers would do anything to please us. Honestly, I was a little uncomfortable at first, but the guys told me to take all the perks thrown my way. And last year, when Martha and her husband Ron learned I was Brock's brother, they treated me like a celebrity. Brock was The Man on campus. Everyone in town knew his name, pretty much bowed before his feet. But the great thing about my brother is that he didn't let any of that stuff get to his head. He knew he was a talented quarterback, but he was humble about it.

"Barrington," a guy from the team, Giorgio, calls, throwing an empty cup at my face.

"He's not here," another guy, Andrew, tells him. "Who are you thinking about today?" He chuckles. "Your secret college girlfriend?"

"He's dating that loser," Teagyn's friend says. "You should really dump her, Brayden."

"Bet he's got two girlfriends!" Giorgio says, holding out his hand for a slap. "My man Barrington is a legend!"

I give him a look. The guys are my friends, but sometimes it feels like they don't know me at all. I'd never date two girls at the same time. As for a real girlfriend? As much as I'd like one, football is my top priority right now. Sure, if the right girl came along, I'd give her my full attention. But so far? I haven't connected with anyone. I told Kara at the interview that I'm looking for someone special, and that's the truth. Honestly, I'm not really sure what that entails, but I figure I'll know when I find her.

"Brayden's not dating anyone," Teagyn says with a flirty grin. "He's waiting for football season to end so he can ask me out. It's great how dedicated you are, Brayden." She bats her eyelashes.

I try not to glare at her. I don't like the way she spoke to Kara at tryouts. No one deserves to be treated that way.

DeAngelo chortles, lightly punching my arm. "Ooh, you hear that, man? Teagyn just called you out. What you guys say? Think it's time for Edenbury High's It Couple to finally get together?"

The table whoops and cheers. Teagyn continues to bat her lashes, and I'm about to lose my mind at how careless she is of other people's feelings. Kara may not be popular or run in her circles, but she's a *human being*.

"I have a girlfriend, and she's amazing." Getting to my feet, I mutter that I'm going to the bathroom. Before I even make it to the door, heels clack behind me and a hand latches onto my arm, stopping me in place.

"Brayden, is something wrong?" Teagyn asks with eyes as large as the lights dangling from the ceiling.

I yank my arm free. "Why did you treat Kara like that?"

She purses her lips. "Like what?"

I throw my hands up. "Like she was less than you. You purposely dissed her in front of all the other kids. You embarrassed her."

"But Brayden, you were there. You saw she wasn't good enough. I'm sorry, but I can't worry about someone else's feelings. I'm trying to build a strong team here, a team that will take us to nationals." She places her hand on my arm again. "You know what that's like, don't you? Wanting to be the best, hoping to be the best."

I pull free again. "Yeah, I get that, but you didn't have to be a jerk about it. She's human, she has feelings. And she's my girlfriend."

Sure, maybe she's my fake girlfriend, but she's a good friend. A good person. A good person who didn't deserve that from Teagyn.

She rolls her eyes. "I still don't know what you see in her."

I rake my hand through my hair. "This conversation is over, Teagyn. And don't talk to my girlfriend that way again."

I make a move to leave, but she grabs my arm. "Admit it, your girlfriend doesn't have what it takes to be a cheerleader. I wasn't a jerk about it, I was just being honest. It's better for her to learn that now. I did her a favor."

Even if Kara didn't perform well today, cheerleading is important to her. I don't know why, but I could read it on her face. And yes, building a strong team is important and so is winning competitions, but I'm sure Kara *does* have what it takes, she just needs practice. And some confidence.

"You know what favor you could have done for her?" I ask. "Given her a chance."

I'm about to leave again, but she calls after me, stopping me in place. "It's sweet that you're so protective of her, but you're only hurting her instead of helping her." She steps closer to me. "I'm sorry, but your girlfriend didn't make the cut and she needs to accept that. You need to accept that. Felicia Montgomery will make a great cheerleader and she'll take us places." She taps me on the chest, gives me a smile, and walks off.

I frown after her, wishing I could do something, but what can I do? I can't convince or force Teagyn to give Kara a chance. I can't do anything.

But one thing I know for sure? I can't stay at the diner a second longer. After returning to my table, I tell everyone I'm heading out.

DeAngelo, who's in the middle of laughing at something Giorgio says, stops and looks up at me. "You okay, man?"

"Fine. Something came up at home and I need to jet. See you guys tomorrow."

A few slap me on the back or give me fist bumps before I leave the diner, thanking Martha for the meal. I walk through the door and let the warm late September breeze wrap around me.

I get in my car and pull my phone from my pocket, scrolling through my texts until I find the person I'm looking for.

I haven't spoken to Kara since she ran out of the gym a few hours ago. I chased after her, but she slipped into the girls' locker room. I could have waited outside, but I figured she wanted to be left alone. I'm not her real boyfriend after all, and something told me she wouldn't have appreciated my coming after her.

But as I sit in my car, replaying the conversation with Teagyn and the events that happened, I *know* I'd be a real jerk if I at least didn't ask her if she's okay. Real boyfriend or not, it's definitely something a friend would do.

Brayden: Hey, Kara. What's up? How are you?

Her response arrives a few minutes later.

Kara: Hi! I'm okay.

Brayden: Just okay?

Brayden: Because if you want to talk about what happened today, I'm here.

She doesn't respond and I stare down at my phone, wondering if maybe it was a bad idea to bring it up. I don't want to hurt her feelings.

Kara: Really?

Brayden: Sure. What are boyfriends for?

A pause.

Kara: But you're not my boyfriend. Not my real one anyway.

Brayden: So tell your fake boyfriend how you're doing. If you want to, of course. If you want to just forget the whole thing, I'm game.

Another few minutes of silence. I'm about to ask her again if she's okay, when her answer comes.

Kara: There isn't much to talk about. I made a fool of myself and that's that. I don't have what it takes.

Brayden: I wish you wouldn't give up. I thought you were great.

Kara: You did?

Brayden: I mean, I'm no expert, but I would definitely want you cheering me on at my next game. But you don't have to be a cheerleader to do that.

Kara: I just...

I wait for her to say more, but she doesn't.

Brayden: You just what?

Kara: Nothing. It's stupid.

Brayden: Nothing you say can ever be stupid, but if you don't want to tell me, it's cool.

Kara: I just wanted to…cheerleading was important to me. But I guess I just have to accept that it'll never happen. That girl they chose? Did you see her? She was amazing. She didn't make an idiot of herself like I did.

I tap out a text, telling her not to be so hard on herself, but stop when she tells me she doesn't want to talk about it anymore.

Kara: I have lots of homework. Thanks for texting me, boyfriend. I'll see you tomorrow.

I'm left with half a text written, unsure if I should send it. She wishes to drop the subject and I'd be a jerk if I continued the conversation. So I delete it, wish her a good night, then toss my phone onto the passenger seat.

The drive home takes about fifteen minutes. The kitchen is in chaos with Mom and Bailey cleaning up the mess they made baking cakes and cookies.

Bailey waves me over. "Bray! Look what we made!" She points to the racks of cookies cooling off, her face smeared with batter. Chuckling, I make my way over to her, wipe the mess off her cheeks with my thumbs, then bend over her to reach for a cookie, making sure not to hurt her.

"These look and smell delicious," I tell her. "Were you Mom's good little helper?"

She nods vehemently.

Mom laughs. "She helped make the mess, that's for sure." She grins at my sister, though the smile doesn't quite reach her eyes. "I think she inherited the baking gene."

Bailey lifts her arms over her head, cheering.

My parents smile at one another, but it's lacking the warmth it did years ago, before Brock died. Things have been continuing to go well between them, but I know that could always change. Maybe they're finally coming to terms with my brother's sudden death, or maybe they're pushing it aside for my and my sister's sake. Either way, I hope they don't return to shadows of their former selves like they did the months following Brock's death. Mom was so broken I had to take care of my sister, make sure she got to school on time, that she had enough to eat, that she was happy. Dad helped, too, but he was just as broken. Eventually, my parents got back into the rhythm of things. I often wondered if the only reason they got up in the morning was because they had two other kids to care for.

"Brayden!" Bailey tugs my sleeve. "You didn't taste the cookie."

I glance down at it. I've been holding it in my hand for so long the chocolate chips are starting to melt and stain my palm. "You're right." I bite into it and my eyes light up. "Perfect. Just like Mom's."

She beams.

Smiling, I ruffle her hair. I take another bite and I'm brought back to a few days ago, when Kara and I did that interview for the school paper. It's weird how we're fake dating now, that all it took was for one interview to possibly change my life forever. If not for Kara, I wouldn't have a chance to get close to a recruiter. And if things work out with her dad…

"Brayden! You only took one."

"Brayden just ate dinner at Mikey's, honey," Dad tells my little sister. "Let's not stuff him, all right?"

She giggles. "A stuffed Brayden, like my bunny."

I wrinkle my nose, imitating a rabbit. "Can your stuffed bunny do this?" I grab her by the waist and swing her onto my shoulders.

"Fun!"

I spend the rest of the evening playing prince to her princess and granting her every wish she desires. Later, she sits with me at my desk, watching with wide eyes as I work on my math homework.

"That looks hard," she says. "Am I gonna have to do that stuff?"

I slide her onto my lap. "Sure, but not for a few years."

She stares at my trig. "But what's all this mean?"

I laugh, rubbing the back of my neck. "Honestly? I don't really know. But I know how to do the work and that's all that matters."

She continues to stare at it. "I'm gonna be smart when I'm old like you."

I give her a face. "Who you calling old?"

"You're sixteen and I'm five. That's old."

I laugh, shaking my head. "Enjoy being a kid, Bay. Because before you know it, the years will fly by and you'll find yourself doing everything you can to get into the school of your dreams and make your parents and brother proud of you."

She blinks at me. "You're weird." Then she climbs off my lap and hops out of my room.

Chapter Sixteen

Sleep slowly leaves my body as a strange sound comes from my bedroom window. Rolling onto my stomach, I open one eye. It's still dark out on a Saturday morning, so whatever that was, I probably dreamed it. Shutting my eyes, I try to catch some more sleep. Weekends are the best because it's an excuse to be lazy, to forget my problems for a little while. The worst part about sleeping in? Is that I remember all the terrible things that happened the past week. Like the debacle at cheerleading tryouts. I try to shove it to the recesses of my mind, but that's kind of impossible when I remember that Brayden was there. He saw the whole thing. He was so nice to text me after and ask if I was okay, but I was so embarrassed about the whole thing. And yesterday at school, we didn't broach the subject, which I was so grateful for. And I sat with my friends at lunch instead of at the popular table. But the memory didn't stop torturing me throughout the entire day.

The sound comes from my window again and my eyes pop open once more. Is that a branch or something?

Quarterbacks Don't Fall For Invisible Girls

Shutting my eyes, I try to let the sleep wash over me, but it's knocked away when I hear that sound again. It's too soft to be a branch. Ugh. Now I have to climb out of my comfortable bed to make sure my window isn't cracking.

I pad over to the window and squint through the fuzziness of sleep. And my eyes bulge out. Because standing outside my window is none other than the man of my dreams, my fake boyfriend, star quarterback Brayden Barrington. Throwing rocks at my window.

He's wearing a tight white tank that exposes his delicious muscles, a band on his forehead that pushes his gorgeous hair out of his eyes, and shorts.

He grins up at me, his eyes flashing with excitement. That look alone can make any girl go weak at the knees.

He waves, his smile growing larger.

I open my window and lean out. "What are you doing here?" I hiss.

He waves again. "Come running with me."

I glance at the time, then scowl at him. "It's five in the morning! Are you insane?"

He chuckles. "Come run with me!" he calls.

I cringe. He's going to wake up my dad. He's always been a light sleeper, but it's gotten worse ever since Mom died.

"No!" I nearly bark. "It's Saturday."

He shakes his head, laughing. "Move those lazy bones and come with me, Kara."

Did I mention I love when he says my name? I'm almost tempted to drop everything and do whatever he asks me.

Almost.

"Come on!" he presses. "It'll be fun and it'll get you in shape."

"Are you calling me fat?"

"No way! But it wouldn't kill you to go for a run and spend some time with your awesome boyfriend."

He's cute when he's cocky, isn't he?

I give him a crooked smile. "Who said you're awesome?"

He laughs. "Just get your butt down here, girlfriend!"

I shake my head resolutely. "No way am I going for a run at five in the morning on a Saturday."

He pouts, locking his fingers together and lifting them over his head. "Pweaty Pwease?"

I can't stop the giggle bursting from my mouth. I never knew this guy could be so goofy. He's always so calm and cool, so comfortable and sexy. But he's got this fun side that I love. He makes me laugh.

"Kara! Please!"

"Why is this so important to you?"

"Kara?" a voice says from behind me. Whirling around, I find my dad standing there, rubbing the sleep from his eyes and yawning. "What's all that shouting?"

I freeze. "Dad! You're up."

He takes in my leaning out the window. "Who are you talking to?"

I giggle like crazy, like I always do when I'm nervous. "It's nothing. I was just yelling at a raccoon."

He looks at me like I fell from Mars. I definitely feel like I have.

He approaches the window and peers out. His eyes widen when he notices the hot guy standing there bent over and pleading. "Is that…?"

"My boyfriend, yes," I say loudly enough for Brayden to hear.

Brayden's head shoots up and he jumps to his feet, placing his hands at his sides like he's in boot camp.

"Hello, sir," Brayden greets, and I note the nerves on him. So, so cute.

Dad nods in greeting.

"Brayden wants to go running with me," I tell my dad. "So I'm going. Apparently, it's important to keep fit."

"All right." He glances at Brayden for a bit, like he's studying him, before removing himself from the window. Before he leaves my room, he faces me. "Honey, I'd like your boyfriend to come over for dinner tomorrow night. I think it's time we were introduced."

My hand flies to my hair, where I pull on the strands. "Oh! Yeah, sure. Of course. I mean, I'll need to ask him, but okay. Sure, yeah."

Dad chuckles. "No need to be so nervous, Kara. If you like the boy, I'm pretty sure I will as well."

"Right."

Panic seizes me because this isn't about me. It's about Brayden. And if he messes up his chance to make a good impression on my dad, then I don't know if I can forgive myself. It's all because of me that Dad woke up. If I would have just agreed to run with Brayden, then we wouldn't have woken up my dad. Darn it.

"He's amazing," I gush. "The best boyfriend I ever had." The only (fake) boyfriend I ever had, but who's really counting?

Dad smiles. "Then I'm really looking forward to meeting him tomorrow night."

My chest heaves as he leaves my room. I zoom over to the window and find Brayden pacing, running his hand through his hair.

"Brayden," I hiss. He glances up. "I'll be down in a few minutes."

"Okay, girlfriend."

I giggle more than I should before shutting the window and rummaging through my closet for something to wear. What does one wear when they go running? I'm about to text my friends, but remember it's freaking five in the morning and most people are still in bed.

But despite the early hour, this is exciting, isn't it? To run with Brayden, feel the wind in my hair, to be so close to him...

I snap out of it and grab a sweatshirt and sweatpants, throw them on, then rush downstairs and fling the door open. Brayden sits on the front porch, elbows resting on his knees, and chin on his hands.

"You okay?" I ask.

His head snaps up and he gives me a weak smile. "I'm sorry I woke up your dad. Did I screw up my chance to impress him?"

I drop down next to him. "I don't think so. He wants you

to come over for dinner tomorrow night."

His eyes widen. "Really?"

I laugh. "Yeah. Now's your chance to knock him off his feet with your charm and talent."

He laughs, too. "Thanks. I'm really looking forward to it. And please tell him I'd love to come over for dinner."

"Yep." I stand. "But first we have some running to do. Am I dressed right?"

He scans me from top to bottom. "Perfect. Have you ever done this before?"

I gesture to myself. "Does this look like a body that works out?" I'm not fat, but I'm not as skinny as Teagyn and her cheerleaders. But I'm fine with my weight.

"I'm not sure if that's a trick question," he admits.

I wave my hand. "I never run. But I guess it could be fun, if it wasn't five in the morning. Do you always do this?"

He nods as he leads me away from my house. "Pretty much. It was something my dad always did with me and Brock when we were kids. It was our dad/son bonding time. And after my dad hurt his knee and couldn't run anymore, my brother and I kept the tradition. Even my little sister wishes she could come, but she's too young."

I gape at him. "Every morning? Talk about dedication."

He nods as we meet the main road and he starts increasing his pace. I follow his every move. So far so good. "I'm very dedicated to things that are important to me. Like my family, friends, football."

"That's great. You'd totally be a dedicated boyfriend." My

eyes widen when I hear what left my lips. Why do I sometimes blurt out my thoughts? They're meant to be private.

His smile is warm. "Thanks. Is it okay if we go a little faster?"

"Sure."

We up our speed, but only by a little.

"Is it okay if I ask why you don't have a girlfriend?" I say after a little bit. "Off the record, of course. I know you mentioned you wanted someone special, but haven't you found anyone at school who fits that description?"

He's quiet as he mulls it over.

"Sorry if that's too personal," I say. "I tend to get a little nosy sometimes." Blame that on my lack of experience in the friendship department.

He shakes his head. "It's fine. I'd rather talk about the article, though. How's it coming along?"

"I'm nearly finished and need to give it to Martina to read before it can go to press. The issue should be out next week."

"Next week? Nice. I'm looking forward to reading it." He gives me a sideways smile. "Any chance I can steal a peek at it before you send it in?"

I twirl some loose strands of hair that escaped my ponytail. "Uh...wow. I don't know. I bet Martina wouldn't like that."

"No worries, just thought I'd ask." He grins. "I'll read it along with all the other kids and teachers and faculty."

"Assuming they'll read it."

He turns his head to me. "Why do you say that?"

I shrug. "You know the paper doesn't reach many readers.

Quarterbacks Don't Fall For Invisible Girls

Most aren't interested or think it's so outdated. But I like that we have a physical paper. It makes it feel more…real, you know?"

"Yeah, I get it. It's something you can hold in your hands, turn the pages and get sucked into the words on the page."

I nod. He gets it.

We decide to go even faster and I know my partner wants to zoom ahead. But he keeps close to me, making sure I'm okay. He's not doing it in a macho, condescending way because I'm some weak girl. No, he's just making sure I'm not overdoing it on my first run.

When an hour passes, he leads us into a park a few miles away from my house. Wow, I didn't realize how long we've been running. If I keep this up, I'll be a pro at this. Yeah, sure. But it's definitely fun. I can see myself doing this again with him. Maybe not at five in the morning, though.

"Come, I want to show you something," he tells me.

He motions for us to take a turn toward an area where there are a few trees and large boulders. There's a clearing in the center and I gasp as I take in the beautiful orange and red colors of the sunrise.

Brayden takes hold of my arm and lowers us on one of the boulders. I can't take my eyes off the magnificent sunrise. Nature is seriously the most wondrous thing in the world.

"Wow," I breathe, slowly bringing my eyes to him. "Is this what you wanted to show me?"

He grins. "Why do you think I asked you to run this early?"

I playfully slug his arm. "You could have given me an extra

hour of sleep and just brought me here instead of running." I shake my head. "Just kidding. It was actually lots of fun. Thanks. And thanks for sharing this with me. It's spectacular."

He leans back on the boulder. "It really is, isn't it? My dad used to take Brock and me here. And when he and my mom were dating, he brought her here. They didn't run, though. He was never able to get her out of bed for that."

I laugh. "Your parents sound like good people."

His smile is strained. "They are." He averts his gaze to the sunrise, suddenly uncomfortable. I hope I didn't offend him. Or pry too much. I just love listening to him talk. About anything.

We watch the sunrise together, and my breath is knocked out of me. Sometimes I get annoyed when the sun blinds me in the morning, but I'm not going to feel that way anymore. Because this is the most amazing thing I've ever seen.

Glancing at Brayden, I wonder how many girls he's brought out here and shared this with, then I remember it doesn't matter.

He turns to me, his smile dropping. "What's wrong?"

"Nothing. You never answered me why you don't date anyone at school. It's none of my business, but I'm curious."

He sits up. "I can ask you why you don't have a boyfriend."

"I do." I wink. "He's sitting right beside me."

He chuckles. "Touché."

He and I stare at the sun that has already risen in the sky. Then I keep my eyes on him, loving the way he marvels at the world.

Quarterbacks Don't Fall For Invisible Girls

We remain sitting for a few more minutes, not saying much to each other, but loving each other's company. Well, at least I am. I hope he's enjoying mine, too.

When we've had enough of the sun beating down on us, Brayden takes me to a small coffee shop a few blocks away, where we buy milkshakes and donuts. Settling down at one of the tables, we talk a little more about the newspaper and how I got into it. He listens intently as I tell him how important it is for me to be part of something that matters.

"Not that the newspaper matters to most kids at school," I say with a laugh as I take a bite of my donut. "But who knows? Maybe after next week, after kids read about our *amazing* quarterback, we'll have more readers."

He chuckles. "I hope so, too." He stands. "Ready to go home?"

"Sure."

Our run back to my house is slow because we both just stuffed our stomachs and don't want to get sick. He tells me some memories of when he, his dad, and brother ran together. Like when Brock nearly tumbled down a hill or when his dad thought he heard a bear in the woods.

When we reach my house, I wish I could turn back time. Just to give me and Brayden some more time to spend together. But then it hits me that I'll see him tomorrow for dinner with Dad.

Brayden must share my thoughts because he swallows as he glances at the closed front door. "Tell your dad hi for me and that I'm looking forward to meeting him."

"Okay."

We just stand there looking at each other. He seems to be deep in thought, probably about my dad. I need to keep telling myself that all of this isn't about me—it's about him. We're trying to pave an amazing future for him.

I shift from one foot to the other, causing the boards on the porch to creak. Brayden's eyes snap to mine, knocked out of his thoughts. "So I'll see you?"

I nod. "Yeah, see you."

He watches me as I step to the door and twist it open. Before I slip inside, I give him a small smile and wave. He returns it, the corners of his lips trembling a little.

Tomorrow is very important to him, and I'll do whatever I can to help.

Chapter Seventeen

"Maybe I bit off more than I can chew," I mutter as I squint at my phone. I found a recipe online for chicken alfredo, one that didn't look too complicated. But I have zero knowledge of cooking. At least I know he'll like the chocolate chip cookies I baked.

"You need help there, pumpkin?" Dad calls from the living room, where he's watching a football game.

"No!" I call. Which is a total lie. I'm drowning here. But I want to do this all by myself. I know how nervous Brayden is to meet my dad, and I thought I could soften my dad up by preparing a delicious meal. Don't they say good food cures everything? But if he gets poisoned...yeah, not good.

"Ugh," I groan as I read over the directions for the millionth time. Why is this so hard?

I know, I'm putting way too much pressure on myself for a fake boyfriend. I mean, Brayden should win my dad over on his own, right? By being his kind, charming self. But I won't lie that a part of me isn't trying to impress him. The way to a man's heart is through his stomach and all that. Not sure if it's true or if I believe that, but good food always helps.

When all fails, turn to your friends.

Kara: Help! Brayden's coming in less than two hours and I have no idea what I'm doing!

Charlie: You should have just made mac and cheese. That's the easiest.

Kara: Mac and cheese for my boyfriend???

Charlie: Not your boyfriend.

Kara: You know what I mean!

Ally: Sorry, I don't know how to cook.

Dani: My mom's an awesome cook, but she's not home right now. I'll see if I can text her.

Kara: Thanks, you're a lifesaver!

And a lifesaver, she is. Her mom gives her some pointers, which she passes over to me. And lo and behold, I actually have a dish.

How on earth did I survive all these years without friends?

"Something smells really good," Dad says as he enters the kitchen. He reaches for a cookie, but I slap his hand away with a spatula.

"Hands off the cookies!"

"This boy must be something special," he says with a laugh. "I've never seen you so bent out of shape."

"Yeah," I mutter as I turn to the stove. If only he saw me the way I see him.

"Can't wait to meet him," he says, then returns to the living room.

Just to make sure everything's going to plan, I shoot off a quick text to Brayden.

Kara: **Still on for 7:00 tonight?**

Brayden: **For sure. Already got my tux on.**

Kara: **Haha.**

Brayden: **I hope he likes me.**

Kara: **He'll love you.**

Brayden: **I don't know. Sometimes my nerves get the better of me.**

Kara: **Just be yourself and you'll be fine. That's what my dad loves most in players—seeing the real person inside. And you've got a great personality and a kind heart, so you have nothing to worry about.**

Brayden: **You really see me that way?**

My cheeks turn bright red. Ugh, why did I text that? I guess it's easier to let go when I'm texting and not standing face to face with him.

Kara: **Sure.**

Brayden: **Thanks. That means a lot. And you have a kind heart, too, Kara. I can't imagine many people agreeing to do this like you are. If this works out, I'll be forever in your debt.**

Kara: **Don't see it like that. I don't want you to feel like you owe me anything.**

Brayden: **We're kind of getting ahead of ourselves aren't we? Tonight might not go the way we want.**

Kara: **Fingers crossed.**

Brayden: **See ya at 7:00 on the dot. Because I know**

your dad likes punctuality.

Kara: You bet.

Once everything is in order in the kitchen, I race up to take a shower and then dress into a pretty dress. Not too formal, but not too casual, either. As for makeup? Ugh, I still haven't figured out most of it, but I do put on some lipstick and eye shadow. That's the best I can do for now.

For the next hour, I pace in my room, imagining different scenarios. My dad falling in love with Brayden and recruiting him on the spot—would that mean our arrangement would be over and we'd return to ignoring each other at school? Or would he at least say hi?

The next scenario is my dad hating him. That would definitely put an end to our arrangement and Brayden would avoid me at all costs. Ugh, I hope that doesn't happen.

The doorbell rings, nearly sending me flying to the ceiling. Is it time already?

"Is that him?" Dad calls from downstairs. "He's twenty minutes early."

"Don't answer!" I yell as I race out of my room and nearly tumble down the stairs. "I got it."

"Okay, okay," he says, holding up his hands. "I'll be in the living room. You must really like this boy," he mutters as he lowers himself on the couch.

I run my hands down my dress, straightening out the creases. Then I quickly glance in the hallway mirror to look at my reflection. Ugh, my hair is so flat. I tried using a curling iron, but that didn't help. I wish my hair was like Dani's—long and wavy and glossy. Mine just sits on my shoulders like a lazy cat.

The doorbell rings again.

"Are you going to let the poor boy just stand out there?" Dad calls with a chuckle.

Taking a deep breath, I close my fingers over the knob and pull the door open. Brayden stands there with a bottle and flowers in his hands. He's dressed in a dark blue dress shirt and black pants.

"Hi," he says with a nervous laugh.

"Hi! You look great! I love your shirt."

"Thanks. You look great, too. I don't think I've ever seen you in a dress."

I stare down at my outfit. "You haven't? Oh, I guess not."

"I like it." He holds out the bottle. "For your dad."

"You brought wine?" I gasp. That will so not make a good impression on my dad.

"Wine?" he asks with wide eyes. He quickly studies the label. "For a second, I thought I grabbed the wrong bottle. It's sparkling water."

"Oh," I say, laughing stupidly. "Yeah, that's better than wine."

"I didn't know what to bring for your dad. And this is for your mom." He holds up the flowers.

"Oh…" I take them from him. "My mom, um…"

"So there's the famous boyfriend." The door widens and Dad appears. "Hello again. Nice to see you from the door and not my daughter's window." Dad laughs.

"Mr. Gander, it's such an honor to meet you. I brought you sparkling water." He holds out the bottle. "And flowers for your wife." He nods to the flowers in my hands.

"My wife?" Dad asks, eyes flitting to mine. Ugh, this is such a mess. As my boyfriend, he should know my mom's dead. I didn't want to tell him because I didn't want him to feel sorry for me.

Brayden's confused eyes travel from me, to my dad, back to me.

"Unfortunately, my wife passed away three years ago," Dad says. "But I'm sure my little pumpkin would love the flowers."

"Dad," I groan. "Do you have to call me that in front of Brayden?"

"I sure do," he says as he teasingly tugs on my ear.

"Dad!"

Brayden laughs. "You guys seem very close."

"We're all each other has," Dad says. He motions with his hands. "Come in, come in."

Brayden smiles at me as he steps into the house and scans around. On the outside, he looks cool and calm. But I notice the way he clenches his hands at his sides, and how he's constantly rubbing the back of his neck. He's so nervous. It's kind of adorable. But it's my mission to help him achieve his goals.

"Your home is lovely," he says.

"My wife designed it all," Dad says with a pained smile. "If you knew my wife, you'd know this was her touch."

"I'm sorry I never met her. She must have been an amazing

person, especially to have raised a daughter as special as Kara."

Special? Does he really think so? Or is he just trying to butter Dad up? Either way, I feel like I might turn to jelly.

Dad nods approvingly at me before giving Brayden a tour of the house. I take the time to check on the food to make sure it's not burned. Thankfully, it's not. I also want to give them some alone time. I know Dad will love Brayden once he gets to know him. Everyone loves him.

"Food's ready?" Dad asks as he and Brayden walk into the kitchen.

"Yeah," I say.

"Are those the same cookies I had the last time I was here?" Brayden asks as he eyes them. The way his eyes light up—it's so cute.

"Yep," I say with a laugh. "You can have some."

"You'll spoil your dinner," Dad says.

"Dad, we're not five."

He shrugs helplessly to Brayden. "It's hard raising a teen all by myself. Everything I say is wrong."

I gently slap his arm. "I'm not that bad."

He grins. "No, you're not. I think I got lucky." He wraps his arm around me and kisses the side of my face.

I know I should be a little embarrassed in front of Brayden, but I'm not. I just love these moments with Dad. Like he said, we're all each other has. I'm glad he and I are still close after the ordeal of losing Mom. We could have pulled apart, but we stuck together like glue.

"You hungry, Brayden?" Dad asks.

161

"Honestly? I'm starving."

"Then let's dig in."

We settle down at the table, with Dad at the head and Brayden and me side by side.

"Smells delicious," Brayden compliments.

"Let's hope it tastes as good as it smells," I say as I pass the dish to Dad. He takes a helping before passing it over to Brayden. But Brayden doesn't take a helping for himself. Holding the dish before me, he says, "Can I serve you?"

"Y-yeah," I stammer as I hold out my plate. With a large grin, he places quite a helping on my plate. My eyes trek to Dad, who wears a pleased smile on his face. Brayden is definitely winning brownie points.

Once my plate is full to the brim—literally—he serves himself and places the dish back on the table. I wait until both men take a bite of the food, too nervous to taste it myself. What if it tastes like mud? A bad meal could ruin tonight, and I can't let anything get in the way of Brayden fulfilling his dreams.

"Mmm," Brayden says after taking a bite. He cuts himself another piece and stuffs it into his mouth, like he can't get enough.

"Delicious, pumpkin," Dad says over a full mouth.

They're just being nice, right?

Tentatively, I cut a small piece and nibble on it. "Holy crap, it *is* good!"

Brayden and Dad laugh.

"It's because of Dani's mom. I have to thank her later."

"I think you inherited your mom's cooking talent," Dad says with a wink.

"I wish I inherited some of her other talents," I mutter.

Suddenly, I feel a warm hand rest on my knee. My eyes flit to Brayden, who gives me a sympathetic smile. He doesn't know exactly what I'm referring to, but oh my gosh, his hand is *on my knee*. Okay, not really because the fabric of my dress is in the way, but I feel the warmth of his skin. It radiates to every single part of my body, making me feel like I'm in a cocoon.

And just like that, it's over. He removes his hand and continues to eat.

"So tell me about your family, Brayden," Dad says as he cuts another slice of chicken. "Barrington rings a bell, but I can't place it."

"You probably heard of my brother, Brock Barrington," Brayden offers. "Or maybe my dad? He tried to go pro, but life was a little hard."

"Oh?" Dad asks.

"My grandfather was paralyzed when my dad was twelve, and my dad had to help support the family. He tried to balance football and a job, but it never really worked out. He had to say goodbye to his dreams. That's why my brother followed in his footsteps—he wanted to make my dad's dream come true." His gaze falls to his plate. "Now it's up to me to fulfill both their dreams."

Dad looks at him. "Did your brother quit playing?"

Brayden swallows hard before raising his head to Dad. "No. He died in a car accident two years ago."

"I'm so sorry. What a tragedy."

"It's been hard without him, but my little sister is a lot like him. Well, I guess she's trying to emulate me now. I don't know how much she remembers about Brock, since she was three when he died. But she's a little firecracker." He smiles. "Her dream is to follow in my footsteps and try to go pro. I know she can do it. She's the toughest kid I know."

"After two brothers, I'm sure she is," Dad says with a smile.

"Oh, but I baby her, too," Brayden says with a laugh. "She definitely is the princess of the family. A tough princess, though. If she were in a fairytale, she'd be the one riding a horse and rushing to save her prince."

I can't help but stare at him in a total daze. Can this guy be any more perfect?

"It sounds like you love your sister very much," Dad says.

"Yeah." Brayden plays around with his food. "After losing Brock, I guess I've grown attached to her. Maybe I'm a little overprotective. But the kid doesn't need anyone looking after her. She's a beast."

"Maybe I'll recruit her one day," Dad says as he takes another bite.

Brayden glances at him and smiles a little. "Yeah, hope so."

I can see the question in his eyes—what about me? Studying Dad, I have no idea what he thinks of him. Then again, I don't think he's ever seen him play.

"Brayden's such a good QB, Dad," I gush. "You need to watch him."

ome the opportunity will present itself."

How frustrating. I wish I could order Dad to come watch the game next Friday. But I know things aren't so simple. Brayden and I need to be patient.

"What are your goals, Brayden?" Dad asks.

"Well, my ultimate goal is to play for a pro team. As for other goals? I want to do well in school, enjoy my last two years of high school with my friends. Make the most of the experience. And be the best brother and son I can be."

"Great answers." Dad turns to me. "This was delicious, pumpkin. You should cook more often."

"No way! After such an ordeal, I swear I have some gray hair."

Brayden laughs softly. "I hope you didn't go through all that trouble just for me."

"I think my daughter likes you a lot," Dad teases.

My face probably redder than the reddest tomato, I gasp, "Dad!"

He shrugs. "My job is to embarrass you, honey. Especially in front of your boyfriend."

"Oh my gosh." I cover my face.

"Now, am I mistaken or did I see chocolate chip cookies?"

"I've been thinking about them since I got here," Brayden admits with a laugh.

My face still bright red, I slide off my chair and head to the counter, where I placed the cookies. Ugh, if I knew my dad would embarrass me like that, I would have ditched the meal

165

and let the two of them get to know each other.

Once I'm sure my face has regained its natural color, I return to the table with the plate of cookies and place it in the center of the table.

"They look even more delicious than the last time," Brayden says as he reaches for one and takes a bite. He sighs, his eyes fluttering shut. "Heaven."

"Last time?" Dad asks, eyebrows furrowed. "You two were alone here?"

"B-before we were together," I quickly say. "I wrote an article on Brayden for the school paper. Martina wanted me to dig deep and get to know the Lions' QB."

"You meant to say the Lions' *amazing* QB."

I laugh. "You still didn't forget that, huh?"

He grins and winks. "Never."

"I must say," Dad says as he leans back in his seat with another cookie, "you two make quite the cute couple."

I freeze, my face scorching hot. "No we don't! I mean...ugh." I cover my face again.

Dad chuckles. "It's fun teasing her."

"I'm so lucky to be your daughter," my muffled voice says.

"Can I offer to do the dishes?" Brayden asks, starting to collect my plate and Dad's.

Dad waves him away. "You two hang out in the living room. Mind you, I'll be right next door in the kitchen, so no funny business."

Funny business? Can someone please take that knife from the table and stab me through the heart? Thank you.

"I insist, sir," Brayden says.

Dad waves him away again. "I appreciate it, son. Go have fun with my daughter."

Brayden nods and smiles at me. "Wanna talk in the living room?"

I kind of want to run up to my room and disappear, but of course I can't do that. We need to pretend we're a real couple, and a real couple would sit on the couch and talk. I nod and walk into the living room, lowering myself on the couch. Brayden sits down next to me and smiles sweetly.

"Sorry about my dad," I whisper. "He's like so cool in front of all the guys he recruits, but at home he's a total goof."

"He's awesome, actually," Brayden says. "I really like him."

"Let's hope the feeling is mutual."

His forehead creases. "Do you think he doesn't like me? Did I do something wrong?"

"No, no," I quickly say. "You were perfect. The perfect gentleman, the perfect boyfriend. You even offered to do the dishes! You did great, dude."

He smiles in relief. "Thanks." His smile suddenly vanishes, his face growing serious. "Sorry about your mom, Kara. I didn't know."

"It's okay. You couldn't have possibly known if I didn't tell you." I grab a cushion and hug it to my chest. "It's um…hard to talk about her with strangers, you know? Sorry I didn't tell you…"

"No, I get it," he assures me. "It's sometimes hard to talk about Brock. But it feels good, too. Like I'm keeping his

167

memory alive. Everyone knew him and loved him, so they love talking about him."

"You must really miss him."

He nods with a pained look in his eyes. "Yeah. You must really miss your mom."

"That's why I wanted to try out for cheerleading," I admit. "My mom was a cheerleader at Edenbury High. Her picture is in the hallway."

His eyebrows lower. "Is that the same photo Coach Myers is in?"

"Yeah."

He thinks about it for a second, and then his eyes rove around the room, focusing on the photos of Mom hanging on the walls or in the picture frames. "You look like her."

"I do?"

"Yeah."

Warmth fills my insides. I know I look a lot like her—some people used to joke that we could be twins—but it's different hearing it from Brayden. I don't know why. Maybe because he *sees* me? But that's just wishful thinking. We barely know anything about each other.

Shifting on the couch, I say, "Do you want to watch something? There's this new show on Netflix I'm dying to watch."

"I should probably head home," he says. "Bailey's waiting for me to read her a bedtime story."

Disappointment washes over me, but at the same time I'm glad he's such a great older brother. "She must love when you tuck her into bed."

"She's the number one girl in my life," he says as we get to our feet.

We stand awkwardly at the door.

I reach for the knob and pull the door open. "Good night, Brayden."

He smiles sweetly. "Good night, Kara. And thanks for all this. Is your dad still around? I'd like to wish him good night and thank him for hosting me."

"One second. Dad?" I call.

There's some shuffling and then footsteps, and then Dad appears. He looks a little surprised, probably wondering where my boyfriend is running off to so early.

"Brayden's going home to tuck his little sister into bed and read her a bedtime story," I say.

"How sweet." I can see it in his eyes—Dad approves of him. I don't think Brayden notices it, since he seems a little nervous.

"I want to thank you for hosting me, Mr. Gander." Brayden holds out his hand. "I had a really great time."

Dad shakes his hand firmly. "Good grip there, son."

"Thanks," Brayden says with a nervous laugh. "Good night, Mr. Gander."

"Good night, Brayden."

Brayden nods to me before slipping out the door. I watch him make his way to his car and fold himself inside. The windows are tinted, so I can't see him, but he doesn't pull out of the curb. I can imagine him sitting in there and thinking about this evening, wondering if he made a good impression on Dad. I wonder if I'm in any of his thoughts, or if it's only Dad.

"What are you staring at, pumpkin?" Dad sticks his head out.

"Nothing," I say, closing the door. A second later, I hear Brayden drive away. I turn to face Dad, studying his expression closely. "So? What do you think?"

Dad heads back to the kitchen. "I think he's a good boy," he calls over his shoulder.

"What do you mean by that?" I ask as I follow him inside.

"He cares about his family, he has goals, he was very well behaved and well spoken. He's a good guy, honey. You chose well."

"Do you like him?" I press.

"Yes, I do."

My whole body sags with relief. "Will you come watch him play?"

"I told you, pumpkin. When the opportunity presents itself."

I know I need to be patient, but it's so frustrating! Then an idea pops into my head. "Dad, you should watch him at homecoming."

"Homecoming?" he asks as he loads the dishwasher. "Is that in two weeks?"

"Yep. You'll love watching Brayden play—"

"Sorry, honey. I'll be out of town that weekend, checking out a promising player in San Diego."

Ugh, seriously? Talk about rotten timing.

He rubs my arm. "I know you want to help him achieve his dreams, but if it's meant to happen, it'll happen. If he's as good a player as you claim, I guarantee it won't be long before I attend one of his games." He kisses my forehead. "Can you take care of the rest of the cleanup? I want to rest a bit on the couch."

"Sure."

As I finish tidying up, something once again dawns on me. If I push Dad to watch Brayden play and he recruits him, my arrangement with Brayden will be over. We wouldn't have a reason to hang out anymore.

But it would be selfish of me to stretch it out. Even though I want to spend eternity with him, I'll do whatever it takes to help him get recruited.

I guess I have to try to cherish every moment I have with him before it's gone.

Chapter Eighteen

The girls and I decide to get together at Dani's house. After school on Monday, we meet at her locker and head to the city bus, since she lives a few miles away from school.

"You're so lucky you live near school and can walk," Dani complains as we wait with all the other people for the bus. Kids from school and people from work, and many others.

"Sorry you have to take the bus every day," I tell her.

She waves her hand. "I'm used to it. Sort of. Not really."

"Sometimes it's not so bad," Ally says.

"She's trying to look at the positive," Charlie says with a frown. "But I don't think there's anything positive when it comes to the city bus."

It doesn't take too long for the bus to arrive. And like we expected, it's packed. I don't know why I'm surprised—our small town of Edenbury has only one bus route. And the school is located in the busiest part of town.

"Are we going to fit?" I stare at the people packed in like sardines.

Quarterbacks Don't Fall For Invisible Girls

"You'd be surprised how many people can fit on these things," Dani says as we wait in line. And like a miracle, we get on.

Let's just say the ride isn't a pleasant experience. I can't remember the last time I rode on one of these things—maybe when I was a kid?

"Bet you can't wait until you get a car, huh?" I say to Dani.

She smiles, but it looks like it's forced, and then she tears her gaze away. Huh. I wonder what that's about. I glance at Ally and Charlie, but they don't seem fazed by it.

We finally reach the stop and get off. I gulp in the delicious smell of fresh air.

Dani laughs at my expression. "Now you know why I prefer to get together at your houses." She nods to the right. "My house is this way."

I examine the neighborhood as I follow the others to her house. It's pretty obvious this is not the richest part of town. Dani leads us to a small house at the end of the block, one that seems slightly rundown.

She stops and turns to me. "So if it isn't obvious...this is how my family lives. I'm not embarrassed by it or anything. My parents are hardworking people."

I put my arm around her. "You have nothing to be embarrassed about."

She smiles thankfully. "Okay. Ready to see the inside? I promise it looks much nicer than the outside."

We walk up the few steps and Dani sticks her key in the lock. She wasn't kidding—the interior looks beautiful. There isn't a lot of space, but everything appears homey and inviting.

"It's beautiful," I tell her.

"Thanks. Mom?" she calls. "Are you home?"

Footsteps sound, and then a familiar-looking woman enters the hallway. "The lunch lady?" I ask. Then I catch myself and say with a smile, "Sorry. Hi, Mrs. Wood."

"Yeah," Dani says, looking slightly guilty. "Sorry I didn't tell you before. I guess I…I don't know, it was stupid."

"I told Danielle she could keep the secret if she wanted," Mrs. Wood says as she extends her hand to me. "I know it's not cool for your mom to be the lunch lady."

"But you're the best lunch lady in the world!" I say as I shake her hand. "You always ask me how my day is going. You have no idea how good that makes me feel."

"I noticed you seemed a little lonely," she admits. "I thought I could brighten your day."

"You did," I tell her. "It really made my day better."

I take a moment to study mother and daughter. They don't look very similar, other than that beautiful dark, wavy hair. But Mrs. Wood usually keeps it in a hairnet. It's no wonder no one at school could figure out they're related.

"And Mrs. Wood makes the most delicious food on the planet," Charlie says with a smile. "That's the only reason our school lunch doesn't suck."

Mrs. Wood waves her hand. "Oh, hush."

"I agree," Ally adds. "Sometimes I look forward to lunch because I know I'll eat something yummy."

Mrs. Wood's cheeks grow pink. "Thanks, sweetheart."

"By the way, thanks so much for helping me with my chicken alfredo," I say. "You seriously saved my butt."

"I heard this was to impress a boy?" she teases.

I give Dani a look.

"What?" She laughs with a shrug. "I don't keep any secrets from my mom."

I feel a pang in my chest as I watch the two of them giggle with each other. I miss having a mom to share secrets with.

"There's peanut brittle in the kitchen if you girls want a quick snack," Mrs. Wood tells us. "I'm heading out now to the Reyes's." She kisses Dani's cheek. "There's a casserole in the fridge. Can you bake it?"

"Sure. See you later, Mom."

She blows her a kiss and leaves.

"My mom cleans other people's houses," Dani tells me. "Lunch lady by day, cleaner at night."

"I love her," I say. "She's always so nice to me. She was the only person at school who noticed the Invisible Girl."

"She tries to stay out of the students' business," Dani says as she leads us to her room. "But she's also kind to everyone, even the jerks who barely look her way." Dani bounces on her bed and motions for us to join her. "She and I agreed on my first day of freshmen year that she wouldn't get involved in my school life. She said it was hard at first because she couldn't stand to see me so miserable without friends. But she never overstepped."

"She really is awesome," Ally says. "She secretly gives me an extra slice of cake. And that started before Dani and I were even friends."

I smile as I glance around. Dani's room is pretty small. There's a bed against the wall, a small dresser and matching closet, and a bookcase packed with books. There are posters of famous dancers all over the walls.

"What about your dad?" I ask Dani.

"He's a janitor for a huge office building. He works from morning to night. I don't know if you'll meet him, since he comes home pretty late." She leans back against the wall and stretches her arms over her head. "I sometimes work after school and on the weekends. Though my mom always tries to convince me not to work. She wants me to hang out with my friends and have fun. But it sucks to see my parents working so hard."

It really does suck for her parents. I know I'm lucky that my dad has a good job that pays well.

"Anyway, on to more interesting things," Dani says. "How was dinner last night with your dad and your boyfriend?"

"Fake boyfriend," Charlie reminds her.

"Whatever."

"Pretty great," I tell them. "He was perfect. I think my dad was taken by him."

Dani claps her hands. "Awesome."

"It would be if he didn't have selfish intentions," Charlie says.

I hold up my hand. "Don't accuse him of being selfish, Charlie. I agreed to the arrangement."

She sighs. "I know, you're right. I just don't like seeing my friend being used."

I give her a wry smile. "Even if this friend is a willing participant?"

She returns the smile. "Even if my friend is hopelessly in love with her assignment."

I chuckle lightly and start to fan myself. "He looked so sexy in dress clothes."

"I'll bet," Dani says with a grin.

"This would be so romantic if he was secretly in love with you, too," Ally says.

I sigh heavily. "Wouldn't it? But it's pretty obvious he only sees me as a means to an end. Maybe not even a friend."

"What do you mean?" Charlie asks the same time Dani says, "I'm sure he at least sees you as a friend."

I puff out some air. "I asked him if he wanted to watch Netflix with me after dinner, and he said he had to read his little sister a bedtime story."

"Ouch," Charlie says.

"That was sweet of him," Ally supplies. "That he wanted to hurry home to read to his sister. It was probably past her bedtime."

"Yeah." Charlie rubs her chin. "That *is* kind of sweet."

I moan as I face-plant on Dani's bed. "See why my crush on him only grows the more I get to know him?"

Ally rubs my back. "Maybe you should tell him how you feel."

My head springs up. "No way! He'll run for the hills faster than a cheetah."

"You don't know that."

"Sorry, Ally, but I'm with Kara on this one," Dani says. "This isn't one of your romance novels where both the guy and the girl secretly have feelings for each other. Kara will have to ride this out until it's over."

"And not get the guy," I say with a groan.

She gives me an apologetic smile.

"Join the club," Ally says. "Who knows if I'll ever have a boyfriend?"

"Me, either," Dani says.

"Count me out," Charlie grumbles. "I don't want a boyfriend."

I gape at her. "You don't?"

She shakes her head. "I don't do drama. And everyone knows boys are drama, drama, drama."

"But they're so worth the drama," Dani whines.

"That's what you think." Charlie throws her arm around Ally, who's the closest to her. "I have everyone I need right here."

"Thanks," I say. "I feel the same."

"But your life would be more complete if you had Brayden," Dani teases.

I sigh as I stare up at the ceiling. "Heck yeah." I look at all of them. "He asked me to go running with him on Saturday. At five o'clock in the morning. But it was so worth it because we watched the sunrise. It was so pretty. And romantic. Well, it would have been romantic if we were actually a couple. Could have been the perfect place to make out."

"Sucks," Dani says.

"It's fine," I say with a brave smile. "I'm just glad I was able to experience it with my crush."

"Are you sure you're okay, Kara?" Ally asks.

"I'm keeping my heart in check," I assure her.

She doesn't look so sure, but she doesn't say anything.

"And I'm so freakin' sore!" I complain. "I knew I was out of shape, but sheesh."

"Is that why you were ambling like a little old lady?" Charlie teases.

I grab a pillow and throw it at her face.

"No!" Dani cries. "No pillow fights. My room is too small!"

"Sorry." I put it aside.

"So," Dani says, "your fake boyfriend didn't want to watch Netflix with you. Will you settle for second best?"

"You guys are not second best," I say firmly.

"Shouldn't we do homework?" Charlie suggests.

Dani groans. "No! I want to watch Netflix with my friends."

"You guys go ahead," she says as she zips open her backpack and yanks out her notebook. "I'll get started on my homework. I have three papers to write for the cheerleaders and jocks, and then trig for a guy in theater."

My jaw hangs open. "Are you ditching us to do other people's homework?" I demand.

She shrugs. "Sorry."

"No. That is so not happening."

Dani rolls her eyes. "It's a doomed battle. Charlie loves school more than anything."

"You love school more than us?" I joke, though I'm not really joking.

"Of course not," she says. "But Netflix is a waste of time."

I clutch my heart like she stabbed me. "Did she just call Netflix a waste of time?"

Ally and Dani giggle. "You have a lot to learn, my friend," Dani says. She reaches for the remote and logs in to Netflix. "One hour, then we'll do homework."

I glance at Charlie.

She groans. "Fine. Just one hour."

But one hour turns to three. Then we freak out that we didn't do our homework and scramble to do it.

For the first time in a while, I don't think about Brayden. The epiphany knocks me hard over the head. I was having so much fun with my friends that he slipped my mind. Maybe getting over him won't be as hard as I thought.

Chapter Nineteen
Brayden

"Dude, what's up with you lately?" DeAngelo asks as he lightly punches my shoulder.

I glance at him and Jerry sitting at the table in the cafeteria. The cheerleaders went off to take care of something and some of my teammates ran to help them.

"Nothing," I mumble as I stab my fork in my meat. It's a little rubbery today, or maybe I'm not myself right now. I keep thinking about the dinner I had with Kara and Nigel Gander. Kara assured me I did well, but I'm not so sure. He didn't even consider watching me play—said he would when "the opportunity presented itself." What does that even mean? Everyone claims I'm an amazing quarterback, but if I can't get the attention of a recruiter like Mr. Gander, then what am I?

"Dude." Jerry slaps my arm. "Whatever it is, you've got it bad." He bends close so the other guys can't hear. "Is it the fake relationship? You suffering *that* much?"

My eyes shoot to the table at the back of the room, where

Kara is laughing with her friends. Suffering? I wouldn't call it that at all. Kara's cool and fun. And kind beyond measure. And the way she's smiling and laughing with her friends? Her entire face radiates joy. It makes me smile, too. It makes me want to make her smile more often, to see her face light up every moment of every day.

DeAngelo grips my shoulder, yanking my mind away from Kara. "Don't tell me you're falling for her, man."

"No way." Jerry laughs. "She's cool and all, but so not for you. She's smart and you're...well..."

I lightly punch him in the chest. "I'm smarter than your dumb butt."

He chuckles. "Finally, he's back. I was worried there for a second. What's got you all coiled up?"

I sigh, puffing out my cheeks. "I had dinner with Kara and her dad on Sunday."

DeAngelo asks, "How did it go?"

I want to shrug, but my shoulders are stiff. "I think it went well, but he didn't seem interested in me...as a potential recruit."

My friends glance at one another.

"Maybe you just need time," Jerry muses. "The man just met you and you can't expect him to drop whatever he's doing to watch you play. Be patient and it'll all work out." He slaps my arm. "You'll see."

I hope he's right, though I'm not really listening to him. I'm focused on Kara and that smile. For some strange reason, it does something to my stomach, something that's never happened before. I can't describe it because I'm not sure what it is.

"The girl knows it's fake, right?" DeAngelo asks. "You're not stringing her along and then going to break her heart, are you? Because from what I see, it's a fragile heart. Girls like her are like that."

I face him. "Like what?"

He shrugs. "You know, the ones who cry at those sappy romance movies and wait for their knights in shining armor to sweep them off their feet."

I furrow my brows as I watch Kara some more. She's not like that. Kara is strong and smart and driven. She lost her mom three years ago, and I know how difficult it is to lose someone close to you. I might be the only one who understands what she's been through.

"Don't tell me she's fallen for your charm," DeAngelo continues.

Jerry chuckles. "Wouldn't be the first time. How many girls have fallen for you? Got enough fingers to count them on? Maybe use your toes."

It's true that many girls have given me attention, but I've only given it back to a few, to ones whom I thought were special. Turned out most just wanted me for my looks or my reputation. I haven't been able to find a girl who sees past the quarterback, who gets to know me for me.

But it doesn't matter. Like I said, I'm focusing on football now. I wouldn't lie and say I wouldn't mind having that special bond with a girl, though.

Kara laughs from her table that's so far away, but somehow I hear it. I wish we could have been friends when we each experienced our losses. We would have been there for each other. I would have helped her get through her mom's death, even though I hadn't experienced something similar back then. And maybe she could have helped me deal with Brock's death. Maybe I could have done something to prevent my parents from growing so distant. They're much better now, but I know it'll take a while before they're back to themselves. If they ever get there.

"We're just teasing you, man," Jerry says.

"You mean you're jealous of him," DeAngelo corrects. He bends close. "Dude, you can have any girl here. *Any* girl. You can have Teagyn Myers, the hottest girl at Edenbury High. Yet you choose to remain single."

I give him a look. "I *do* have a girlfriend. And I'm focusing on my dream of going pro."

Jerry rolls his eyes. "I'm sure Kara won't mind you dating someone else. It's not like she likes you or you like her. And besides, how do you know she doesn't have a real boyfriend?"

My eyes shoot to her table, where she and her friends are huddled together in a heated conversation. I wonder about what.

And I also wonder if my friends are right. Kara told me she doesn't have a boyfriend, but maybe she's keeping him a secret. I don't know why the thought of her with another guy bothers me. I have no right.

"Yes!" Jerry cheers when he notices the cheerleaders and

the rest of our team enter the cafeteria and head this way.

I can't look at Teagyn. I know we run in the same circles and share friends, but I'm still not over how she treated Kara. I'll tolerate her because I have to, but as far as she and I are concerned? We're nothing to one another. Not even friends.

"Hey, Brayden." She shoots me a smile as she and the others settle down at the table. She stabs her fork in her lettuce. "Wasn't that history test insane?"

I nod pleasantly, only because I don't want to make a scene or split up our group of friends. If I wasn't quarterback and had a reputation to uphold, I'd march over to Kara's table and sit with her and her friends.

I quickly shake my head. What am I thinking? Who said they'd even want me? I might be a jock, but those girls don't care about that. They're intelligent and good students. They don't want someone who barely averages Bs among them.

Wow. Where is all this insecurity coming from? I've never felt like this before. I have doubted myself here and there, but never to this extreme.

Teagyn squeezes my bicep. "Brayden, it's such a shame you can't watch me practice. I feel like we'll win the competition if you're cheering for me in the stands."

I pull my arm free. "Sorry, got football." I busy myself with my pudding so she'll take the hint and leave me alone. I don't want to be rude about it, even though she deserves it. I'm not that kind of person.

The bell rings a few minutes later and Teagyn complains she hasn't finished her food. I shoot to my feet like I've got rockets attached to my sneakers and make way for Kara's locker. She's leaning against it, surrounded by her friends.

I rest my shoulder on a locker, watching her for a little bit, that smile so contagious I want to etch it into my memory forever. I know we'll go our separate ways once our arrangement is over, but I hope we'll remain friends. If we don't, at least I'll always remember that smile.

One of her friends, a girl with long dark hair, looks at me and grins. "Your boyfriend is waiting for you."

Kara's gaze flits to mine and she smiles. "Hi, Brayden. Want to meet my friends?"

"Sure." I head over and smile at each of them. They return friendly grins and greetings.

Kara motions with her hands. "This is Dani, Ally, and Charlie. Guys, this is Brayden."

Hmm. She didn't refer to me as her boyfriend. Is she embarrassed to be seen with someone not up to par with them academically? I don't know why that hurts me. I know she's way above me on the academic ladder. Girls like her would never choose the dumb jock.

Not that it matters. We're just friends.

Are we even that, though? Or are we just two people who have an arrangement where one gains and the other is doing it out of the goodness of her heart?

"Hi, nice to meet you all," I say. "You mind if I escort my girlfriend to her class?"

They step aside to allow Kara to pass. Dani grins at her, Ally nods, and Charlie just watches us like she's not sure about us or something.

I smile at Kara. "Ready?"

She shuts her locker, tells her friends she'll see them later, and follows me down the hall, hugging her books to her chest.

"Your friends seem nice," I tell her. "I like them. Though I don't think Charlie likes me. She seems suspicious and guarded."

She hugs her books tighter. "Yeah, she's not one hundred percent okay with our arrangement."

I lift a brow. "Oh, so they know we're faking."

She nods. "Don't worry, they won't tell my dad the truth. They know this is important to me because it's important to you."

I'm about to ask her why it's so important to her, but she continues, "Charlie thinks you're using me." She quickly holds up her hands. "But you're not, don't worry."

I stop walking. "But there's a truth to it, isn't there? You're not gaining anything from this."

She glances away, the tips of her ears growing red. "We've talked about this. I want to help you fulfill your dream. Here's my class. You're so sweet for walking me here."

I smile. "Thanks." My smile drops. "I hope Charlie doesn't think too low of me. She must not be a fan of jocks, huh?"

"I don't think that's true. She likes doing their homework, so I doubt she hates them. She needs them to satisfy her thirst for extra school work."

I blink at her. "What?"

She giggles loudly. Then her eyes widen and she covers her

mouth. "Sorry." Her face is beet red now.

"Don't be sorry. Your laugh is really cute."

Her face grows even redder, something I didn't think possible. "Oh, um. Thanks." She clears her throat. "Charlie does your friends' homework for them because she loves school and wants more work."

"Wow. I've never met anyone like her. Some of my friends told me a nerd does their homework for them, but I didn't know it was her..." I stop talking and shake my head. "I'm sorry. I shouldn't have called her a nerd."

Kara waves her hand. "She's fine being called that. She wears it like a crown."

"Still, it was rude of me."

"Have you ever asked a nerd to do your homework for you?" she asks.

I shake my head. "Never. I might not be the sharpest penny in the bunch, but I know the value of schoolwork. Coach would kick us off the team if we fail a class. That's probably why my friends just dump it on your friend. They can't be bothered with it."

Her smile is small, but I see so much in it. "It's great that you're so honest. You're different from the others."

I rub the back of my neck. "Sometimes I feel like I'm too different. I mean, I love my friends and we get along great, but sometimes I feel like they don't understand me."

Like they'd never imagine I actually have fun spending time with Kara. They assumed I was suffering. Why would I ever suffer with someone as amazing as her?

Quarterbacks Don't Fall For Invisible Girls

The bell rings before she has a chance to respond. I hate that I have to pull away from her, but I need to focus on my classes or else I'm off the team.

I stretch my arm over her shoulder, hauling her close to my chest like any boyfriend would do. "Catch you later, girlfriend." Then I turn on my heels and hurry to my classroom at the other end of the hallway.

Chapter Twenty

Martina was blown away by the article I wrote on Brayden when I handed it to her yesterday. It was a little last minute—the paper's coming out tomorrow!—because I kept rewriting it and rewriting it and rewriting it. Brayden is so much more than just words on a paper. He's...he's perfect. And no amount of words could capture that.

But Martina gave me a final deadline yesterday and I had no choice but to hand it in. She read it immediately, swallowing up the words. She told me I nailed the article and it's sure to be a success when it's released tomorrow.

I'm not so sure, but I'll try to be hopeful. Maybe she's right. Maybe we'll have more readers and the Edenbury High Times will finally be recognized.

I leave the newsroom and go out to the football field to watch Brayden practice. He's in his element right now, owning the field like it's his playground. He's seriously so good at this, so talented, so driven. It's a shame my dad can't see this, but I know we have to be patient. If I pressure my dad, it might mess up Brayden's chance.

Brayden's head shoots up as if he feels me watching him, and he waves enthusiastically. My heart picks up speed and my stomach does countless summersaults. I wave back, not able to hold back from beaming at him. Is it so terrible to admit he makes me feel really, really good? I know it's not healthy because we'll eventually end this, but I'll bask in it for the time being.

When practice is over, I wait for him at his locker. He smiles as soon as he sees me, wrapping his arm around me and pulling me close to his chest.

I'm definitely going to miss this when we're done with our arrangement, but I won't think about that now.

"You were amazing as usual," I tell him.

"Thanks." He pushes his fingers through his wet hair, droplets dripping down his cheek. "I was wondering if you want to hang out after school? Or do you have plans?"

"No, no plans," I quickly say. "My afternoon is totally free."

He grins. "Cool. Maybe we can go to the mall or to Mikey's or the park or something." He reaches into his locker for his phone and unlocks it. "Sorry, I just have to read this text from my mom." He scans it. "Oh, my parents are going out and I need to babysit my sister." He looks at me. "I guess we'll hang out another time...unless." His eyes light up. "Do you want to meet Bailey? She'll love you."

My mouth opens and closes, but no words come out. He wants me to meet his little sister? Isn't that something real girlfriends do?

I'm thinking way, way too deeply into this.

"Okay. But are you sure she'll like me? I don't have a lot of experience with kids."

He stuffs his phone into his jeans pocket. "Of course she will. What's there not to love? You're nice and funny and great to hang out with."

My face feels so hot I need to dump it in ice-cold water. He thinks I'm fun to hang out with? Me? Invisible Girl?

He leads me out the doors, to his car that's parked in the student lot. I freeze as it dawns on me that I'll be alone with him in his car. Just a few days ago, I wished to be in an enclosed space with him and now it looks like it'll finally happen.

He turns to me, holding open the passenger door. "Kara, you okay?"

I blink and nod. "Yeah, of course I'm okay. Why wouldn't I be?"

He laughs. "Then get in."

"Right." I slide in and he shuts the door, then runs around to his side and climbs in. Why did that feel so intimate? Like a real date?

"Buckle up," he tells me, nodding to my belt. I stretch it over my body and snap it shut. Then he pulls out of the lot.

"You have a nice car," I say, taking everything in. He's not the kind of driver who makes a mess in here and treats it like his second home.

"It was Brock's," he says, voice soft, eyes on the road. He

slowly brings them to me, smiles, then returns them to the road. "I wasn't sure if I wanted it at first. My parents were about to sell it, but I changed my mind last minute. Brock took such good care of it and I swore I would do the same. He saved up for it and bought it on his own. He didn't have to do that—my parents planned to surprise him on his sixteenth birthday, but he surprised them first and got it all on his own. And he told me he'd help me save up for mine when the time came."

"I wish I could have known him," I say. "He sounds like he was a really good person. I only know he was QB and very popular. Like you."

He shakes his head. "No, I'm not like him. Brock was friends with everyone. He had a way about himself—you know, like those people who can command a room? That was him. Everyone loved him."

"Everyone loves you."

He grins wryly. "Your friend Charlie doesn't." He sighs. "I don't think Brock would have done what I'm doing—fooling everyone into thinking I'm dating you just for a chance to be recruited into a good school."

I want to place my hand on his knee like he did to me at dinner, but I curl my fingers into my palm. I'm not brave enough.

"I don't see it that way," I tell him. "I mean, we're pretending, but it's not like anyone is getting hurt. And it's not *that* shocking that we're dating, is it? What am I saying? Of course it is." I shut my eyes, wishing I hadn't said that.

Seriously, I need more control over my mouth.

Brayden looks at me, then at the road, not saying a word. I have no idea what he's thinking, but it's obvious that he agrees that someone like him and someone like me have no business dating.

"It doesn't bother me that we're faking," I tell him. "And I don't think it should bother you either. Because at the end of the day, all that matters is you getting recruited."

He nods slowly. "But you're missing out on meeting a good guy."

"And you're missing out on meeting a great girl. Besides, no one would ever…" I press my lips together. Nope. I won't tell him that no one could ever like someone like me.

His eyes flit to mine for a second. "No one would what?"

I quickly shake my head. "Nothing. I forgot what we were talking about."

He stops by a red light and gives me his full attention. "You think guys wouldn't like you?"

My hand shoots to my hair and I pull on the strands. "Well…truth?"

"Off the record."

I take in a deep breath. "It's hard being the Invisible Girl."

"The what?"

I give him a look. "Don't tell me you've never heard of the Invisible Girl."

"No, I haven't. Who calls you that?"

The light turns green and he continues to drive. I just stare at his profile. I don't understand him. Is he telling me he genuinely has no clue what people call me, or is he just being nice?

He glances at me. "Kara, who calls you that?" His tone is full of concern and...care. He cares? Why?

I wave my hand. "Just some kids."

"Like Teagyn?"

I shrug. "Whatever. It is what it is."

"It's not," he insists. "You shouldn't let them call you that."

"But it's the truth. You didn't even know I existed until I asked you to do that interview." As soon as the words are out, I wish I could take them back. Darn it. I never meant to say that. The last thing I want to do is attack him.

He's quiet, his eyes on the road. I busy myself with looking out the window.

"You're wrong," he says after a little while. "You were never invisible to me. Maybe I didn't know you were on the paper or that you're so kind and fun and a great friend, but I knew you were smart and studious. I noticed you in class last year, how you were always the first to raise your hand when a teacher asked a question. Or how you nearly always handed in your test paper first, putting the rest of us to shame."

My heart skips a beat. He...noticed all that?

"I'm sorry I never talked to you," he continues. "You were just...at the top of the brain tower. You were so smart. And me? I was one of the dummies of the class."

"Brayden."

He laughs. "It's not like it's a lie. I barely average Bs and I'm okay with that. I know my strengths aren't in school.

Honestly, Kara, we're so different and run in different circles and our paths never crossed. But I wish they would have. I would have liked to have a friend like you."

I just stare at him. "You…you really mean that?"

He nods with a smile. "At least we can be good friends now."

I nod. Right. Friends. Because there's no chance in heck we can ever be more than that. He said it himself, we run in totally different circles. He belongs at the popular table and I'm with the…not popular kids.

"We're here," he announces.

I take in his house. It's larger than mine with a small garden in front, and a fountain designed as a football.

He gets out, runs around the car, and opens the door before I have a chance to get out. "You don't have to do that," I tell him as he shuts the door. "We're not really dating."

"So?" He nods to his house. "That's my home. What do you think?"

"That football fountain is so cute."

He laughs. "My mom got that for my dad as a gift. She had someone custom make it."

"Wow. Your parents are probably so in love."

He brushes his fingers through his hair. "They were…before my brother died. It's been tough on them, but they're pulling through." He smiles. "We'd better go inside so they can get to their meeting."

I follow him up the steps, where he stabs the key into the lock and pushes the door open. His house is pretty typical, not too rich, not too poor. Just normal.

The first room we enter is the kitchen, where a man and woman are working on dinner. The woman has the same sandy brown hair as Brayden.

"Hi, Mom and Dad. This is Kara," Brayden tells them, gesturing to me.

They both greet me warmly, and I notice their eyes are filled with pain and loss. But they go out of their way to make sure I'm comfortable, offering me something to eat and drink.

"You have to try my mom's cookies," Brayden says with a wink. Then he turns to his mom. "You've got some competition there, Mom. Kara's cookies are amazing."

His mom chuckles. "That's great to hear." She offers me and her son some. Brayden grabs a handful, winking at me again. The guy sure does love his cookies.

I bite into one and my eyes widen. "So good. Definitely better than mine."

Brayden shakes his head. "It's super close."

His mom smiles, though it doesn't reach her eyes. "Thank you."

"Kara's going to help me babysit Bailey, if that's okay?" Brayden asks. "I know Bails will have lots of fun with her."

"Sure, son," his dad says. "We'll be home in a few hours, but we prepared dinner. It just needs to be warmed up."

Brayden nods. His mom reaches up to kiss his cheek and his dad slaps his hand. Then they tell me it was nice to meet me, wish us a good day, call out goodbye to Bailey who must be upstairs, and leave the house.

Brayden watches them go with longing, lips pulled down in a frown. I inch closer to him, stretching my hand toward his, then yank it back. I wish I could touch him, comfort him, but I can't. It's like my heart is telling me to, but my brain is warning me it's a bad idea.

Brayden turns to me, shooting me an uncertain smile. "Sometimes it's hard to see them like this. They used to be so in love, so happy."

"They still love each other. They just need some time."

He nods unsurely, then his lips curl into a wide smile. "I think it's time we find the little princess."

I follow him up the stairs and into a room that's painted half pink and half blue. There are dolls scattered around and posters of many different football players and athletes adorning the walls.

"Bailey," Brayden sing-songs as he steps into the room, motioning for me to follow him. I walk close behind him as he ambles toward what looks like a fort made of pillows and bedding. "Where are you, Princess Bailey?"

He stops at the fort, chuckling, then turns around and pretends to search around the room for her.

"Where could the princess have run off to?" he says loudly. "It looks like she doesn't want to play with Prince Brayden and his new friend today."

A head peeks out from the opening of the fort. A little girl with identical hair as Brayden stares at me. She's wearing a Cinderella dress. "Who's that?"

Brayden whips around and his eyes widen in mock shock.

"There's the princess!"

She doesn't take her eyes off me. "Who is she?"

Brayden wraps his arm around me, gently pulling me close to his side. "This is my friend, Princess Kara. She's here to play with us."

Friend...he called me his friend. Well, I guess he wouldn't want to lie to his sister.

Bailey blinks at me, scanning me from top to bottom. "Do you like tea parties?"

"I guess?"

"Sports?"

I nod, even though I never play. But I like watching her brother, so that must count, right?

She scans me again. "Okay, you can play. I'll get you a tiara." She vanishes into her fort.

Brayden pulls me aside. "Sorry about the whole friend thing," he whispers. "I didn't want to tell her you're my girlfriend because she gets very attached to my girlfriends and I don't want her to get hurt when we, you know, break up."

I nod. "Right. Of course. That makes total sense."

He keeps his eyes on me, as if he wants to say more, but Bailey emerges from the fort with a golden tiara. She pushes it into my hands. "You have to wear it," she commands. Then she frowns at her brother, small hands on her hips. "Where's your crown?"

He holds up his hands defensively. "Sorry, I left it in my room. Be right back." He dashes out.

Bailey studies me. "Are you Bray's girlfriend?"

"No, just a friend."

She pulls over a chair, gets on, takes my tiara from my hand, and places it on my head. "Timmy from school said there's no such thing as boys and girls being friends. He said they can only be boyfriend and girlfriend." She climbs down and lugs the chair back to its place.

"Oh, there are lots of platonic relationships."

Her eyebrows furrow. "What's that?"

"Friends who are opposite genders."

She nods slowly. "Oh. So Timmy's wrong?"

"Yeah. Your brother and I are great friends. But just friends," I quickly add.

She narrows her eyes like she doesn't believe me. Am I *that* obvious that I'm into her brother?

Brayden sweeps into the room, a golden crown on his head and a royal red cloak around his shoulders. "Do I look presentable, Your Highness?"

Bailey nods with a lifted chin. "I want a tea party now."

Brayden salutes. "Sure thing. Why don't you girls have fun while I prepare everything?"

Bailey slips her hand into mine, giving Brayden a bright smile. "Yeah. Kara's nice. I like her. She told me Timmy was wrong about prognic relaships."

His eyebrows knit. "Huh?"

"Platonic relationships," I clarify. "I told her guys and girls could be just friends."

His eyes meet mine and it feels like he's staring at me for hours. But then he leaves the room.

"Wanna see the fort Bray made for me?" Bailey asks, jumping in place. "I helped, too, but I think I got in his way. He's *so* good at building stuff."

I smile at her. "Sure. I'd love to see your fort."

She yanks my hand to pull me inside. I hang back, my eyes on the small opening. "I don't think I'll fit. Maybe it's best I just peek in."

"Okay!" She disappears inside, holding the door open for me.

Bending on my knees, I peer inside. The floor is covered with pillows and cushions and she's got many toys lying around, dolls as well as action figures and electronic toys. It's like her own personal playroom.

"You like it?" she asks eagerly.

"I love it."

She slides out and hands me a piece of paper. "I drew that."

I glance down at it and see a man, woman, two older boys, and a little girl all holding hands. Their colors match their hair—all except for the dad have sandy brown hair. "It's beautiful," I tell her. "Is this your family?"

"Yeah, Mommy and Daddy and Bray." She taps the older brother. "That's Brock. I don't really remember him so much, but we have lots of videos with him. He taught Brayden how to build forts. And one time he was supposed to be watching me in the pool but he forgot and I almost drowned."

My eyes widen. "Really?"

She shrugs. "Yeah, but then he remembered me and everything was okay. He died when I was really little."

"I'm sorry."

Her eyebrows furrow. "Why do people say that? It's not their fault he died, is it?"

I shake my head. "No, but it's a way to show compassion and sympathy."

"Oh."

Footsteps sound in the hallway and then Brayden steps inside with a tray carrying a kettle and three cups. He sets the tray on the small table in her room and we gather around it. The chairs are kid-size and I have no idea how we'll sit down without smashing them to bits. But I'm surprised when Brayden lowers himself on one of them like it's no big deal.

"Princess Kara sits near me because I like her," Bailey says as she pulls me down on the chair beside her.

Brayden pouts. "Don't you like me?"

"Yeah, but she's the guest," she hisses to her brother. "And Annie will sit next to Brayden." She nods to the empty chair near her brother."

"Annie?" I ask.

Brayden bends close to whisper, "Her new imaginary friend from England. Her other friend Sally ran away, so we need to be nice to Annie so she'll stay."

I nod in understanding and smile at the empty chair. "It's so nice to meet you, Annie."

Bailey beams. "She likes you!" Then she straightens up like royalty. "Please pour the tea, Prince Bray." She says it with the most adorable British accent I've ever heard.

"Yes, milady," Brayden says, bowing his head. He, too,

speaks with a British accent.

He's about to pour some tea into her cup, but she holds up her hand, gesturing to me. "Where are your manners? The new princess first. And then Annie."

He bows his head. "Forgive me."

"Thank you," I say once he pours my drink.

"British accent!" Bailey demands.

I look from one sibling to the other, insecurity washing over me. "Oh, I'm not good at that. I don't know how."

Brayden smiles. "I'm sure you can do it. Besides, it's all fun. No one will judge you."

Bailey nods vehemently.

I clear my throat and try my best to form a British accent. "Thank you."

Bailey nods, pleased. Then she starts talking about her day, from morning to this very moment. Brayden watches her as if she's the most interesting person on the planet and my heart skips a beat. He's so...wonderful. Perfect. Oh, man. I'm totally in trouble now. If I thought my crush on him was massive before, now it's the size of the Grand Canyon.

As his sister talks, Brayden's eyes move to mine. I quickly avert my gaze. Does he know I was ogling him?

We drink and talk for about twenty more minutes before Bailey demands we do something fun.

"Like what?" I ask.

She jumps up and down. "Basketball!"

"You play basketball?"

She lifts her chin proudly. "Yes. And I wanna play. Please,

Bray?"

He laughs. "Sure, kid. Anything you want. Tonight is your night. Go change out of your princess clothes."

He and I slip out of the room so she can get changed. He leans in close to whisper in my ear, "Every night is a Bailey night." He chuckles, his breath warm on my cheek. I'm trying not to freak out that he's *this* close to me. It's not the first time, but every time seems new.

I smile at him. "You're such a fun older brother."

"Thanks. I try."

Bailey appears in the doorway a few minutes later. "I'm ready. And Annie's going to watch us. She's too scared to play."

"Are we going to the park?" I ask as we go down the stairs.

"Nope. Got our own hoop in the backyard."

Bailey takes my hand, pulling me toward the door leading to the backyard. Brayden follows close behind. He pulls the door open and I take in the pretty yard behind the house. There's a large pool, a barbeque, a small garden, and a basketball hoop.

"I didn't know you play," I say to Brayden. "You're not on the school basketball team, are you?"

Laughing, he shakes his head. "No. I'm not good. I just play for fun." He taps his chin. "How are we doing this?"

"Girls vs. boy!" Bailey says as she bounces in place.

Brayden and I exchange a glance. He raises an eyebrow. "What do you say, Kara?"

"I'm game, but I've never done this before. You're going to

have to teach me, Bailey."

"Okay." She spends a few minutes going over the rules, making sure to be clear and meticulous. She really is so adorable and I kind of feel a little lonely that I'm an only child. But I'm glad to spend time with Bailey now. And Brayden of course.

We start playing and right off the bat I see we're no match for Brayden. But he's so obviously letting us win. Not for my sake, but for his sister's. When it's her turn to make a shot, I lift her in my arms so she can reach the basket.

"Yay!" she cheers.

He laughs and I laugh and then we're having so much fun I don't pay attention to the time until my phone dings.

"It's my dad," I say as I glance at the screen. "He wants to know when I'm coming home for dinner."

"Eat with us!" Bailey says.

I glance at Brayden and he lifts a brow. "We'd love to have you."

Warmness fills every part of me. "That's really nice of you guys, but dinner…it's important to my dad that we eat together and I don't want to upset him."

Brayden nods in understanding. "So I'll see you tomorrow?"

"Yeah." I turn to his sister. "I had so much fun playing with you, Bailey."

She flings her arms around me. "Me, too. You're my favorite of Brayden's friends." As I hug her, my eyes find Brayden's. He looks away, fully aware that after our arrangement is over, I most probably won't hang out with his sister again. That hurts me more than I thought it could. I won't just lose this amazing guy when we break up—I'll lose all the great things that come along with him.

Chapter Twenty-One

I'm on pins and needles as I watch the students read the Edenbury High Times's October issue the next morning. I, as well as the rest of the team, have been handing them out the second they were available and so far, no one has thrown them to the floor. A good sign, right?

I guess Martina was right—putting Brayden's picture on the front page sparked people's attention. Our photographer did a great job catching my fake boyfriend in just the right light to make him look even sexier than he is. And more than that, you can see the fire and passion in his eyes, not just for football, but for life. Just staring at his picture, I see him in a whole new light.

I smile as the kids read it, most of them even moving on to the articles and topics that are not football related. But as I walk through the hallway and the throngs of students, I spot several kids shrug and toss the paper on the floor like it's garbage. My stomach drops to my toes. I guess I shouldn't have hoped we'd reach *all* the students. I should be glad about the people who are interested—hopefully they'll pick up more copies in the future.

I turn toward my locker and my eyes widen when I catch a tall, buff guy bending down to sweep the discarded newspapers off the floor. He walks over to those who threw them away, speaks a few words to them, then hands them the paper.

What in the world is Brayden doing?

The crazy part? The people actually listen to him. The guy has a way with people…must be all that charisma.

And the even crazier part? Brayden has his own stack of papers that he's handing out. I didn't know he volunteered to pass them around.

I can't help but stare as he moves from student to student, either returning their discarded papers or handing them a new copy. I stand in the middle of the hallway in such shock, I don't pay attention to the kids knocking into me on their way to their lockers or classrooms.

"Hey," a voice says.

Glancing up, I find Brayden smiling at me. His stack is gone. Wow. He handed them out pretty quickly. I still have over half of mine.

"What are you…I mean, you're handing out the newspaper?"

He grins. "I told Martina I wanted to help out. Figured people might be more swayed to read it if I gave it to them."

I nod, my mind still not able to believe he…cares this much. Does he, though? Am I ever going to understand his complex mind?

"Do you want me to help you?" he asks.

I look at him. "What?"

He slides half the stack out of my hands. "We can pass them around together," he suggests.

I nod again, and we head down the halls.

"I read your article," he tells me, then laughs. "Twice actually. I loved it."

My walking comes to a halt. "You did?"

"Yeah." He stops a girl and guy passing by and places two newspapers in their hands. They start reading as they continue to where they were going. "You painted me as this driven, hardworking, positive, kind, caring person."

"That's what you are. I just wrote the truth."

He smiles as we resume our trek down the hall. No one accepts a copy from me, but the second Brayden asks them to read it, they rush to comply.

"It's crazy how popular you are," I say. "Though I'll admit it has its advantages right now."

He chuckles. "Yeah it's great, I guess. But sometimes I wish I could just fade into the background and be…"

"Invisible?"

He laughs again. "Yeah."

"Trust me, being invisible is not fun. But I think I'm starting to realize that being so popular isn't a walk in the park, either. Always being in the spotlight can't be easy."

He shakes his head. "No."

I smile. "But it still beats being a nobody."

"Maybe you won't be a nobody anymore once everyone

reads your article."

"No, I'm pretty sure people still won't know who I am."

He playfully jabs his elbow into mine. "You never know." He lifts his eyes and catches a few kids throwing their copies on the floor. He chases after them and convinces them to give it a shot. Like with the others, they agree.

Brayden returns to my side. "People can be so rude sometimes. You and your team worked so hard to get this done. The least they could do is appreciate it." He runs his hand through his hair. "Sorry, it bothers me when hard work goes by unnoticed."

"Thanks for that. But I don't know if there's a point. Those who want to read it will, and those who don't won't."

"Maybe they just need some convincing. Hey!" He heads over to some of his football buddies and hands them each a paper. "Read it." He comes back to me. "I think we're almost done. And look…no papers on the floor or in the garbage."

"Why do you care so much?"

His eyebrows furrow. "Like I said, it bothers me when hard work goes by unnoticed or unappreciated."

My insides deflate. I don't know why I was hoping he'd say he was doing it for me. That's selfish.

"And I want them to read your awesome article," he says, voice so soft it touches every part of me. "Not because it's about me, but because it's a great article. I felt like I got to know myself better." He laughs. "I know that sounds weird, but it's the truth." He places his hand on my shoulder. "I'm sorry I never paid attention to it. The past few weeks…I feel like I've changed. I notice things I haven't noticed before. Like the paper and all the hard work you put into it. That you're pretty cool and not just a smart girl whom I have nothing to talk to about. I think we get along great."

I smile. "We do. And we make one heck of a fake relationship."

He chuckles. "Yep."

My eyes widen. "Oh my gosh! I totally forgot. I have something for you."

His eyes light up in curiosity as I reach into my pocket and retrieve the small piece of paper.

"Close your eyes, boyfriend," I say.

He looks at me suspiciously.

"Come on!" I urge.

He shuts his eyes and I can't help but stare at how beautiful he is. Everything about his face is perfect, his chiseled jaw and smooth skin, his long lashes and beautiful mouth. But there's more to this wonderful guy than a pretty face. He's kind and deep, cares about his family and his friends. He's so desperate to make his parents and dead brother proud of him. My article doesn't do him justice. If I was able to, I'd write a whole book on this amazing person.

"Uh, Kara?" he asks. "What's going on?"

Dang it! I forgot he's still standing there with his eyes closed. "Sorry, just one more second."

He waits patiently as I take him in one more time. "Hold out your palm."

He twists his lips like he doesn't trust me.

"I won't hurt you or anything," I assure him.

"I know you won't. Okay." He holds out his palm.

I try to hide the excited giggle bubbling up inside me before I carefully place the piece of paper on his palm. "Okay, you can look now."

His eyes pop open and he glances at his palm. With wide eyes, he scans the words. "A ticket to the Falcons game this Sunday?" His eyes grow even wider and his jaw is about to sweep the floor. I've never seen anyone so shocked and excited before in my life. And it makes me feel so warm and good and excited for him.

His eyebrows furrow as he looks at me. "Just one ticket?"

"My dad has the other one. I was supposed to go with him, but I think you should go instead. You're still trying to win him over, right?"

"Yeah, thanks so much. But are you sure he's okay with my taking your place? I don't want to impose. And you're okay with it, too?"

I nod. "I've been to many games with him. And my dad is really looking forward to going with you. But he'll be tough. You *are* my boyfriend after all and he's very overprotective of me." I roll my eyes. "But don't let any of that discourage you. Show him the amazing and talented person that you are."

"Thanks. That means a lot." His face changes. "Hey, I was wondering if you want to go to a party with me this Saturday at DeAngelo's house?"

He's inviting *me* to go to a…right, of course. As his girlfriend, we should go places together. "Okay, it sounds like fun."

"Cool. Great. Ready to head to class?"

I'm about to tell him for the millionth time that he doesn't have to walk me, when the football team comes out of nowhere and sweeps Brayden along with them, talking about my article. Brayden's eyes catch mine as he's whisked away and he smiles. I wave.

Then I glance around. Wow, the kids are actually reading the newspaper. I'm not sure how many will be returning customers, but at least we have this win. Martina and the rest of the team are probably so excited. The hard part? Figuring out what to write for our next issue.

"What do you think you're doing?" a voice demands from behind me. Whirling around, I find Teagyn standing before me, flanked by most of the cheerleading squad.

Her arms are crossed over her chest and she flares her nostrils. She steps closer to me, her heels clacking on the floor. "Who do you think you are? Trying to worm your way into the popular group? You can date Brayden and you can try out for cheerleading, but you'll never be like us. *Never.*"

I ignore her and turn around to head to my locker, but she grabs my arm, spinning me around to face her. "I'm not done yet. I don't know how you did it, how you manipulated him into thinking he's into you, but someone like *you* has no business dating someone like *him*. You're trash and he's gold. Trash goes with trash and gold goes with gold. Know your place, loser."

I know this—of course I know this—but hearing her say

that stings. Brayden's a good person, a good friend, but that's all. Sometimes I get so swept up in him that I forget we're just that. Friends who will go our separate ways once my dad recruits him.

Teagyn steps even closer to me, forcing me to back into the wall. "He'll come to his senses and break up with you. Maybe you should save yourself the heartache and tears and end things with him first. I mean, we wouldn't want you to cry in front of *everyone* again."

She's referring to cheerleading tryouts, but I shove that memory away. "No," I tell her. "I'm not going to break up with him. And it's none of your business." The bell rings. "I need to get to class."

I make a move to leave, but she steps in my way. She glares at me, her lips pressed in a tight line. She can get as mad as she wants, but she can't do anything about it. It's on the tip of my tongue to tell her that Brayden loves me and will never leave me, but of course I don't say that. First, that's not true. Second, I'm not that brave.

But I do manage to slip past her death glare and head to my classroom. Luckily, I don't share any classes with her or I don't know how I would get through the lessons. I get very uncomfortable when someone hates me.

It's ridiculous that she's getting so worked up over my fake relationship with Brayden. Does she even know him? Like him? Does she want him only because he's the quarterback?

Okay, I'll admit that I didn't know anything about him and initially had a massive crush on him due to his looks. But now I know him. He's more than just good looks and talent. He has a huge heart, a never-ending amount of kindness and care. He's what I always imagined my perfect guy would be.

But what does it matter? At the end of the day, he and I are just two strangers who have an agreement. Once that's over, Teagyn is free to sink her claws into him.

The thought of that makes me feel like someone is stabbing my stomach over and over again.

"Kara?" the teacher asks.

I blink up at her. "Yes?"

"I asked the class if anyone worked on the chemistry homework. Seems like no one bothered. Why don't you enlighten your classmates? Oh, and I read your article in the Edenbury High Times. Very fascinating and well written. I enjoyed it immensely."

I smile, my cheeks heating up. She's never complimented me before, probably never even read it. It's a great feeling to know people are enjoying my hard work.

Chapter Twenty-Two

Would it be lame to admit that I've never been to a high school party? Maybe, but the fact that Dani, Charlie, and Ally haven't been to one either makes me feel better. Charlie was adamant about not going at first, but she wants to be my moral support. Dani has always wanted to go to one but was never invited or had no one to go with, and Ally is a little freaked out by it. She doesn't do crowds. But she is very curious. And isn't it every teenager's rite of passage to at least attend one high school party in their lifetime?

Since none of us have our licenses yet, Ally convinces—bribes?—her sister, Amanda, to drive us to the party. Brayden said he'd meet me there.

"This is exciting, isn't it?" Dani gushes on our way to DeAngelo's house. "Our first high school party."

"Meh," Charlie mutters as she works on a kid's history report on her phone.

"I'm excited, but super nervous," Ally admits. "I hope I don't get lost in the crowd."

"You can hang onto me," Dani offers.

"Or me," I tell her.

She shakes her head with a smile. "You'll spend the whole night with Brayden."

I'll admit, the prospect of being at his side the whole night makes my heart float to the sky.

After twenty minutes, I hear music in the distance. Is that the party? Sheesh, you can hear it from so far away. Will one of the neighbors call the police? Will I get arrested? No, I'm being ridiculous. But I hope nothing happens because I promised Dad I would be okay. Too bad the party is this weekend and not next, when he'll be out of town. But I'm almost seventeen—he can't treat me like a little kid forever. I know it's hard raising me on his own, but I wish he wouldn't be so overprotective.

"Is this it?" Dani asks when Amanda slows down in front of a large house. Wow, DeAngelo's parents must be super rich.

"Will you pick us up?" Ally asks her sister once we're on the pavement.

She scowls at her from the driver's window. "The deal was to get you here."

Ally groans. "I'll do your chores for another week."

"Sold." She speeds away.

"I wish she'd move out already," Ally grumbles.

"But then who would be our ride?" Dani asks.

"How old is she?" I ask Ally.

"She'll turn eighteen next month. She was supposed to go to college this fall, but decided to take a gap year to…" She makes air quotes. "'Figure things out.' I swear, my parents love her more than they love me. Maybe if I wasn't so shy…" She shakes her head. "Never mind."

I put my arm around her. "You're perfect just the way you are."

She smiles. "Thanks."

"Ready to party like there's no tomorrow?" Dani asks as she shakes her body awkwardly.

"Please don't do that," Charlie mutters with a laugh.

"Was it really that bad? Darn, I'll never be a good dancer. I can kiss Broadway goodbye."

"You still have time to practice," I assure her. "I think you have rhythm, you're just, um…"

"Too clumsy?" she offers. "But can any of you do this?" She steps back and does an amazing pirouette.

Charlie whistles. "Impressive, Wood."

"I know." She does an exaggerated bow. "Thank you ever so kindly. Took me years to master that."

We all laugh as we make our way toward the entrance of the house. Many kids are drinking and talking outside. We squeeze through them, Dani and me grabbing hold of Ally's hands so she won't accidentally get lost. And when we get inside? Absolute madness. Okay, maybe that's exaggerating a little, but there are so many people here and the music is so loud. The house isn't too messy, but it's obvious things have been pushed and kicked around.

"I feel so out of place," Charlie says as she gapes at everything.

"I feel naked," Dani says.

"Same," Ally agrees.

"Anyone see Brayden?"

"Is that him with the football players?" Charlie asks.

I'm about to head over to him, when Dani closes her hand around my arm. "Wait. Let him come to you."

"What?"

She playfully knocks her shoulder into my mine. "I know you guys are just pretending, but play a little hard to get. Let the man chase after you."

My eyes grow large. "But what if he doesn't come to me all night?"

She gives me a face. "And I thought I was the clueless one in the romance department."

"She's right, you know," Ally says. "Boys love the chase. Let him play his part."

"Okay," I say unsurely. What if he forgets he has a girlfriend because—newsflash—he *doesn't*? Does that mean I won't hang out with him the whole night?

And then I realize how ridiculous I am. He would only hang out with me for the pretense. While I could have a great time with my friends.

"Do you guys want to dance?" I ask them.

"What?" Ally looks like I asked her to sell her soul to the devil.

I nod toward the kids dancing in the large room next door.

"I can't dance!" Ally gasps.

"I don't do dancing," Charlie tells me.

"I'm in!" Dani takes my hands and tugs me to the dance floor. "I'm going all out now. Don't make fun of me."

"I would never."

"I don't get to freestyle often," she says as she starts moving her body. "Can't fit it into my dance schedule."

"What classes do you take?"

"Ballet, hip-hop, tap, and musical theater dance. I get free lessons in exchange for work, since my parents can't afford them."

"That's cool. What kind of work? You give lessons to little kids?"

"I wish," she says. "No, I clean the place."

"Oh."

"It's not so bad," she assures me. "Well, if you don't count cleaning the toilets." She wrinkles her nose and laughs. "But I'm thankful they let me take the classes in exchange for work. But it does push me back behind the others. My instructors see potential in me, but I don't know if I can be as dedicated as the other dancers. And because I have no coordination, I have to work ten times as hard as them."

"I'm proud of you, you know that?" I ask as the DJ switches to a faster beat and Dani and I up our moves. "You know what you want and you're going after it. I still have no idea what I want to do with my life."

"You still have time," she assures me. "But right now, all that matters is Brayden Barrington." She winks.

I laugh. Then my face grows serious. "Has he even noticed me?"

She cranes her neck right and left. "I don't think he's even in here."

I sigh dramatically. "I'm even invisible to my fake boyfriend."

She giggles as she takes my hands and spins around. "Forget him. Have fun with me."

I am having fun with her, of course, but it still stings that Brayden's not even looking for me. I mean, I know he invited me here only because we're supposed to be seen together in public, but does he like my company at all?

I catch Charlie making her way over to us with Ally hanging onto her arm. "We decided to give this dancing thing a shot," she tells us.

"You decided," Ally mutters. "You forced me to come."

"You don't want to be left alone, so you had no choice but to come with me."

"I'm so happy you guys are here!" Dani takes both their hands and dances with them. "We'll have so much fun!"

And fun we have. I never thought I would ever attend a high school party, let alone have a good time. Everything changes when you have friends to go with. I feel like I'm finally acting like a regular teenager.

"Kara?" a deep voice says from behind me.

I spin around and come face to face with Brayden. Oh gosh, he looks so yummy in his tight green T-shirt and dark jeans. And his smile is so warm it sends tingles down my back.

Dani gives me a nudge.

"Oh! Hi, boyfriend," I say.

"Were you here long? I was waiting for you."

"You were? Sorry. I was just having fun with my friends."

He grins. "It looks like it. I don't want to interrupt. I'll be in the next room if you want to catch up."

He walks away.

"Ugh, isn't he the sweetest or what?" I groan.

"I'll admit, that was pretty cool of him," Charlie says. "He could have gotten annoyed at you for hanging out with us instead of him."

"Don't encourage her," Ally says with a laugh. "She's already hopelessly in love with him."

That would be an understatement.

"What are you waiting for?" Dani hisses as she gently pushes me. "Go to your man!"

"He isn't really my man…"

"Whatever, just get out of here."

"Okay," I say with a laugh. "See you guys later."

I enter the next room and find him laughing with the football team. And the cheerleaders. Including Teagyn. Ugh, I can't forget what she said to me on Thursday in the hallway. Even though she basically confirmed what I always believed— that someone like me couldn't possibly be with someone like Brayden—she was still a jerk for saying it. I'm glad I'm not on the cheerleading team and decided not to sit at the popular table anymore. Even though I do miss eating with Brayden.

She's the first one to notice me approach and bristles like I'm a Dementor and turned the room cold. I ignore her and place my hand on Brayden's arm. Wow, talk about being bold.

It takes all I have to keep my hand there and not remove it with a startled gasp.

Brayden turns to me and smiles. "Kara, hey."

"Hi."

Jerry, DeAngelo, and some of the other football players greet me, some slapping me on the back a little too strongly. Sheesh, what's with that? I try not to cough.

"Your home is so cool," I tell DeAngelo.

His eyebrows furrow. "Thanks, I guess? This your first time here, Gander? I throw parties like every weekend."

Teagyn scoffs. "This is her first party. *Ever.*"

They all gape at me. "You've never been to a party before?" one of the guys asks.

"Of c-course I've been to parties before," I lie. "I go all the time. I'm like the party queen."

"Cool." Jerry fist bumps me. "Kara's surfing the crowd once this party really gets started!"

"Surfing what?" I ask.

"Ignore him." Brayden takes my arm and pulls me to the side, a place devoid of people and where the music isn't too loud. "Sorry, is this too much for you?"

"What are you talking about? This is totally cool," I lie again.

He studies me for a bit before saying, "Is this your first party, Kara?"

I sigh. "Yes, it is."

He runs his hand through his hair. "Sorry. I didn't realize it wasn't your scene. You should have told me. They can get a bit too wild sometimes."

"No, it's totally okay!" I assure him. "I brought my friends with me. We're having fun."

"You *were* having fun," he mutters to himself. "And I pulled you away."

"What?" I ask.

"This arrangement," he says. "It's more to my benefit than yours. You're missing out on hanging out with your friends because of me."

"No, no, no," I quickly say. "It's fine. We talked about this already. How about you show me how to have fun at a high school party," I suggest. "Uh, not the drinking part. Just the dancing."

His brows shoot up. "You want to dance?"

Heck yeah! I've been dreaming about it for years. Okay, maybe in my dreams there was a white dress involved…

"Sure," I say, trying to act all nonchalant. "Show me your sick moves, Barrington."

He chuckles. "I wouldn't call them sick. But sure."

He slides his hand into mine and guides me to the dance floor. More like he's dragging me, because I'm frozen in place. Because sexy Brayden Barrington is *holding my hand.*

True, he's touched me before, but he's *holding my hand.* That's like one of the most romantic things in the world.

I just hope my hand isn't sweaty…

He finds an empty spot on the dance floor and faces me with a smile, starting to shake his body. I mimic his movements, but I'm so uncoordinated that I trip over my feet.

"Sorry, I have two left feet."

He waves his hand. "All that matters is that you're having fun."

I am, I really am. Because I'm dancing with Brayden Barrington. At this moment, it doesn't matter that he's my fake boyfriend because we're having fun. We're *both* having fun. As friends.

"There you go," he says with a laugh as I get in the groove of things. I don't know what my body is doing, but it seems like I've lost control of it. It's dancing to the beat of the music, not caring that I'm probably making a fool of myself. Because I'm having a blast.

I catch sight of my friends dancing together. They smile at me and give me thumbs up. Some of the other kids are watching us, especially Teagyn. She's got such a scowl, she looks so unattractive. I ignore her and grin at Brayden. "This is fun."

"Super fun," he agrees. "I didn't know you had such awesome moves."

"Oh please," I say. "Hey, watch this. Dani taught it to me."

I try to pirouette, but as I'm doing it, I hear the song switch out to a slow one. I gasp as I trip over my feet and crash toward the floor. But my body doesn't hit the ground—I land in strong protective arms.

I gaze up into Brayden's gorgeous blue eyes.

"You okay?" he whispers.

I untangle myself from his arms. "Yeah," I say as confidently as I can, though I know my voice quakes. "Totally okay. Other than the fact that I failed the pirouette and embarrassed myself…I think I'm going to drown my sorrows in some Coke." I turn and walk away.

"Kara?" he calls.

I shut my eyes for a second before slowly twisting around to face him.

"Do you want to dance with me?"

"What?"

He gestures to the couples on the dance floor wrapped in each other's arms. Does he mean…? He wants to…?

Oh, of course. As a couple, we should dance in each other's arms, too. Like all the other couples are doing. Real couples who aren't faking it.

I know. I agreed to do this. But to slow dance with my crush? I want to do it so badly. It's like a dream come true. But in my dreams, he was my real boyfriend.

I should refuse and walk away. Why torture myself like this? He's a good guy and would never hurt me, but he doesn't realize that he *is* hurting me. It's not his fault of course. The only one at fault here is me.

But everyone is looking. Watching. Waiting. How could I reject him like that?

"Sure," I force out. "I would love to dance with you."

His smile can chase away everyone's greatest fear as he wraps his arms around me and gently yanks me to his chest. With shaky hands, I snake them around his neck and turn my face so my cheek is pressed against his chest. And then we join the many other couples dancing in this intimate way.

Quarterbacks Don't Fall For Invisible Girls

I hope he doesn't hear my thumping heart. Hope he doesn't feel my trembling body. His heart doesn't thump, his body doesn't tremble. All I feel is his strong, hard chest and warm body so close to mine.

We're just actors in a play, I tell myself. Putting up an act, nothing more.

"Is this okay?" he whispers. "Because we can stop if it's not."

I swallow the tears threatening my eyes. "It's fine."

And so we sway in each other's arms to the beat of the soft music. All the while, I try not to burst into tears.

Finally, the DJ switches to an upbeat song. I step out of his arms and paste on a normal face, smiling at him. "That was fun."

He watches me for a bit with a look in his eyes that I can't explain or understand, then nods. "Yeah, it was."

"Cool. So I'm going to hang out with my friends for a bit."

He nods again. "Yeah. Cool. Have fun."

I'm about to turn around, but Teagyn blocks my way. Flanked by Macy and Felicia.

"You guys look *so* cute together." Overly-sweet honey drips from Teagyn's tongue. "And that dance? *So* romantic. But…" She squints at me and Brayden. "I can't help but notice that I've never seen you guys kiss."

My wide eyes flit to Brayden's shocked ones before returning to Teagyn. "What?" I croak.

She folds her arms over her chest as she regards the two of us. "If you guys are actually together, shouldn't you kiss?"

Every single person in the room stares at us now, including my friends. Their expressions? Shock and bewilderment. Probably the same look I have on my face.

Teagyn motions toward everyone. "We're all waiting for Edenbury High's most talked-about couple to lock lips."

I swallow before glancing at Brayden again. He looks frozen and tongue-tied.

Teagyn taps her shoe on the floor like she's impatient.

Taking a deep breath, I say, "That's private."

She scoffs. "Are you a prude? Or does Brayden *not* want to kiss you?" She makes a face like the thought of kissing me will make her vomit.

"We *don't* have to prove anything to you."

She throws her head up as she snickers to her friends. "I knew it. They can't possibly be dating. Who would want to date someone like her? I bet she's using Brayden to be popular. And Brayden's too nice to say no."

"That's not true," Brayden's quiet voice says. "She's not using me."

Teagyn's brows lift. "So you're using her?"

A whole array of emotions passes over his face. The one thing that stands out most is his concern for me. Because he thinks he put me in this position. I also can tell it's on the tip of his tongue to just tell everyone the truth. For my sake.

But we can't tell them the truth. Because then everyone will know he and I just got together so he could get closer to my dad, which means my dad might find out. He would think the worst of Brayden for using me like that. No, over my dead body would I ever allow anything like that to happen.

As Brayden opens his mouth to say something, I step over and move closer to him, so close that there's barely any space between us. "Don't," I whisper so only he can hear. "It's not worth you losing your shot."

"We don't have to do this," he whispers back. "Like you said, we don't have to prove anything to them."

"It'll be okay," I tell him with an assuring nod, letting him know I'm totally okay with this and he has nothing to worry about.

He searches my eyes one more time before nodding.

"What's the holdup?" Teagyn's annoying voice demands. I wish I could slide off my shoe and chuck it at her face.

Giving Brayden another reassuring nod, I step even closer to him until our chests touch. Now there is literally no space between us. I move my face closer to his.

His gaze drops to my lips before he dips his face to mine.

As our mouths glide toward each other, my eyes flutter shut. This might not be the way I've fantasized about this, but holy heck, I'm about to have my first kiss. With none other than Brayden Barrington.

It feels like forever until our lips touch, but finally, his warm breath is on my face and then his soft lips press against mine. They're hesitant at first, but then they start to move over mine, slowly, leisurely. Perfect.

And then it's over.

He steps back and my eyes flutter open. Our gazes don't leave each other's, as though our eyes are glued on one another.

229

Some of the football players cheer. I feel the intense scowl on Teagyn's face before she stomps away with the other cheerleaders. Some kids whisper. But I don't look at any of them because my gaze is still locked on Brayden.

That was the best kiss in my entire life.

Okay, it was my *only* kiss and I don't have anything to compare it to, but man, that was the best thing that could have happened to me. Even though it was forced upon us.

There's nothing but concern in Brayden's eyes. Concern for me. I wish I could tell him he has nothing to be worried about—that was *awesome*—but I know he doesn't feel the same. How can he when he doesn't feel about me the way I feel about him?

And that's when the reality of the situation really hits home. Brayden was just forced to kiss me. Someone he doesn't like. Someone he never imagined he would kiss in a million years. Is he disgusted? Upset? I can't read any other emotion in his eyes other than concern. Which is now morphing into sympathy. No, pity.

He feels sorry for me.

I turn on my heels and weave through the crowd staring at me. "I'm leaving," I tell my friends.

They hurry after me as I exit the house. I hold up my hand as each one of them opens their mouths to say something. "I don't want to talk about it. Can you call your sister, Ally?"

"Sure." She fumbles for her phone. "I'll text her to pick us up right away."

I hug my arms as I battle tears. The kiss meant the world to me, but the only thing Brayden feels is pity. He feels sorry that a loser like me could only get a kiss through a dare. Because there's no way on this Earth someone like Brayden Barrington would ever want to kiss someone like me.

Chapter Twenty-Three
Brayden

I toss and turn all night, the memories of what happened only a few hours ago running around in my head. Kara so close to me. Kara's soft, warm lips pressed to mine. Kara fleeing with her friends as though the devil chased her.

My head isn't here as I get ready for the Falcons game with Mr. Gander, or when I climb into his car.

Kara was so kind to give me her ticket, but the truth is, the game is the farthest thing from my mind right now. I keep replaying the party, wondering if I hurt her. Who am I kidding? Of course I hurt her. She was forced to be in a situation she didn't want to be in all because of me. I *hate* forcing anyone to do something they don't want to do. I'd never force a girl to kiss me when she doesn't want to.

Why did Teagyn have to do that? Put us on the spot like that?

It was wrong. I feel terrible and hope she doesn't think poorly of me. I'm not that kind of person.

The kiss, though? It was the most amazing thing I have ever experienced in my life. She wasn't my first, but it was *wow*. More than fireworks on the Fourth of July. When she and I locked lips, the world stood still—no, it poured all its goodness onto us. Showered us.

And then it was over. She looked at me like she was horrified. Embarrassed. She wanted to get as far away from me as possible. And I wanted to chase after her, to apologize for forcing her into this.

I don't regret kissing her at all, I just wish it were under different circumstances. And I wouldn't lie and say I wouldn't mind kissing her again, wrapping her in my arms, feeling like…

No. We're not really together.

"Son, are you all right?" Mr. Gander says. "I've been calling your name, but it doesn't seem like you heard me at all."

It takes me a second to remember where I am and who I'm with—on the way to the Falcons game with Kara's dad. I'm trying to make a good impression on this man, but how would he react if he knew I pretty much forced his daughter to kiss me? He'd toss my butt into the street.

"Yeah, I'm fine," I lie. "Just have a lot on my mind. Football and school and the future." And your daughter who's become such a good friend. And I wish she'd…that we'd…

No. Kara would never choose a guy like me.

Mr. Gander nods in understanding. "For sure. I remember how I was at your age. The pressure you're under." He places his hand on my shoulder. "You'll be fine. Just take a deep breath. Why don't you tell me about your intentions with my

233

daughter?"

My eyes widen. "My intentions?"

He nods. "She's very precious to me. And I don't want her to get hurt. Do you understand what I'm saying?"

I nod, my throat tight. She's not the one who will get hurt when we end our arrangement. I'm so invested in her, it's like she's become part of me. Weird as that sounds. And after reading the article? It just made me more excited to see her, her smile, hear her laugh. It makes me want to spend more time with her.

But after that kiss yesterday? I have no idea where we stand or what will happen to us. And about the arrangement, but that's the least important thing right now. Sure, I want to get recruited, but I care more about her feelings.

What can I do to fix this? I haven't texted her since the party. I guess I'm worried she'll reject me. I wouldn't be able to handle that.

"Good, as long as we're clear on that," her dad says. "I want you to know I approve of you."

I rub the back of my neck. "Oh. Thanks. That means a lot."

Her horrified face floats before mine, but I squeeze my eyes shut. I can't let it tear me apart. I need to make a good impression on her dad or everything we've done so far would be for nothing.

I start a conversation about football and he's completely immersed in the topic. He reminds me a little of my dad— they both love football. Mr. Gander was quarterback in high school and college, and he laughs when he tells me he had all the girls wrapped around his finger.

"I was The Man," he says with another chuckle. "I thought I was invincible. King of the school. If my son behaved that way? I'd kick his rear end. But you're not like that. You're very humble."

"Thanks." My throat is tight again. If he knew I was using his daughter to get close to him, would he approve of me? No.

What if I'm starting to…to maybe see this as more than just a fake relationship?

But what does it matter anyway? She *ran* away from me.

The truth is, I was starting to feel more than friendship toward her before the kiss, but now that we've shared that, my feelings for her have only grown.

We reach the stadium, get out of the car, and find our seats. I try to be pleasant and a good conversationalist, but I can't get his daughter out of my head. I never felt this way about a girl before. Is she…is she that special one I've been waiting for? I always figured I'd know when I met her, but now I'm not sure about anything. What if I found her but let her slip through my fingers?

Mr. Gander talks more about football before the game begins. Normally, I get so swept up in the cheers and the excitement I don't think about anything else. But not today. No matter how much I try, I can't forget about Kara and what happened between us.

But then I tell myself I need to pull it together or I won't make a good impression on Mr. Gander. So as hard as it is, I force myself to push Kara to the back of my mind.

We have a good time and our team wins, so that's great. Definitely a positive to my gloomy day.

Her dad peers at me once we're back in the car. "You haven't texted my daughter once," he observes.

My eyes widen. He'll see through the lie. "Yeah, Kara didn't want to bother us. She wanted us to focus on the game and have a good time."

He grins. "That sounds like my pumpkin. But please feel free to text her now. She really likes you, Brayden. But don't tell her I told you that."

I force a smile, the corners of my mouth trembling. Kara's a very good actress. And I guess I am, too, since her dad doesn't see through my lie.

I pretend to text her, though, my thumb hovering over her name. But I don't contact her because I figure she needs time. Or maybe she doesn't want to talk to me.

"Thanks for taking me to the game," I tell him once he pulls up before my house. "I had a great time and I'm glad we got to know each other better."

He smiles. "Thank you, Brayden. I feel the same."

Normally, my body would perk up at his positive words—does this mean he'll come to one of my games?—but because of what happened with Kara, all I feel is guilt. The only reason her dad likes me is because of her, and I put her in such an uncomfortable position.

Her dad waves and drives off. I enter my house and go up to my room, plopping down on my bed and staring at the ceiling.

As guilty as I feel, I can't get that amazing kiss out of my head. And honestly? I don't really want to.

Chapter Twenty-Four

The last few days have been…weird.

Brayden and I have been avoiding each other since the party on Saturday. Or should I say since the kiss. I feel him looking at me sometimes, like he wants to say something, but he never does. And I have no idea what to say to him, even though this strain between us is killing me.

When I walk through the school doors Wednesday morning, my eyes immediately search for Brayden—whether to ignore him or stare at him, I'm not sure. Maybe a bit of both? Either way, he's not here and a sigh of relief escapes my lips.

I head over to my locker to grab my chem textbook, and after shutting my locker and turning around, I come face to face with Teagyn and her friends. The queen stands before me with her arms crossed over her chest and a glint in her eye. Her minions have similar glints as well. Not in the mood for whatever BS she has planned, I try to push past her. But she blocks my way.

"Where you off to, Gander? To make out with your

boyfriend? Wait a minute." She chuckles. "He ran for the hills after that pathetic kiss on Saturday."

Her friends snicker.

It feels like a metal hand closes around my heart and squeezes.

"Brayden should have known invisible girls like you don't know how to kiss. I bet he'll dump your sorry butt by the end of the week, if he hasn't done so already."

She and the girls snicker again.

My fists clench at my sides as I try—so very desperately—to keep my tears at bay. Teagyn's just a bully, and I shouldn't allow her words to affect me this much. But she's echoing the thoughts that have been racing through my mind since that awful night.

With the glint in her eye growing evil, she steps forward and hisses, "You got what you deserve. You really think someone as pathetic as you can be popular? Learn your place on the social ladder, invisible girl. And don't ever try to go for someone like Brayden again."

With a toss of her stupid hair, she spins around and marches away. Her friends toss their hair identically and hurry after her.

But Teagyn doesn't make it far. A guy with a massive chest and sandy brown hair steps in her way.

My heart nearly catapults out of my chest. The last few days, I was on my guard in case I bumped into—or even locked eyes with—Brayden. But Teagyn had me so frustrated that I didn't have a chance to put on my armor. His eyes flit to mine and remain there for a few seconds before landing back on Teagyn. I involuntarily step back, until I hit my locker.

With his lips pressed tightly together, he narrows his eyes at Teagyn. "Leave Kara alone," he says in a quiet yet commanding voice.

"Brayden!" Teagyn gushes. "Hi. Walk me to class." She wraps her claw around his arm.

He closes his hand over hers and plucks it off. "I said, leave Kara alone."

"Brayden—"

"None of it is true," he says, still in that quiet but commanding voice. "Stop spreading rumors, Teagyn."

His eyes slowly find mine again. And he keeps them there for a few seconds. A few seconds *too long*. I spin around and run to my chem class.

***

The only good thing about today? The book club. My friends have been very supportive, not bringing up the party or the kiss once, giving me the chance to talk about it if I wanted to. But I didn't want to up until this point. Now? I guess I just need to get all this tension off my chest.

"But she has more power than you think," Ally says, referring to the heroine in the regency romance, *A Lady of True Honor*, we started reading this week. "She's smart, resourceful, and she's not afraid to go after what she wants."

"She's still under her brother's control, though," Charlie replies.

"That's how it was at that time. You know women didn't

have any power."

"I like her," Dani muses. "She knows she could screw up her life by going after the stable boy, but she *does* go after what she wants. She chooses love."

"A luxury most women didn't have at the time," Ally adds.

"So now she's stuck." Charlie snaps the book shut with a frown. "I really don't like regencies."

Ally's gaze flicks to me. "What do you think, Kara?"

I stare at the space in front of me. "I haven't been able to stop thinking about the kiss."

Dani frowns. "But the hero and heroine didn't even kiss yet."

Charlie gently smacks her shoulder and hisses, "She's talking about Brayden."

"Oh. Duh."

They all look at me.

"Thanks for not bringing it up," I say with a forced smile. "I've been avoiding it and my feelings. But I feel like I'm going to explode."

"You can talk to us if you want," Ally offers. "You know we'd never judge you."

Of course I know this. I've only been friends with the girls for a few weeks, but they understand me. Still, I'm not used to opening myself up like this and baring my soul. It's been so long since I've done something like this, since Mom died.

I clear my throat and shift in my seat. "I hate the way he looks at me. Like I'm some pitiful girl who can only get kissed if someone forces him."

"I doubt he looks at you that way," Charlie says.

"You didn't see his face."

"Maybe it's all in your head?" Dani offers. "I mean...you don't have to talk about this if you don't want to, but...how was the kiss?" From the look in her eyes, I know she's bursting to know every little detail. So is Ally, the hopeless romantic. Charlie, like usual, seems guarded and suspicious.

Squeezing my eyes shut, I say, "It was the best thing that's ever happened in my life."

Dani squeals and claps, but then she remembers there is nothing remotely romantic about this whole situation. "At least the kiss was good," she says.

"On *my* end," I stress. "From the way he looked at me..." I shake my head.

"Well, it was your first kiss," Charlie says, matter-of-factly. "Cut yourself some slack."

"How can I? He probably has lots of experience kissing girls. Then he was forced to kiss someone with the kissing knowledge of a ten year old. Ugh!" I cover my face. "I should never have agreed to go to that party. Nothing will ever be the same between us. He'll always look at me as the pathetic girl he was forced to kiss."

"Stupid Teagyn," Dani grumbles.

Her words immediately conjure up what happened this morning in the hallway. I try to shove it out of my mind. It's been playing in there over and over for the last seven hours. I'm done dissecting it.

"I was worried something like this would happen," Ally's

soft voice says.

I lower my hands from my face. "I'm fine. Let's get back to the book."

"Does this mean the arrangement is over?" Dani asks.

"I don't know. I mean, I still want to help him get recruited by my dad, but…I have no idea how it's going. He and my dad went to the Falcons game on Sunday, but I have no idea if anything came out of it. My dad just said Brayden is a nice boy, and I obviously didn't hear anything from Brayden."

Suddenly, the room is stifling. I tuck my legs beneath me, but that doesn't help. I lower them back to the floor, but I'm still uncomfortable. Getting to my feet, I say, "Can we end early today? I want to go home."

"Sure," Dani says, eyes full of worry.

Ally gently puts her hand on my arm as I pass her. "Are you sure you're okay?"

I close my eyes for a second to regulate my emotions. "Thanks for worrying about me," I say, glancing from her to Dani and Charlie. "All of you. I think I just need to be by myself for a little while." Although I have no clue what good that will do. I was basically alone the last four days and that didn't do a single thing to help. I laugh lightly. "I'm not exactly the best company right now."

"We don't mind," Charlie says with a smile.

"Books heal the soul," Dani adds.

I give her an apologetic look. "Sorry, Dani, I don't think a book can make me feel better. But don't worry about me, this will pass. Just give me some time, okay?"

They all nod.

"I'll see you guys tomorrow."

I push the door open and march toward the exit, my head still a jumbled mess. My friends are being super cool about the whole thing, I just wish I wouldn't push them away. But I don't know how to deal with all these emotions passing through me. I'm upset at myself for so many reasons—why did I let Teagyn push me around like that? I could have said no to kissing Brayden. Then he and I would still be friends and I wouldn't be such a mess.

"Oof!" I crash into a bus and tumble to the floor.

"Kara?"

Looking up, I find Brayden standing over me. Sheesh, that bus was *him*? He must have gotten stronger since the last time I bumped into him because *ouch*.

"You okay?" He holds out his hand.

The kiss flashes before my eyes.

I scramble to my feet and stumble away from him. "Yeah," I stammer. "I'm good."

He slowly lowers his hand to his side. "You sure? Because the last time I bumped into you, you told me I felt like a brick wall."

"You've been upgraded to a bus," I mutter.

His eyes widen. "Sorry."

I shrug. "It's cool. I should really watch where I'm going."

We stand in the middle of the hallway in utter silence.

"Shouldn't you be at practice?" I ask, eyes anywhere but on his face.

"Yeah. I just had to get something from my locker."

"Oh."

Quiet.

"Cool," I say before turning around and walking away.

"Kara?" he calls.

I release a breath before slowly twisting around to face him.

He lifts a shaky hand to his head and runs it through his hair. "Can we talk?"

My heart bounces around in my chest. "Um…sure."

He moves to the closest classroom and pushes the door open, peeking inside. "This one's empty." He widens the door for me.

"What about practice?" I ask.

He waves his hand. "This is more important."

Again, my heart bounces in my chest. Did he just imply that talking to me is more important than football?

He sits down at a desk in the front, and I take one a few rows away. I don't know why. I guess I'm used to separating myself from the crowd. Brayden glances at the space between us and gets up, heading over to the one next to mine and sitting down.

"Sorry," I mutter, shaking my head. "I didn't mean to make you feel like a leper."

That causes a small smile to tease his lips. "You didn't make me feel like a leper. But I'll return to my original seat if sitting next to you makes you uncomfortable."

"No!" I practically yell. "Sitting next to you does *not* make me uncomfortable. It's the complete opposite. I—" My lips snap shut as I lower my head. "I'll shut up now."

He laughs softly. "You're funny, do you know that?"

"No."

"But you are."

I shrug. "If you say so."

The smile teasing his lips grows stronger. "I'm glad we're talking again," he admits. "Things have been really weird the last few days."

Yeah, talk about a *major* understatement.

He leans a little closer, his eyes growing soft. "Look, Kara, I'm really sorry about what happened at the party. I shouldn't have let Teagyn…what I mean is, I shouldn't have kissed you."

"We kissed each other," I correct him.

"I know. But the only reason we were in that position to begin with was because I asked you to pretend to be my girlfriend. If not for that, you wouldn't have been uncomfortable."

But then I wouldn't have hung out with him all these weeks. We wouldn't have exchanged so much as a hello.

"I'm glad to help, Brayden." I finally look him full in the face. "I want you to get into the school of your dreams."

"And that's what makes you so unbelievably awesome."

But not awesome enough for him to see me as anything more than a friend.

"I hope I put Teagyn in her place this morning," he says as he leans back in his seat.

"Why do you even hang out with her?" I ask.

He sighs. "I don't like her, but she's friends with my friends and we all hang out. I try not to judge her. She's under a lot of pressure from her mom. Not that it excuses her behavior at all, but if Coach was my dad and put all that pressure on me..." He shakes his head. "I can't imagine."

I think about his words for a few seconds. "I guess I never considered that."

"You never know what a person is going through, so I don't think it's fair to judge them."

My heart won't stay still. He's making it super hard not to fall madly in love with him. "You're a good person, Brayden," I say.

"You're the good person."

I shake my head. "I'm not."

"I disagree."

Tears threaten my eyes. I don't know why. I bite hard on my cheek because I don't want to cry in front of him. Not because I think he'll get uncomfortable—he's not like that—but because I want him to see me as strong.

"I'll understand if you want to break our arrangement," he says.

My gaze snaps to his. "What? I don't want to do that."

"You don't?"

"No. I promised I'd do whatever I could to help you."

The smile he gives me is so sincere, I think my heart just exploded. "Thanks, Kara. That's so sweet of you. But I promise I won't let Teagyn or anyone else get to me. Whatever happens, you come first."

How I wish those words were said in a different context.

I shift in my seat. "How did it go with my dad on Sunday? Did you have a good time?"

"Amazing," he gushes, eyes lighting up like the sun is buried in his skull. "Your dad has so much football knowledge, it's crazy. He kept spouting statistics and information on the players—I felt like I was in football school."

I smile. "That sounds like my dad."

His face grows a little anxious. "What did he say about me?"

"Oh…um, he didn't really say much."

His face falls. "He didn't?"

"Just that you're a nice guy."

He stares down at his knees. "Maybe he doesn't like me."

"He does," I assure him. "He told me after dinner that night that he likes you a lot. Maybe he just needs to see you play?

"Maybe he'll come to the homecoming game."

I give him an apologetic look. "He's out of town this weekend."

"Oh."

"But we just have to be patient," I say with the most confidence and assurance I can muster. "Just have faith that everything will work out, okay? I know he's impressed with you. It's just a matter of time before he sees you in action."

He nods as my words enter his head. "Yeah. You're right."

We're both quiet. I don't mind the silence this time, though. Because Brayden and I are talking again. We're friends again. It feels like everything is right in the world again.

"Um, I should probably let you get back to practice," I say reluctantly. "Your coach will probably skin you alive if he knew you ditched to talk to me."

"Yeah," he mutters with a frown, like he doesn't want to leave. Then his eyes snap to mine, "Hey, Kara?"

"Yeah?"

"I've been wanting to ask you something for a while now, but things got weird with...well, you know, and I wasn't sure..."

Okay, why is he so adorable rambling like that?

"What I mean to say is..." He laughs as he rakes his hand through his hair. "Why am I so nervous to ask this?"

"Ask what?"

"If you want to go to homecoming with me."

A large, goofy smile conquers my face. Wow, the thought never even crossed my mind. Maybe because I never imagined I'd actually go to homecoming. I didn't have friends to go with in the past, let alone a boyfriend. But now I do.

Except, it's fake. Why does my brain—and heart—constantly forget that little detail?

With a shrug, I say, "Sure. I am your girlfriend, after all."

He frowns and is quiet for a short while. Then he says, "Right. But can we forget the fake couple thing just for one night? I'd like us to go as friends."

Disappointment nearly knocks me over the head. What's worse—a fake relationship or just being friends? Both hurt either way.

"Oh, sure," I say. "Going as friends would be great. But we

still have to pretend to everyone that we're together."

"Right," he quickly says. "We still have to pretend."

It takes everything I have not to sigh like the world is coming to an end.

"So, thanks," he says as he lightly punches my arm. "Friend. *And* girlfriend."

I force out a laugh. "Friend *and* boyfriend."

He stands. "I should get back to practice before coach fries my butt. I'll see you tomorrow."

"Okay, bye."

He smiles with a nod before leaving the room.

I bang my head into the desk. I guess I'm glad we're back friends instead of awkwardly avoiding each other, but I still find myself in the same dilemma. Brayden will forever only see me as his friend.

Chapter Twenty-Five
Brayden

I look at the bleachers during today's practice, scanning each and every person carefully. Hoping my eyes are playing tricks on me. But no, Kara's not here.

I try not to be disappointed. She doesn't owe me anything—it's *me* who owes her everything—but I miss seeing her out there. She doesn't have book club and I don't think she has the paper this afternoon, either. I guess she has better things to do than watch her friend practice.

I shake my head, silently scolding myself. Who said she even sees me as a friend? I put her in such an uncomfortable position at that party, all because of a selfish agenda to gain her dad's attention. Had I known it would have led to that, I wouldn't have asked her to do it.

But then I wouldn't have gotten to know her. Wouldn't know there was a sweet, smart, kind, amazing girl who went to the same school as me. A girl who's become such a big part of my life. I can't imagine what will happen when we part ways.

I won't hang on to her. I caused her enough trouble already. If she won't want to be friends once our arrangement comes to an end, I'll respect her wishes. I just want her to be happy.

"Good practice!" Coach Papas yells. "Hit the showers, boys!"

I race along with everyone else toward the locker room, when Coach yells, "Not you, Barrington! Need a word with you."

Darn, did I screw up? I didn't mean to get so distracted...

"Yeah, Coach?" I ask as I sprint over to him. My eyes widen in surprise when I see Coach Myers, the cheerleading coach, standing next to him.

Coach Papas claps me on the back. "You did good out there, Barrington. Ready to smoke Starview Grove High this weekend?"

"You bet," I say, my eyes gliding toward Teagyn's mom, not sure why she's standing there and why she's got a weird grin on her face.

My coach nods to her. "You know Coach Myers, right?"

"Of course," I say with a pleasant smile. "You're doing an amazing job with the squad. They're great."

She tilts her head from side to side. "They could be better."

Ouch. Talk about pressure.

Coach claps me on the back again. "Who are you taking to the homecoming dance?"

"What?" I stare at him. It's a little odd for my coach to ask me a personal question like that. He's never done that before.

"Uh…my girlfriend," I say.

"Who is your girlfriend?" Coach Myers asks.

"Kara Gander. She's with the Edenbury High Tim—I mean, she's the awesome girl who always cheers for me at my games and practice."

Coach squints and then shrugs. "Never heard of her." He waves his hand. "Forget about her. I want you to take someone else to the dance."

I just gape at him. "You what?"

"Oh, there she is." Coach Myers waves her hand like she's flagging someone down. "Teagyn! Teagyn, come over here."

My gaze snaps to her, watching her dump her pom-poms on another cheerleader and race over to us. "What's up, Mom?" She notices me standing there and smiles with a wave. "Hi, Brayden." She has a certain look in her eye, but I can't quite make out what it is.

"The Atlanta Daily wants to do a feature on the school, specifically the football team and the cheerleading squad," Coach Papas tells me and Teagyn. "Just in time for homecoming."

My heart rate spikes. Did he just say The Atlanta Daily? One of the most well-known and respected newspapers in America? If I'm featured in the article, it could grab the attention of recruiters all over the country. "Wow," I breathe. "That's amazing."

"But they want a good story," Coach Myers says. "Something deeper than an amazing football team with an exceptional QB, and an equally amazing cheerleading squad."

My eyes move from her to my coach, not sure what they're getting at. Teagyn looks confused, too, but why do I have the feeling she's putting on an act?

"Imagine the headlines." Coach Myers waves her hands before us. "'Edenbury High's star QB Brayden Barrington and his beautiful girlfriend and head cheerleader Teagyn Myers head off to the homecoming dance together hand in hand after demolishing Starview Grove High School. They spend a wonderful night celebrating with their friends, then after receiving the coveted title of homecoming king and queen, they tangle themselves in each other's arms and lead their classmates into a beautiful dance.' It's sure to grab every reader's attention. And it would be a great representation of our school. It could very well open many doors and give the sports department more funding. The cheerleaders can do with new uniforms."

"The football team can do with new equipment," Coach Papas adds.

I look from one to the other. "Wait. You want Teagyn and me to…?"

"That sounds amazing!" Teagyn nearly bounces on her feet. "I would love to represent our school like that."

"Wonderful," Coach Papas says. Then he looks at me. "I don't need to tell you what a feature in The Atlanta Daily can do for your future, son."

My heart beats so loudly and wildly in my ears that I'm having trouble making sense of my thoughts. They want me to take Teagyn to the dance? To be crowned king and dance with her on the stage? But I just asked Kara to homecoming yesterday.

"I have a girlfriend," I say.

"She's a nobody," Teagyn says. "Just some wanna-be loser who's put her dirty paws on Brayden. But he's too nice to shake her off. You have nothing to worry about."

Kara is *not* any of those things. I shoot Teagyn a hard look, but she ignores me.

Her mom nods. "Good. Because Coach Papas and I are relying on you to paint our school in the best light possible. The reporters will be at the game and they will attend the dance as well. Do not disappoint us."

She says it to the both of us, but her eyes are pinned on Teagyn. Biting her lip, she quickly nods.

"Great." She smiles. "You two have a good day."

She and her daughter walk away.

"Coach, I just asked Kara yesterday to homecoming."

He rests his hand on my arm. "I know girls seem important to you right now, Barrington, but the hard truth is that in five years' time, you won't even remember her name. What's more important to you—playing for a college team or a girl?"

My heart once again hammers in my ears. I suck in a deep breath to calm it so I can think clearly. I don't want to admit it, but my coach is right. Kara isn't even my girlfriend. Should I sacrifice everything I worked for just because of this fake relationship I convinced her to be in?

She shouldn't be upset by the news, though, right? It's not like she likes me. Maybe as a friend, sure, but definitely not more than that. She would understand, wouldn't she? Because

255

she's so unbelievably kind. And she did say she would do whatever she could to help me fulfill my dream—and maybe this is the way. Maybe her dad will read the article and finally come to one of my games. Of course Kara and I would have to assure him I took Teagyn to the dance only because of the article, which I'm sure he'd understand…

Coach claps my back again. "Make the right decision, son. Your future is on the line."

I swallow hard as he walks away. My future *is* on the line. I need to do whatever I can to make my parents proud, to make Brock proud, to make Bailey proud. But most importantly, to make myself proud.

After I'm done with my shower, I shoot Kara a text, asking her if we could get together later. She responds a few seconds later that I can come over to her house whenever I want. I reply that I'll be there in a few minutes.

As I get in my car and drive to her house, I can't help but worry she'll be hurt by the news. But I reassure myself that she won't be—we aren't dating for real. Even though sometimes…it does feel like it's real.

I shake my head. That's a crazy thought.

I park the car in the driveway and ring her bell. She answers it with a smile. "Perfect timing. I have cookies."

"You do?" I ask as I close the door behind me.

"Yeah. I baked them for my dad to snack on the plane. He just left for San Diego to check out a potential recruit."

That's why he's missing the homecoming game. I try not to let that sting. It is what it is.

"Is that why you weren't at practice?" I ask. Then I mentally curse myself. Way to be cool, Barrington.

"What?" she asks as she holds out the plate of chocolate chip cookies. "Oh, yeah. I watched you practice for like a second before I went home. Had to make sure my dad packed enough underwear." She laughs lamely.

Why do I feel warm at the thought that she did come to see me practice, even if it was just for a few minutes?

"Cookie?" She pushes the plate closer to my face.

I smile. "Of course." I grab two and bite into one. "Mmm. Even better than before."

Her cheeks grow a little red. "Thanks. So…did you want to talk to me about something?"

"Yeah. Can we sit?"

She leads me to the living room, where we sit side by side on the couch. I busy myself stuffing another cookie in my mouth, avoiding the inevitable, I guess. I just don't want to hurt her.

She laughs lightly. "I'm on pins and needles here."

I nod, washing the cookie down with a can of Coke she placed on the coffee table. "Sorry. It's just that what I'm about to tell you isn't good news."

She tucks her hands underneath her thighs. "I'm listening."

"Okay, so my coach and Coach Myers had a talk with me and Teagyn. The Atlanta Daily is interested in doing a story on the football team and the cheerleading squad."

"The Atlanta Daily? That's awesome!"

"I know." I shift in my seat. "The thing is, they want both

Teagyn and me to represent the school. So the coaches thought it would look good for us to…go to the homecoming dance together. And be crowned king and queen. So…I can't go to homecoming with you. Sorry. I know I just asked you yesterday."

She's quiet for a moment. Then she says, "You're going with…Teagyn?"

"I know." I roll my eyes. "Out of all cheerleaders, it had to be her. I feel like a selfish, self-centered jerk here, Kara, but if I'm featured in the article, it can do wonders for my career." I lower my gaze to my knees. "Maybe your dad will finally notice me. I know he'd understand why I had no choice but to take Teagyn to the dance and not you."

She's quiet again. I don't want to raise my head and look at her. It'll kill me if she's upset.

She rests her hand on my hand that's on my knee. "I totally get it."

My eyes spring to hers. "You do?"

"As someone who works on a paper, I know how hard it is to find a good story. And the captain of the football team and head cheerleader dating and going to homecoming together? That's a good story. Overdone, sure, but our small town needs something like this."

My brows furrow. "So…you're not upset?"

"Why should I be upset? I told you I'd do whatever I can to help you fulfill your dreams. And it's not like I'm your real girlfriend."

"Right," I mutter, my mind miles away. Why am I

disappointed that she's not upset by this news? Does that make me sound like a jerk? I guess she doesn't like hanging out with me as much as I like hanging out with her.

I force a smile on my face. "Thanks for being so understanding."

"Of course. Friend. Boyfriend." She gently punches my arm.

We sit in silence.

"Is there something else you wanted?" she asks after a little while.

"What? Oh. Yeah, another cookie." I reach for one and bite it.

"Take the whole plate home," she offers.

I shake my head. "No way."

"It's just me here for the whole weekend. You'll be doing me a favor by getting rid of them."

"You'll be here all alone?"

She waves her hand. "My friends are dropping by. Don't worry, I won't be alone."

"Okay. Good. I guess I'll head home now." I stand.

"In case we don't have a chance to talk tomorrow, good luck on the game." She stands and sweeps the plate of cookies into her hand. "I'll put these in a container for you."

She leaves and returns a few minutes later with a semi-large container. And the cookies inside? Much more than the ones that were on the plate.

"Thanks," I tell her. "I know Bailey will love them."

"And a certain quarterback?" she teases.

I laugh. "He'll probably eat more than his little sister."

She walks me to the door and opens it. "Good night, Brayden."

"Good night."

As I place the container on the passenger seat and buckle up, I glance back at the house. Is it just me, or did the curtain shift, like someone was looking out?

I was probably just imagining it.

I'm glad Kara wasn't hurt by the news, but...why am I?

Chapter Twenty-Six

"I don't think this is a good idea," I mumble as I glance at my reflection in Ally's bedroom mirror. "He's taking someone else to homecoming. I can't show my face…can't watch him with his arms wrapped around her…" I swallow, averting my gaze.

Ally rests her hand on my back. "If it's too hard, maybe you should skip."

Dani shakes her head resolutely. "You *have* to go, because if you don't, you'll show Teagyn she won."

I roll my eyes. "This isn't about Teagyn."

Charlie frowns from where she's tapping on her laptop. Looks like she's got some extra homework to do. "Apparently it is. In our school, it's all about Teagyn."

Dani turns to me. "No one's forcing you, but don't you want to have some fun, normal high school memories? We'll be graduating next year and I don't want you to miss out. What do you say, Kara? Come with us? The Four Musketeers?"

I glance at Charlie whacking at the keys. "Only if Charlie

comes, too."

She waves her hand. "I don't do dances."

I head over to her and place my hand on her arm. "Please? We're a team. Either we all go together or we don't go at all."

She scowls. "This requires me putting on a dress."

Ally heads over to her closet and flings it open, exposing rows and rows of dresses fit for royalty. My jaw drops. "How do you have these?"

She shrugs. "Hand-me-downs from Amanda. She bought a new dress for every dance. So take your pick, guys."

Dani and I run to check them out while Charlie remains on the bed, working. Dani, Ally, and I exchange glances, blinking at each other.

"Uh, does anyone know anything about dresses?" Dani asks.

Ally shakes her head with wide eyes, while I say, "Not a clue." We all turn to Charlie.

She glances away from her laptop to us. "Have you seriously lost your minds? Does it look like I do dresses and dances?"

Ally groans. "Looks like we'll have to call the expert. I already owe her so much in chores, now she'll demand more." She smiles shyly. "But it's worth it, isn't it? Like Dani said, let's be regular high schoolers for once."

Charlie snorts. "Regular. Sure."

"As regular as we can be," Dani says. She nods to Ally. "Get your sister's butt in here so she can make us pretty."

"Prettier," I correct. "We're all beautiful."

Dani wraps an arm around me. "Aw, how sweet! I love this girl."

I laugh, my cheeks heating up. Sometimes I still need to pinch myself to check if this is real and I have friends. "And I love you."

Dani wiggles her eyebrows. "And you love Brayden, too. Too bad he can't take you to homecoming."

I sigh. "The negative side of being popular. But as much as this hurts me, I have to remember what's important—Brayden getting recruited by my dad. Did you see how well he played last night? It was like his best game ever." I frown. "Too bad my dad was out of town and couldn't watch him."

"There will be other games," Ally reassures me.

"And at least you have an excuse to fake it with him for a little bit longer."

Ally rests her hand on my arm. "How are you feeling, by the way? About the fake relationship? I mean, after that kiss…"

I force a smile. "I'll be okay. I still can't stop thinking about it, but at least I have that memory to hold onto after we break up. And it's true that we have more time to spend together. But not tonight, though." I sigh heavily. "I just wish I could dance with him again."

Now all three girls pat my arm. Even Charlie gets up from the bed to comfort me. And I appreciate it so, so much. What would I do without these amazing girls?

"No more feeling sorry for myself," I say with a bright smile. "Let's have fun tonight. Ally, call your sister."

She salutes and leaves the room, returning a few minutes

later with a reluctant Amanda. She takes one look at us and says, "You owe me big for this. Because all this?" She motions at us. "It's going to take a lot of work."

Ally scowls. "Just make us look pretty."

"Sure thing. Who wants to go first?"

All four of us blink at one another. Charlie steps back. "Don't look at me. This wasn't my idea. And I don't do dresses."

Amanda grabs her. "You're totally going first."

It takes hours before all of us are ready. Amanda checks out her work, hand on her chin. "Not bad, if I do say so myself. Who knew under all that nerdiness are actually pretty girls?" She turns us to the mirror so we can see her work. Wow. She's right. We look good. Different, but amazing. She didn't cake us up too much, just put on enough makeup to enhance our natural beauty.

Dani's wearing a dark purple dress with two slits on the sides, Ally's is a little more conservative—rose gold that covers most of her skin—Charlie's is an emerald green that shows a lot of leg and brings out her eyes, and mine is teal that reaches just above my knees.

Ally's cheeks are bright red, Dani smiles, Charlie huffs as she pulls on the hem of her dress, and I picture Brayden wrapping his arms around me at the dance. But then the reality hits me. He won't be doing that because he'll have his arms full of Teagyn. The thought of that makes me want to vomit. How can I go there and watch them? Maybe I should hide away in my room.

No. I'm going to the dance to have a good time with my friends. Tonight, I'm not Brayden Barrington's fake girlfriend. I'm just Kara from the book club and high school newspaper. And I'll make sure to enjoy every second of tonight.

Amanda puts some last-minute touches on us before we're good to go. Well, Ally, Dani, and me. Charlie on the other hand? She keeps muttering how this is so not her and she's going to rip the cursed thing off. Amanda threatens she'll smash her laptop if she dares. I don't know why Charlie is so against the dress—she looks amazing.

Amanda will be our chauffeur tonight, though she doesn't seem to mind it one bit. I think she feels like a proud mom sending her kids off to kindergarten.

"You know something, Ally?" She tells her sister as we get in the car, Ally taking the passenger seat while the rest of us climb into the back. "Tonight is free of charge."

Ally's eyes widen. "You serious?"

Amanda smiles. "You made me realize my calling. What I want to do with my life. I want to go to cosmetology school. I've always loved makeup, but tonight I realized I want to do it for a living. Giving makeovers to women is something that speaks to me. I mean, look at you and your friends. You went from drab to totally fab."

Dani's eyebrows furrow. "Gee, thanks a lot."

Amanda shoots her a look. "You want to look good for the dance or not? Hot guys will snatch you up within seconds."

Charlie snorts. "Doubt it. You might dress up the nerd and put makeup on the nerd, but she's still a nerd."

Amanda shakes her head in disbelief. "At least try to have a good time."

"That's the plan," Ally tells her.

The drive is a short one and we get there within minutes. I wring my hands in my lap, not ready to face tonight. To face Brayden with his arms around the girl who thinks I'm less than the ants on the ground. But it's not his fault. It's his duty. I've accepted it. I've told him I'm okay with it. I have to be.

"Kara?"

I snap back to Earth. Everyone else has already gotten out of the car and is waiting for me. I thank Amanda for the lift, then join my friends outside.

The other students are dressed beautifully and are entering the school gym where the dance is being held. I crane my neck for Brayden, but don't find him anywhere. Is he already inside? We're a little early, so maybe he's not here yet.

"Ready to go?" Dani asks.

Loud giggles prick my ears, and I turn my head to where the sound is coming from. The student lot. Brayden and Teagyn are headed this way, pressed together and fingers locked. A few cameramen and reporters surround them. Brayden has a wide, pleasant smile on his face. Teagyn is shining.

My heart stops pumping for a second. They look like the perfect couple. She with her beautiful golden dress that puts the rest of ours to shame, her updo that looks a million bucks. And Brayden in a suit that makes him look so dashing, like from a Jane Austen novel. His golden tie matches her dress, and he's holding her like she's the most important person in the world.

I swallow hard, my eyes burning a bit. I know this is just for the story they're doing on the school, but why did they have to pick him?

I didn't think it would hurt this much.

Brayden's eyes meet mine and his expression changes. His smile falters, but only for a little bit. He needs to represent the school now, to do what's expected of him. Of course he can't look miserable. But is he? Or is he having a good time?

"Where are you going, baby?" Teagyn says louder than she should. "They're taking our picture."

He turns to me. "I just wanted to talk to—"

"Smile!"

Charlie grabs hold of my arm, pulling me toward the entrance to the gym. "We don't have to see that."

All four of us freeze as we take in the gym. The homecoming dance committee transformed the place into a magnificent fairytale. I can't help but marvel at everything. From the decorations to the music to the lighting. It's like a dream come true.

And I've missed out on this for two years. Well, not anymore. I'll make tonight one of the best nights of my life.

"Who knew our lame gym could look so…" Dani starts.

Ally lifts a brow. "Magical?"

"Wondrous?" I supply.

"A waste of time?" Charlie mutters.

Dani frowns at her. "At least try to be into this. And maybe Amanda's right. Maybe we'll find ourselves some boyfriends tonight."

Charlie rolls her eyes. "What did I say about putting makeup on a nerd?"

Dani throws her hands up. "I'm trying to be positive." She groans as her eyes sweep the room. "What's *that* doing here?"

I follow her gaze and see Easton Knight, our resident billionaire, talking to one of his friends.

"He'll ruin the night for me," Dani grumbles.

"Just stay out of his way and you'll be fine," Charlie tells her.

"More like he needs to stay out of *my* way."

There's a commotion at the entrance, and when I look there, I find the reporters and their crew filming Brayden and Teagyn as they enter the gym. The reporters ask them many questions, tell them to strike a few poses, before they follow them deeper into the gym.

I turn away because I can't watch. It hurts too much. Not only because his arms are around her, but because of the smug smile on her face.

"Let's dance," Dani says, pulling me to the dance floor. Ally and a reluctant Charlie follow.

As I sway my body from side to side, all I can think about is the party and what happened afterward. That wonderful kiss. I haven't stopped thinking about it since. Will I ever kiss him again? Who am I kidding?

Everyone steps aside as the news crew films Edenbury High's IT couple swaying on the floor, tangled in each other's arms. Brayden's eyes are on hers and she giggles and laughs profusely. Then he smiles at her so warmly, and my heart shatters.

Why did I come? *Why did I come?*

My friends try to distract me with crazy moves, but I'm not really feeling it. I keep my eyes on Brayden the whole time. As he swings Teagyn in his arms, as he wraps them around her waist. As she bends her head close to his.

Ally squeezes my arm. "How are you holding up?"

"I'm fine. But I think I need a break."

They follow me as I sit down at a table, where I once again stare at my fake boyfriend. He's so…charismatic, so captivating. I don't think there's a girl here who hasn't stopped to stare at him.

I don't know how much time passes with everyone dancing and having a good time before it's time to crown the homecoming king and queen. Brayden already told me who the winners will be, so it's no surprise when he and Teagyn are called to the stage.

Ugh. They look so good up there together, so perfect. That's how the world works. The Braydens end up with the Teagyns, and I can't change that no matter how much my heart yearns to.

The news crew catches the whole thing on film and love what they see. I don't blame them. Our school will be very popular and well-liked when this story comes out.

The king and queen lead the first dance and I catch Brayden staring into Teagyn's eyes. Then I quickly look away because I can't stand it anymore. Many other kids join them on the dance floor, but I have no heart to. I'm glad I came, glad I was able to experience something regular teenagers do, but it's too hard. I don't know if I can stomach this any longer.

Dani, who sits across from me and is in the middle of talking, suddenly sits up like a spider crawled down her back. Her eyes widen at something behind me.

"Kara?" a deep, familiar voice says.

I turn my head and find Brayden standing there, his crown crooked on his head. But on him it looks perfect.

He holds out his hand. "Want to dance?"

I hear a collective gasp from all the other students who have stopped dancing and are watching us.

I just stare at him, not sure I heard him right. "What?"

His smile is warm and so friendly and sexy and all the good things that make me swoon internally. "Dance with me?" He stares into my eyes, his so mesmerizing I can get lost in them.

Dani kicks my leg from under the table and I jump. "Okay," I squeak.

He smiles again as I place my hand in his and get to my feet. As we walk through the many kids, I feel their heated eyes on me. I feel Teagyn's hard eyes on me.

Brayden tears the crown off his head and tosses it to DeAngelo. I hear another collective gasp from the students. Even the teachers are surprised.

"What are you doing?" I hiss as I take in the news crew who are also gaping at us. "What about Teagyn? The story?"

He shrugs as he twirls me onto the dance floor. My stomach somersaults like a gymnast as he wraps his arms around my waist, gently yanking me to his chest. "They got what they needed. Now I want to dance with you." He lowers my head to his chest before I can demand what the heck that means.

I focus on him and him alone, not the kids staring at us, not at Teagyn sending me what surely are death glares, and not the news crew who don't know what to make of this.

I'm in Brayden's arms, just like I dreamed of. I'm dancing with him, swaying on the floor with him, pressed up against him.

I never want to leave.

"I'm sorry," he whispers, his breath warm on my cheek. "I hated every second I was with her."

I laugh lightly. "The downside of being popular."

"Totally."

His arms tighten around me, securely, protectively, like he doesn't want to let me go. Or maybe I'm imagining it. Either way, I'll take it. I know this moment will only come once, and I want to enjoy it. So I shut my eyes and let the music wash over me, let Brayden's warmth snuggle me up. I just let myself go.

"You look beautiful tonight," he says after a few minutes

I lift my head to his, my heartbeat zooming up. Did he…did he just call me beautiful?

"Thanks," I breathe. "You look beautiful, too. Handsome. I mean, handsome."

He laughs softly. "Thanks."

"And you were amazing during the game," I tell him. "You were out of this world. I'm sorry my dad didn't see you."

"It's okay. I'm trying to be positive. And thanks for being so kind about my performance. I really felt it, you know? I was alive out there."

I smile. "You could tell."

I return my head to his chest and shut my eyes, letting the music flow through me and getting lost in Brayden's protective arms.

I hear Teagyn crying and screaming at the reporters not to leave. But they probably figure they're done here. Teagyn stomps her foot like a little kid, and I can feel Brayden's chest rumble as he chuckles.

"I think you ruined her night," I mumble, keeping my eyes shut as I continue resting my head on his strong chest.

He says something softly, maybe that she ruined his? I can't be sure. He also says something about it being better now? But I'm not sure if I'm hearing things that I want to hear. I mean, we're still faking, so this can't be...real. Can it?

For me, yes. For him? Probably not. I have to keep reminding myself that our arrangement is about him, not me.

We continue to sway and Brayden presses his warm cheek to mine, just as he did at the party. Then he pulls back and gazes into my eyes, his so deep and hypnotic. I gaze right back into his and time stands still. Everyone else fades into the background. It's just me and him on our own dancing island.

But then the music shifts to an upbeat song and the moment is lost. Brayden shakes his head, as if snapping out of the trance, and smiles at me. "Having a good time?"

"Yeah." He has no idea how miserable I was watching him

dance with Teagyn. He has no idea how much this moment means to me.

He bends close. "Me, too."

The music eventually turns slow again and Brayden once again wraps his arms around my waist. I press myself to his chest, my cheek to his.

And then we sway.

Chapter Twenty-Seven

I lounge on the couch Sunday afternoon, sitting on my phone so I won't be tempted to look at it. Specifically at Brayden's Spill It!.

It takes everything I have not to replay the homecoming dance in my head over and over and dissect it until there's nothing left but little pieces. Because I'll just drive myself even more insane than I already am.

How close we were, wrapped in each other's arms. How firm but comfortable his chest was as I rested my head on it. How warm his cheek was when he pressed it to mine...I sigh in contentment.

Don't let it get to your head, Kara, I tell myself. Brayden was just being nice. It's not that big of a deal that he ditched his date to dance with me, right? He was probably sick of Teagyn and her whining. I don't blame him for ditching her. Either way, the reporters had enough footage of Brayden and Teagyn together, so he figured he could dance with whoever he wanted.

Quarterbacks Don't Fall For Invisible Girls

But he chose you, my mind reminds me. *He called you beautiful.*

I shake my head, my cheeks warming. He probably just wanted to continue impressing my dad. Even though he wasn't at the game or at the party, Brayden knows I would tell my dad about it. Which would certainly earn him brownie points. It sucks, yeah, but that's how it is.

My hand acts without my permission and slides under my butt, sweeping out my phone and unlocking it. For the next half hour, I look at Brayden's Spill It!—rather, I look at posts and pictures and *anything* that has to do with homecoming. Teagyn, of course, posted tons of pictures of her and Brayden together. But of course there are no pictures of me and Brayden. It's like everyone wants to pretend it didn't happen.

Because someone like me isn't supposed to be with someone like him.

Keys jingle outside and then the door opens. Dad enters with his suitcase. "Dad!" I say.

His face lights up when he sees me. "Pumpkin! I thought you would be out."

I race over to him and hug him, then help him with his bag. "How was your trip?"

"Let me settle down and I'll tell you all about it."

He parks his suitcase on the side and heads to the kitchen. After preparing himself a cup of coffee, we both settle down at the kitchen table.

"So?" I ask. "Did you recruit the boy?"

"Unfortunately, he wasn't what we're looking for."

"I'm sorry," I say. "You traveled all the way there for

275

nothing."

He shrugs as he takes a sip of his coffee. "All part of the job, sweetie. I heard the Lions demolished Starview Grove High."

"They were amazing, Dad! Too bad you weren't there."

If he would have seen Brayden play, I know he would have recruited him on the spot.

"I'll help you unpack," I say.

I gather all his dirty laundry with mine and start a load. All the while trying to push homecoming out of my head. When I get back to the living room, I find Dad unwinding on the couch with a game. I drop down next to him. I try to concentrate on the game, but all I see before my eyes is me in Brayden's arms as we swayed to the soft music.

"I'm going to watch Brayden play this Friday."

I nod, my thoughts still on the events that happened yesterday. How he ditched Teagyn and held out his hand to me...

I sit forward and gape at Dad. "What did you just say?"

"I'm watching Brayden play at his next game."

"And you just casually threw that out like that!? Oh my gosh, he'll be so excited! I'm going to tell him right now."

I bound off the couch and run into my room, leaping on my bed and scrolling through my contacts. There aren't many people here, though, and I find Brayden's name in no time. I quickly press the green button.

"Kara, hi," he says.

"I have the best possible news in the world!"

Quarterbacks Don't Fall For Invisible Girls

He laughs. "Okay."

"Guess who's coming to watch you play this Friday?"

He's quiet for a bit, then he gasps. "Your dad's coming?"

"Yes!"

"But how? When? Why?"

"The guy he wanted to recruit this weekend was a total bust. I think he heard how well you did at the game and finally decided to check you out."

I hear him blow out a breath and lower himself on his bed. "Oh my gosh, Kara, I don't know what to say. I'm shaking."

"You don't have to say anything." I laugh.

"Thanks so much. I really couldn't have done any of this without you."

"I didn't do anything. It was all you. You're an amazing quarterback and you deserve this."

"Thanks. It means a lot to hear you say that."

"No problem."

Quiet.

He laughs again. "I kind of want to tell everyone."

"Oh! Please, go ahead. I'll see you tomorrow at school."

"Yeah. Thanks again, Kara."

My cheeks hurt from smiling so hard. Finally, Brayden will be given a shot to make his dreams come true. I'm so happy for him.

Then it dawns on me that if he gets recruited, he and I...we will cease to exist.

But maybe that's not true. After all, he told me I'm his friend. Maybe we'll still hang out? He'll really be the big man on

277

campus after he gets recruited. And me? I'll still be the same old me. Of course we can't be friends—we are and always will be from two different worlds.

Chapter Twenty-Eight

"This is so exciting!" Dani exclaims as we make our way to the bleachers. I stop for a moment and scan the crowd, and then I spot him in one of the front rows. My dad. A breath I didn't know I was holding seeps out of my nose. Thank goodness he's here. I can't wait to see the look on his face when he sees what an amazing player Brayden is. I bet he'll be so impressed he'll offer him a scholarship in the blink of an eye.

"Here's an empty spot," Charlie says. We follow her and sit down. There's a huge crowd tonight. Maybe because of the article? The reporters stated Brayden was the best quarterback to play for Edenbury High since his brother two years ago and that you would do a disservice to yourself not to see him play. They weren't lying. They should all get ready to have their socks knocked off.

"Kara!" a voice calls. "Princess Kara!"

I look to my left and spot Bailey with her family, waving a foam finger. I smile and wave back.

"Is that Brayden's sister?" Ally asks.

"Yeah, isn't she adorable?"

"Very."

After what feels like forever, the players finally run onto the field. My heart does a backflip as I take in Brayden. He looks...different. I mean, I can't see his expression because of his helmet, but it's like he has this aura around him. Full of confidence and excitement, and yeah, nerves, too. But it's the good kind of nerves. He's ready to knock this out of the park, that's for sure.

He sees his family first and waves both hands. Bailey squeals and jumps up and down, waving that foam finger. Her dad quickly grabs hold of her before she tumbles off the bleachers. "That's my brother!" she yells. "Bray the Bulldozer!"

I smile at how cute she is.

Then Brayden's head moves to me. I wave and point to my dad. He glances at him for a second before returning his gaze to me, his body growing a little stiff. I give him two thumbs up—he's got this. He nods before focusing on the game.

"The crowd is wild," Dani says. "This is sure to be one heck of a game."

And it is, at least for the first ten minutes. Because after that...things just go south.

"No," I gasp as I fall down on my seat. Brayden...I don't know what's going on, but...he's playing terribly.

I rub my eyes, certain they're playing tricks on me. But no, he continues to do a really bad job.

Coach Papas calls for a timeout. The team gathers and he yells at them, specifically Brayden. My heart hurts as I watch him shake his head, silently scolding himself. He glances at Dad for a second before putting his attention back on his coach.

"He'll do better now," I whisper. "He's probably just nervous."

"Yeah," Charlie says. "Everything is on the line for him now."

"You can do it!" Bailey yells. "My big brother is the best quarterback in the world! Go, go, Bray! Go, go Bray!"

He looks up at her and waves, though I notice his hand quakes. Wow, he's really nervous. He just needs to loosen up and shake away the nerves. He's got this.

Except…no, he hasn't got it. He plays even worse.

His coach yells at Brayden, even threatens to bench him. Again, I can't see his face, but his shoulders are slumped, like he's given up.

No, he can't give up.

Before I can stop myself, I leap to my feet and yell, "You can do it Brayden! You can do it!"

His head snaps to mine and his body perks up. He nods resolutely to himself before getting back in the game.

He plays better, but it doesn't last too long.

"Darn, what's wrong?" I glance at Dad and see him shaking his head as he jots some things down. "Oh no. He's not impressed."

My friends look at him. "There's still a chance for Brayden to turn things around," Dani says.

"The game's almost over," Charlie points out. "Chefield won."

Tears sting my eyes as the game ends. Chefield High is announced as the winner. They all cheer and congratulate each other as half of the stands go wild. As for the Lions? They just look at each other like they have no idea what just happened.

"What has gotten into you?!" Coach Papas shouts at Brayden. "You played worse than a middle schooler."

Brayden says something, but I can't hear from all the way here.

"You'd better!" the coach yells. "Because if you don't, you're off the team."

Brayden stands there staring after him. Then he yanks off his helmet and squeezes it in his hands, so hard his knuckles grow white. He looks up at his family with a haunted expression—like he let them down. No, like he let his dead brother down.

Then he glances at Dad, who's writing in his notepad, shaking his head. A hard swallow makes its way down his throat.

"Look at me," I whisper. "Please look at me."

He turns around and marches off the field.

My heart urges me to spring to my feet and hurry after him. To hug him and tell him it's okay—that it will be okay. That it *has* to be okay. But I keep myself planted on my butt because I don't know if he'd want me to chase after him. After all, we're not really boyfriend and girlfriend. Maybe he doesn't want me anywhere near him. He has his teammates and the cheerleaders and his family. I...I have no place in his life.

The crowd starts to thin out. My friends and I just sit there, still not believing what just happened.

"Kara!" a voice calls. "Kara Gander?"

I peer down and see Dad waving at me. "Let me drive you and your friends home."

Even though they live out of the way, Dad doesn't mind giving them a lift. None of us says a single thing as we drive to their houses. I guess we're all confused by the game. It's not until Dad and I are alone in the car that he says, "He has a lot of potential and raw talent, but he's not what Astor University is currently looking for."

"He's better than that, Dad!" I cry. "Much, much better. Quadruple times better! You should have seen him at homecoming. He was out of this world."

Dad keeps his eyes on the road. "Honey, I can only judge him on what I saw tonight with my own eyes. And tonight, he did not impress me."

"He was just nervous," I explain. "This meant so much to him."

"Pumpkin, if he falls under pressure that easily, he certainly isn't a good fit for Astor University. We can't take a chance on someone so unpredictable. Astor University only picks the best of the best. I'm sorry."

"He is the best, Dad! If you would have just come to the homecoming game instead of traveling across the country—"

"I understand you're concerned for him because he's your boyfriend, but it's a harsh world out there. My best wish for him is that another school sees something in him that we didn't."

There's so much I want to say. I wish I could make him see reason. Brayden's performance was not a reflection of who he is or how he plays. Why can't Dad understand that? Why can't he believe me when I tell him he's amazing?

But I fall back on my seat with a huff because I'm worried I might make things worse if I say another word. I spend the rest of the ride staring out the window, tears gathering in my eyes when I try to imagine how Brayden is feeling right now.

***

I stare at my phone for what must be the hundredth time. Every part of me itches to text him, to make sure he's okay. But how silly is that? Of course he's not okay. What if I upset him further by texting him?

Social media is abuzz with the Edenbury High Lion's abysmal performance, specifically that of the QB. Some people have even made memes of Brayden's terrible passes. I wish I could unleash a digital virus that would shut down the internet for good.

I start composing a text, but then I delete it. Start and delete again. Then I chuck my phone aside. He doesn't want to hear from the Invisible Girl.

With a sigh, I climb into bed and try to sleep. But the only thing I see before my eyes is Brayden's terrible performance and then the look on his face when he looked at my dad. Like he knew at that moment that he shattered his dreams forever.

I don't know how, but I manage to fall asleep. The first thing that enters my mind when I wake up is Brayden. And my whole body aches for him.

Quarterbacks Don't Fall For Invisible Girls

I get dressed and make my way to the kitchen. Dad is reading the morning paper. My mouth opens to say something, to try to plead Brayden's case again, but I force myself to close my mouth. It won't do any good, and I don't want to make things worse.

Dad smiles and offers me some pancakes. As I eat, he chats about many different things, but I can't listen to this. Dad's chatting happily like everything is all fine, when my boyfriend's world just fell apart. Okay, fine, my fake boyfriend, but I still care for him as though he's my real boyfriend.

Then it dawns on me that I've been looking at this all wrong. He might not see me as his girlfriend, but he *does* see me as his friend. I'm probably the only one who understands how he must feel right now because he and I concocted this plan together. I know how much was riding on his performance last night, and I know what it means that he blew it.

After I'm done eating, I tell Dad I'm going out and race out of the house. I call an Uber and ride to his house.

"Please be home," I mutter as I ring the bell. "Please."

No one answers. I try the bell again and knock. Shoot, maybe I should have texted him that I was stopping by.

I'm about to leave, but then I hear footsteps. Slowly, the door opens a crack and a head peeks out. Brayden's head.

I try not to gasp. Brayden looks…not so good. His eyes are bloodshot, his hair is a mess, his clothes are wrinkled like he slept in them, and his body is bent over like he'll collapse from dejection.

"Brayden," I whisper.

He squeezes his eyes shut. "Kara, sorry, I'm not really in the mood for company…"

"Can I talk to you?" I ask. "Please."

His eyes slowly flutter open and he nods, widening the door so I can enter. It doesn't look like anyone else is home. He leads me to his room and we sit side by side on his bed. At any other time, I might hyperventilate that I'm actually in Brayden Barrington's room. But I don't feel even an ounce of excitement. Just pain for what the guy I care most about must be feeling right now.

"How are you?" I ask. Then I hit my forehead. "Dumb question. Sorry."

He doesn't say anything, just stares at the spot in front of him.

"I wanted to text you last night, but…"

He still doesn't say anything. It looks like he might just die from disappointment, and that kills me. What can I say to make this guy feel better? Nothing. Absolutely nothing.

"What did your dad say?" his gruff voice asks.

I bite on my bottom lip. "It doesn't matter."

His head lifts to mine. "It does. Whatever it is, however harsh it is, I need to know."

"I don't know, Brayden."

"Please, Kara? And please don't sugarcoat it. I know I messed up big time."

I sigh, tearing my gaze away from him. "He said you're talented and he sees a lot of potential, but you're not what Astor University is looking for."

A heavy, heart-wrenching breath escapes his mouth. "What else?"

"Brayden…"

"Please."

"Okay. He said Astor University can't take a chance on someone unpredictable like that. That it's a harsh world out there and Astor University only takes the best. He wishes you the best and hopes another school will see something in you that he didn't."

He pinches his eyes shut. "It's over. Darn it, it's over." He scrubs his hand down his face. "Everything I worked for all my life, down the toilet because of one sucky performance…" He takes in a deep breath and releases it. "I guess I have no choice but to hope another school recruits me. But after my crappy performance, I doubt any school would look at me ever again. I don't know what happened. I…I was just so nervous. Felt so much pressure. I…I guess I caved." He hangs his head. "Darn it." He lifts his head and tries to smile at me, but fails miserably. "Thanks for all your help, Kara. You've been so kind and supportive to me throughout all of this. Sorry I wasted your time."

"You didn't waste my time," I try to tell him, but his head isn't here.

We sit in silence for a long time. I know I'm not helping by staying here. As much as I wish I could suck out his pain, the truth is that I can't. Brayden has to deal with this on his own.

"I'll see you," I whisper as I get up and make my way to the door.

The one thing I want to do is help the people I care about. And I'm powerless to do anything to help Brayden. I hate this feeling of being powerless. When my mom was sick in the hospital, I was powerless to do anything. I just sat there and watched her wither away until she was gone.

At the door, I look back at Brayden and find his body still bent over like a question mark, dejected, hopeless, lost.

I won't stand by and be powerless. I *won't*. I march back over and say, "No, Brayden. We're *not* giving up."

His head springs to mine.

"You're the best quarterback Edenbury High has ever seen. You're *going* to be recruited by my dad and you're *going* to Astor University."

"But…"

"I don't care what it takes," I continue, my voice firm and full of hope. "I'm not giving up on you. We'll do this, Brayden—together. We'll show my dad how *lucky* he'd be to have someone like you for his school. I mean, we'll have to figure out what to do about your nerves, but the point is that we'll do it *together*. I won't stand idly by and watch your dream go up in flames. I *won't*."

He just stares at me, totally dumbfounded. Then he shoots up from his bed and throws his arms around me. "Why does it feel like you care more about me than I deserve?"

I internally sigh as I melt against his body. *Tell him*, my voice urges. My heart begs. *Tell him how you feel. Now is the perfect opportunity to lay all the cards on the table. To bare your heart and soul.*

No, I can't do that. The only thing that matters right now is

Brayden. He needs to focus on football, not some girl who has a massive crush on him.

I step out of the hug and smile at him. "One thing my mom taught me was that it's never too late to chase your dreams. If you want something, you have to go for it. *Never* give up."

For the first time since the game, I see a smile on his face, and his body is no longer bent over. "You're right," he says. "I can't give up now."

I nod. "You focus on being the best quarterback you can be, and I'll work on my dad. I promise you, Brayden, I won't ever give up on you."

He wraps his arms around me again. "Thank, you, Kara. Thank you so much. I can't remember the last time someone believed in me this much."

"Now all you have to do is believe in yourself."

Chapter Twenty-Nine

Brayden has a troubled look on his face when I enter the movie theater Sunday afternoon and find him leaning against the wall. Even though we promised not to give up, he's still broken over what happened on Friday. It's hard to have hope when everything seems hopeless. I wish there was something I could do. That's why I invited him to watch a movie with me. To help take his mind off things, to take a break from life for a few hours.

"Hi," I say as I face him. "You okay?"

He shrugs. "I'm trying to be."

I place my hand on his arm. "We'll convince my dad to give you another chance."

He forces a smile. "Hope so. Have you chosen a movie?" He tilts his head to the poster across from us. "That looks good. A comedy is what I need right now."

"Of course."

We pay for our tickets, popcorn, and other snacks, then settle down in the theater.

"Thanks so much for this," Brayden says as he puts his drink in the cup holder. "It means a lot that you care. You're a very special person, Kara."

My cheeks heat up. "You're special, too. And you'll live out your dreams. I know it."

He nods. "Thanks. It's just a little hard. Seeing the disappointment on my parents' faces. They're not upset with me, of course. They're just worried."

"I'm really sorry. I hope this movie takes your mind off it for a little while. Movies always help me forget my problems."

"They do for me, too."

The lights dim and the movie begins. I don't watch comedies often and am pleasantly surprised at how funny this is. Like crazy funny. Not the corny or silly kind, but pure laugh-out-loud funny. Brayden, me, and the rest of the people are rolling in our seats.

My hand is on the armrest the whole time, but during the movie, Brayden places his hand on mine and I feel warm and cozy and tingly all over.

"Sorry," he quickly says, removing his hand. I want to tell him to put it back on, but of course I don't. Today isn't about me, it's about making him feel better.

He's laughing a lot, which makes me laugh, too. And when the movie is over, we take a stroll around the nearby park, discussing our favorite moments from the movie.

"Thanks for putting me in a good mood," he says. But then his face changes as it must dawn on him that he's exactly where he was two hours ago. "So much for that. I'm sorry for being

291

so negative and down."

I shake my head. "No, don't be sorry. I just wish I knew what to say to help."

"You've done so much, Kara. I really appreciate you wanting to convince your dad to give me another shot, but I don't know…I guess I don't want to get hopeful and then be disappointed."

"I understand."

He plows his hand through his hair. "I love hanging out with you, but is it okay if I walk alone?"

"Of course."

***

I plop down on the couch with a sigh. I feel so down, so helpless. Because Brayden's so frustrated with himself. And there's nothing I can do about it. I feel so bad, like I'm taking on his problems. It's not like I mean to do it, I just care about him so much. My crush? It's turned into love. I'm in love with him. Not just infatuated. I've fallen deep and hard for this guy. And I can't stand seeing him so broken.

But other than try to cheer him up, there's nothing I can do. It's not like I can hold a gun to Dad's head and threaten him to watch Brayden play again. I know I promised Brayden I would do whatever I could to convince Dad to give him another chance, but I still have no clue how I'll do it.

Dad shifts from his seat on the recliner and I glance up. I didn't see him there reading the paper. I'm so distracted with Brayden, it's swallowing me up whole. I know it's not healthy. I just care about him so much.

"Hi, sweetie. How was the movie?"

I sigh as I remember how excited and happy Brayden was, then how quickly that morphed into gloominess.

"Was good."

Dad watches me for a little bit with concern. "You've been walking around the house like a ghost the past few days," he says.

I shrug. "I know and I'm sorry. I just…"

He nods. "It's Brayden. You feel bad for what happened."

I sigh again. "It sucks. He's such a good player and just had a bad day. You saw him play at the *one* game he played badly. The universe has an odd sense of humor," I grumble. "If only you could have seen him at the other games. You would have been floored." I grab a cushion and hug it tightly to my chest, biting hard on my lip so I won't cry. Life is so unfair. And I have absolutely no idea how to convince my dad to come to another game. Does that mean I made Brayden a promise I can't keep?

Dad studies me as I continue battling my tears. The only thing I see is Brayden's sad eyes.

"Okay, pumpkin, here's what I'll do. I'll give him another chance."

My eyes leap to his. "What?"

He holds up his hand. "Only because I love you and he's your boyfriend. And because he's a good kid." His face grows serious. "But you tell him he'd better be on his game this Friday. He needs to be flawless."

I jump to my feet. "I will! I will! Thanks, Dad." I rush over

Emma Dalton

to him and throw my arms around him. "Thanks so much! I have to tell him."

I call an Uber to take me to his house and ram my knuckles on the door. Feels like hours pass before it swings open to reveal Brayden.

He must see the animated look on my face because he asks, "What happened?"

I enter the house and the words tumble out of my mouth. "My dad's giving you another chance! He's coming to watch you play this Friday!"

His eyes widen. "What? Are you serious?"

"Yes! He just told me."

"How did you convince him?"

"I didn't. I think he saw how important it was to me that he give you another shot."

He flings his arms around me, squeezing me to his chest. "I can't believe this. Thanks so much!"

I pull free, my face probably as serious as my dad's. "But you have to be your best. You have to play as well as you did at homecoming."

He nods quickly. "I will. I won't let him, my parents, or you down."

I grin. "See? This whole fake dating thing worked out after all!"

His smile drops. "Right."

"What's wrong?"

He shakes his head. "I just don't know how to thank you. I feel like nothing I do will ever be enough." He swallows. "I just need to make sure I'm ready. I can't let anything distract me. No more nerves. I can do this."

"Yeah. You focus only on football for the next few days. Then you'll knock my dad off his feet."

He smiles. "I hope so." He flings his arms around me. "Thank you, Kara. I couldn't have done this without you." He steps back, rubbing the back of his head. "I'm acting like I already got recruited."

"Because you will be. I know it. I can *feel* it. And if you need me to cheer you on from the sidelines, I'm your girl."

His face brightens. "You really are special, Kara."

My heart soars to heaven as he looks at me like I'm his world, but then it comes back to Earth when I remember this isn't real. He's *not* looking at me like I'm his world. I've just helped him get one step closer to his dream.

Chapter Thirty

On my way to my book club meeting Monday after school, I stop when I hear voices from around the corner of the hallway. Familiar voices. I inch closer to take a peek.

Brayden and Teagyn are standing there. The halls are deserted, except for the two of them. Their voices are hushed so I can't hear what they're saying.

They lean toward each other and kiss. I can't see Brayden well because she's blocking him, but I see enough. And it's not just any kiss—it's full of passion and love.

My heart shatters into a million pieces.

He kissed her. He *kissed* her.

Whirling on my heels, I fight tears as I make my way to the book club. How could he? How *could* he? Were they dating all this time? Was he fooling me?

Sure, we were faking all this time, but still. He should have told me he had a real girlfriend on the side.

Or...or did they just get together now? I knew I saw him gazing at her at the homecoming dance. I suspected he had feelings for her, but I didn't want to believe them. But now I know the truth.

I shove the door to the book club open and throw myself down in my seat. I'm too broken, too angry, too upset to hold the tears anymore. They roll down my cheeks.

"Kara?" my friends gather around me, placing their hands on my back and shoulders. "What's wrong?"

I glance up at each of them, shaking my head because I can't get the words out. The others pull their desks closer to mine and sit down. "Talk to us," Dani urges. "Please. We hate seeing you this upset."

Ally rubs my back. "It's okay, talk when you're ready. We're here for you."

They sit with me for a few minutes as I try to make sense of my jumbled thoughts. But there's nothing to make sense of. He never cared for me. Of course he didn't. It was all fake to him.

I look at each of my friends. "I saw Brayden kissing Teagyn," I whisper.

They exchange stunned glances.

I throw my hands up. "Why should I be surprised? Now that my dad is giving him another shot this Friday, he doesn't need me anymore. So he ran to Teagyn." Fresh tears pool out of my eyes.

"Jerk," Charlie mutters. "I knew something like this would happen."

I wipe my eyes with a tissue Dani provides for me. "But he's not a jerk…he was so nice to me. How could he do this?"

Charlie's face grows hard. "He played you just to get close

to your dad. And now that he got what he wanted, he threw you to the curb."

Tears spring to my eyes again and drip down my cheeks. I don't know what to say, what to think. I'm just so lost and confused and I don't want to do anything but cry. My friends know this and stay with me as the sounds of my tears fill the quiet room.

***

When I get home, I put on a brave face for my dad, pretending everything is great and telling him how much I'm looking forward to Brayden's game on Friday. Then I sulk to my room and drop down on my bed. The tears continue to seep out of my eyes as I lay there. Just lay there.

Their kiss keeps replaying in my head over and over again. No matter what I do, I can't forget it.

She's definitely a better kisser than me. Has he compared us? Was I so disgusting that he ran to her? Did he want to forget me *that* badly?

My phone dings and I reach for it, assuming it's my friends texting to try to comfort me some more. But my insides fill with dread and pain. He's texting me after what he did?

Brayden: Hey, Kara. How are you? I think I had a good practice today, but I missed you in the bleachers. How was book club?

His words are so sweet, it's hard to imagine this is the same guy who hurt me so badly just a few hours ago. He's making it seem like he genuinely cares about me. If he cared, he wouldn't have kissed the girl who's been tormenting me since my epic fail at cheerleading tryouts.

Why can't he be the guy I dreamed of? Why does a part of me still believe he is?

With fresh tears flowing from my eyes, I stash my phone under my pillow and turn to my side, closing my eyes. Mom always said things will look better in the morning, but I doubt that's the case here. Because tomorrow morning, Brayden will still be with Teagyn. That won't change.

My phone dings a few more times, and I know Brayden's texting me. But I force myself to ignore him. For my own emotional health, I need to forget him.

***

I'm like a zombie as I enter school the next day. I don't look at anyone, barely talk to my friends—and they understand that I need time—just go to my locker to get my books for first period. The football players are gathered in the distance, and I notice Brayden in the group. I also notice Teagyn there as well.

I rip my gaze away and head for my first class, trying not to cry at how lonely I feel. Brayden used to walk me to my classes, but that feels like centuries ago.

I get through my classes and then it's time for lunch. I don't have it in me to face everyone in the cafeteria, but I do want to hang out with my friends. They've been so supportive and I don't want to shut them out. But as I make my way to the cafeteria, a hand latches around my wrist and drags me aside.

Brayden stands before me, so close I can see just how clear and beautiful his eyes are. But I force my heart to remain calm. He's not who I thought he was.

He searches my eyes. "Are you okay? Why haven't you been answering my texts?"

I glance away from him because I can't look him in the eye without bursting into tears. I thought I shed enough over him, but I guess not.

"What's wrong?" His voice is soft, a little desperate. "Are you avoiding me?"

I should be mad at him, I should yell at him. But I can't. I just can't. There is only one thing I know for sure, though—I can't do this anymore.

Lifting my head, I look him in the eyes. "I'm done, Brayden."

"What?"

I wave my hands around. "All this? I'm done with it. I don't want to do it anymore."

He steps closer to me, causing me to back into the lockers, but I don't have much room to move to. "What are you talking about?"

"What do you need me for?" I ask, holding back tears. "You got what you wanted. My dad's giving you another shot this Friday. Our arrangement is over."

"Kara." He reaches for my hand, but I yank away from him. Turning on my heels, I stalk to the doors. I never left during school hours before, never cut class, never skipped lunch, but I need a break. From him. From everything.

I'll probably be back in time for next period, but right now, I just need some space. As I march to wherever, I let the tears fall freely down my face.

Chapter Thirty-One

I wake up far too early on a Saturday morning. At 6 AM.

I try to fall back asleep, but all I'm doing is tossing and turning. Why can't I fall asleep, darn it! I haven't slept well all week. All because of that jerk Brayden.

Except, why do I still believe in my heart that he's not a jerk?

No, I have to tell myself that he is, or else I'll mourn over him for the rest of my life. I need to cut him out of my heart. But it's been nearly a week already and I still ache when I think about him. And the ridiculous thing is that we were never even together. So I have a broken heart over something that never existed.

It was real in my mind, though. In my heart.

The best way to distract myself is to play on my phone. But I turned off my Wi-Fi and mobile internet so I won't be tempted to look at his Spill It!. I can't even text my friends because they're still sleeping.

Somehow, an hour passes and then another. At 8:30, I can't

301

stand lying in bed anymore. Maybe I'll find a show to binge on Netflix. I go downstairs and pour myself a bowl of cereal, but there isn't any milk left. Maybe Dad went to the grocery.

I curl up on the couch with a show that doesn't have an ounce of romance.

About half an hour later, Dad walks in with a grocery bag, seeming surprised to see me awake. "Hey, pumpkin. You're up early."

I haven't told him that Brayden and I broke up. Even though he hurt me, I don't want to screw up any chance he has of getting recruited.

"You were at the grocery?" I ask.

"We were out of milk." After he deposits it in the fridge, he settles down near me. "Another teen drama?"

"No, I'm sick of those. This is a thriller movie."

He leans back and we watch in silence.

"Dad, how was the game last night?" I ask.

I know I shouldn't care, but I can't help myself. I invested myself in Brayden and his cause and am dying to know how it all turned out. I couldn't bring myself to go last night, and Dad thinks I was sick.

"I was impressed," he says.

"What do you mean by that?"

"Just that I was impressed."

Is he trying to turn all my hair gray? What the heck is that supposed to mean?

But I guess it doesn't matter. It shouldn't matter. He got what he wanted from me.

***

"My turn to pick the next book," Charlie says as we gather at my locker before first period.

"Okay, but nothing too complicated," Dani says. "I'm swamped with so much work and need to use my brain cells on that."

Ally sighs. "*A Lady of True Honor* was far too good."

I laugh. "Well, I'm game with whatever. Just as long as it's a good book."

"Kara?" a voice says from behind me.

My friends and I turn around and come face to face with Brayden. He stands there with an uncertain expression in his eyes. But there's something else in there, too. A bright light that can illuminate the world. Did he and Teagyn just have a hot and spicy make out session under the bleachers?

He takes a small, hesitant step toward me. "Can I talk to you?"

I should say no. Really, I should. But there's something else in his eyes…something that makes me sigh and say, "Just for a minute."

He nods and we walk off to the side. I fold my arms over my chest, keeping my eyes on him.

He smiles unsurely as he rakes his hand through his hair. "I've been recruited, Kara."

I stare at him. "What?"

"I impressed your dad. Astor University wants me to play for them."

A part of me wants to fling my arms around him and give

him a super tight hug. Finally, after everything he's been through, after he worked so hard and…

No, he doesn't deserve anything from me. The only reason my dad gave him another chance was because of me.

"Congrats," I say.

His face falls, like he was expecting me to actually hug him. Why does his expression squeeze my heart?

He moves closer. "Kara—"

"It's great that your dreams are coming true. Good luck." I turn around and walk back to my friends.

"Kara!" he calls after me.

"Let's go," I tell them.

As we march away, it takes everything I have not to look back at him. To glimpse one more time at the guy I thought he was.

Chapter Thirty-Two
Brayden

"Where's the tea?" Bailey's voice calls from upstairs, in her perfect British accent. "Princess Bailey is getting a little impatient."

I smile as I place the teabag in the pot, or I try to. I don't think I've given anyone a real smile the past few days, because all I've been feeling inside is confusion, hurt, hopelessness. Kara is no longer my friend.

I don't know what happened between us. She's been ignoring me, hasn't returned my texts. I just don't understand what I did wrong.

"Prince Brayden!" Bailey calls.

I place the teapot and mugs on a tray and carry it up to her room. She's already sitting at the table in her Belle dress, shoulders raised in importance. "Yay!" she cheers when I walk in.

I try to give her a smile as I place the tray on the table and settle down, but it's hard. I guess I'm not great at hiding my emotions. But I don't want Bailey to sense something's wrong. I want her to be as carefree as possible.

"Thank you," she says when I pour her a cup.

She starts to slurp and chat in her British accent, but try as I might, I can't focus on her. My thoughts are consumed with Kara and what I could have possibly done wrong. I really don't understand. She was so excited when she came over to tell me her dad was giving me another shot. And then she totally changed. She didn't respond to my texts and then dropped the bomb on me—she was done with our arrangement. Done with me.

I thought we were friends. No, I thought…well, I thought we might have been more than friends. But I was wrong. I started developing feelings for her, but I guess she never felt the same. For her, it was all pretend.

I don't know how I pulled off the game last weekend. I was so distraught and confused and hurt by her actions. But I had no choice but to shove it all away. For my parents and Bailey, for Brock, and for myself. But also for Kara. Because she was there for me every step of the way. She was there when I was so broken over my bad performance at that previous game, and she was the one who raised me up. She didn't want to quit on me and refused to let me quit on myself. Because of her, I pushed myself. I believed in myself. Because of her, my dreams were a possibility.

She hadn't shown up to my game. I saw her dad in the stands, but not her. It made my world collapse, but I had to push all my feelings away. Even if it took every bit of strength I had. And I had a knock-out performance.

Thanks to her, I got recruited by her dad. She didn't even congratulate me, not really. I thought she would be happy, I thought the news might have patched up whatever went wrong with us. But she gave me a lame congrats and walked away, not looking back once.

Are she and I...over?

"When's Kara gonna have tea with us again?" Bailey asks as she finishes her tea. "I miss her."

I sigh as I slump forward in my seat. "Me, too." A lot.

Chapter Thirty-Three

A few days have passed since Brayden told me he got into Astor University. I've been hanging out with my friends a lot, accepting their comfort. They really are the truest, dearest friends in the world. I'm lucky to have them.

Now it's Thursday after school and I'm home alone. Dani has dance, Ally has choir, and Charlie's got all her extra homework. And Dad's not home, either.

The house is so quiet. So lonely. I wish Mom were here. She'd know how to help me get through this. Dad doesn't even know that Brayden and I broke up. I guess he'll find out eventually.

I slump around the house, too distracted to do my homework. I miss him. I miss him so much. Going to his games, seeing him practice, texting him. Hanging out. Seeing his eyes light up with a smile. Being in his arms when we danced.

I'll never experience those things with him again. Heck, maybe never again. Because if this is what heartbreak feels like,

Quarterbacks Don't Fall For Invisible Girls

I'd rather remain single.

I go to the living room and turn on the TV for some Netflix. I'm not really in the mood, but maybe a good TV show will distract me. Action and science fiction will be perfect right now.

I must be in the middle of the second episode when the doorbell rings. Maybe my friends are done with their extracurriculars and want to keep me company. Awesome. I could seriously use them right now.

Flinging the door open, I go still when I spot the tall guy standing before me with eyes the color of the sky. It's been days since I've gazed at them, and my heart skips a beat. Stomach swoops with summersaults.

I don't want Brayden. Don't want anything to do with him. I make a move to shut the door in his face, but he presses his palm against it. "Kara, what's going on? What happened between us? Why are you ignoring me?"

The tears are threatening to fall because he sounds so confused and torn up and lost. But it's all an act, right? He knows exactly what he did.

"Why are you so upset with me?" He's nearly pleading now, his voice cracking a little. That just makes the battle with my tears grow stronger.

"Just run off to your girlfriend." I once again am about to shut the door in his face, but he slams his palm against it again.

"My girlfriend? What are you talking about?"

"Teagyn!"

His eyebrows furrow. "Teagyn? My girlfriend? Never in a

million years would I ever go out with that girl. Even if she was the last woman on Earth."

I throw my hands up. "But I saw you kiss her! I saw the two of you in the hallway last week. You *kissed* her."

He gently takes hold of my hands. For a second, I want to melt into them because his touch is so warm. But then I remember how much he hurt me. "Kara, I didn't kiss her. *She* kissed *me*."

I yank my hands free from his grip, rolling my eyes. "That's what they all say. You're lying."

He gazes into my eyes, pleading. "Kara, I swear to you I didn't kiss her. She came onto me, said we deserve to be together. That I was wasting my time with you. But I pushed her away. I never wanted Teagyn. I don't love Teagyn. I…I love you, Kara Gander. I'm crazy about you."

I cross my arms over my chest as more tears drip down my face. "You're lying. How could someone like you love someone like me? Just look at me!"

He takes my hands again. "I *am* looking at you. I see a smart, beautiful, kind, caring, wonderful girl. A girl who means the world to me. A girl who has captured my heart. A girl whom I never want to let go of."

I pull my hands away, turning my head to the side. He doesn't mean that. He's lying to me. Maybe he still needs me around because he's worried Astor University will retract his scholarship.

But then I move my eyes to his and I realize I'm being ridiculous. This is Brayden Barrington. The guy who has a huge heart, who was so kind to me, who never made me feel like I was invisible. And it wasn't only because of our arrangement. He texted me when he didn't have to. He hung out with me when he didn't have to. He became my friend when he didn't have to. He defended me from Teagyn when he didn't have to. He *cared* that I was uncomfortable because of the kiss. He actually took the time to consider my feelings.

I know this guy and I know he would never hurt me.

"I…I…" But no words come out. I'm speechless.

He gathers me close to his chest. "I started falling for you when you played tea party and basketball with me and Bailey," he whispers in my ear. "No, I think it was before that, even. You had such a bright smile that lit up your entire face. And every time you smiled, I felt something. In here." He touches his heart. "I didn't know what it was at first, but now I do. I've found that special girl I've been waiting for. It's you, Kara. When we kissed, my feelings for you grew stronger. Because that was the most amazing feeling in the world. Being with you makes me happy. I can't bear not having you in my life. I can't bear you being upset with me." He gazes into my eyes. "Please believe me when I say there's nothing going on between me and Teagyn. I don't love her. I love you, Kara Gander. You are and always will be my special girl."

I stare into his eyes. "Do you really mean that?"

He rests his forehead on mine. "I do. I want to show you off to the world. I don't want to fake anything with you anymore. I want to date you for real. Please tell me you want the same."

I lift my hand to stroke his cheek, more tears slipping down my face. "I've had a crush on you since middle school."

He wipes my tears with his thumbs. "I wish I could have known that sooner. I've always been in awe of you. You're so smart and I never imagined you'd want anything to do with a dummy like me."

"You're not a dummy. You're smart and so talented. And you got recruited into the school of your dreams. Your future is so bright."

He rests his hand on the back of my neck. "Only if you're in it, Kara. What do you say? Do you want to date me for real?"

I shut my eyes, feeling the tears drip down the sides of my face. Then I open them. "How can we? I'm the Invisible Girl and you're the star quarterback."

He gathers me close again. "I don't care. I don't care what anyone says. I love you and want to be with you. You're my world."

"I love you too, Brayden," I whisper. "I always have."

His mouth dips toward mine, then his eyes scan mine, as if he's asking if this is okay. I bring my head closer to his and close my eyes. When his lips make contact with mine, a spark shoots to each and every one of my limbs. I wrap my arms around his neck, pressing myself closer to him like I can't get enough of him. And he locks his arms around me like he can't get enough of me, either.

He's kissing me so gently and softly, like he wants to savor every moment. Then he draws back and searches my eyes. I smile and kiss him again, this time more urgently, passionately.

Quarterbacks Don't Fall For Invisible Girls

I've waited for this for years and it's finally happened. For real this time.

Brayden Barrington, star quarterback and the most popular guy at Edenbury High has fallen for me, the Invisible Girl.

And they say fairytales don't come true. But I'm having my happily ever after right now. I find myself giggling. I'm just so darn happy.

"Why are you laughing?" Brayden asks.

I shake my head. "Just kiss me."

And he does. We remain in the doorway of my house, kissing like the world is coming to an end and we're the last two people on Earth.

I can totally get used to this.

"Want to know a secret?" I ask him when we finally take a break. "You're the first boy I have ever kissed."

He smiles. "Want to know a secret? You're the first girl I've kissed who actually means something to me."

And we lock lips again. At the back of my mind, I know Dad could drop by any second, but I don't really care.

Chapter Thirty-Four

"Oh my gosh, these burgers are my life," Dani says as she continues digging into her burger. "We need to eat here at Mikey's every weekend."

Brayden grins at me as he dips a fry into ketchup and brings it to my mouth. I bite a chunk off. "The fries are amazing, too," I say.

"Not as amazing as you," he says.

I nuzzle his nose.

"Ugh, you guys are too cute," Charlie says.

"Makes you want to have a guy of your own, huh?" Dani teases her.

"Nope," she says, popping the "p."

"Liar," Ally says with a laugh.

Brayden stretches his arm over my shoulder and I snuggle against him. I can't believe that just a week ago, I thought I hated this guy. I thought my heart would never heal. But here we are together finally. For *real.* And we couldn't be happier.

"My dad wants you to come over for dinner tomorrow

night," I tell him.

"Are you going to cook again?" Brayden asks as he rubs my shoulder.

"Definitely not! I need my hair to stay brown or else I'll look like a grandma when I'm thirty. We'll probably order something fancy."

"Can't wait," he says. "I really love your dad."

"And he loves you," I tell him. "Seriously, he can't stop talking about you. He said he hasn't recruited anyone as gifted as you in a long time."

His brow shoots up. "He really said that?"

I nod. "Your parents must be very proud of you."

"They are. And so is Bailey. And I hope Brock is, too."

I slide my hand into his and give it a loving squeeze. "I know he is."

"Ugh, I can't with the two of you," Dani complains. "You two are relationship goals."

"Well, if you minus out the faking part," I remind her.

"I don't know," Brayden says as he smiles at me. "I think faking it brought us closer."

"We definitely would never have gotten together otherwise."

"That's because of this moron right here." He points to himself. "I can't believe I could have missed out on the most amazing person in the world."

"You know what I love most?" Dani says with a mischievous grin. "Seeing Teagyn's face whenever the two of you walk down the hallway holding hands."

"Don't be mean," I say.

"Admit it, you secretly gloat."

I giggle. "I totally do!"

"Busted," Charlie says.

We all laugh.

"I do feel a little sorry for her, though," Ally says. "The cheerleaders aren't doing that great. They probably won't make it to nationals. Coach Myers is super hard on Teagyn. Maybe she wouldn't be so bad if she didn't have all that stress thrown on her."

Ally has a point. Who knows what kind of person someone could be if they had the confidence to just be themselves? The Edenbury High Times might have introduced me to Brayden, and the fake relationship might have brought us together, but what made us a couple was each other. Our personalities. It doesn't matter that he's a popular jock and I am Invisible Girl. All that matters is what's in our hearts.

"Look who just walked into Mikey's," Charlie says as she teasingly slugs Dani's shoulder.

Dani glances at the door and frowns. "He always shows up wherever I am. It's like he's stalking me."

"I'm pretty sure he's just here to pick up an order," I say as the woman behind the counter hands him a takeout bag.

"He could have gone to any diner," Dani points out.

"You just said yourself that Mikey's has the best burgers," Ally reminds her.

"But what's he doing slumming it down here with us commoners? Don't arrogant rich people like him only eat gourmet food?"

"Maybe he wants to be a normal kid and eat unhealthy food?" Charlie offers.

"Am I missing something here?" Brayden asks. "What's wrong with Easton Knight? The guy's cool."

Dani gapes at him. "Cool? *Cool?* Are we talking about the same pompous jerk?"

"Uh…I wouldn't refer to him as a pompous jerk…"

"He's coming this way!" Ally hisses.

"Hey," the guy in question says, stopping before our table. "How's it going?"

He's always dressed to perfection. A clean-cut dress shirt with no wrinkles, not a single crease in his pressed pants, his chocolate brown hair brushed neatly, not a strand out of place. And not a speck of dirt on his shoes.

And he's hot. Not as sexy as my boyfriend, though.

"Hey, Easton." Brayden slaps his arm. "Picking up dinner?"

He rolls his eyes. "Sneaking it in my car. You know I can't eat this stuff at my house."

"Such a tragedy," Dani mutters sarcastically. Then her eyes widen and she covers her mouth. Clearly she didn't mean to say that out loud.

"Something you want to say, Wood?" Easton asks in an overly sugary voice.

"Nope," she says, glaring down at the table. "Nothing at all."

He keeps his eyes on her for a bit before muttering, "Mmm," and turning back to Brayden. "See you around,

Barrington."

"Catch you later, Easton."

As soon as he walks out the door with his food, Dani grumbles something under her breath.

"If I didn't know any better, I'd think there was some tension between you two," Ally says. "Of the romantic kind."

Her jaw hangs open. "You think he and I…girl, you have no idea what you're talking about."

"Uh huh."

"Can we please enjoy our meal and not talk about the arrogant Easton Knight Jr.?"

After we're done, Charlie, Ally, and Dani go home while Brayden and I take a stroll around the park, hand in hand. His is warm and so large it swallows mine up. I feel protected and loved, a feeling I'll cherish forever.

"How are your parents doing?" I ask as we continue our stroll.

"Much better." His eyes light up with a massive grin. "Things are definitely looking up, and I have a feeling they'll be back to their old selves soon."

I squeeze his hand. "I'm so happy to hear that."

"Thanks. And Bailey requested your presence for tea tomorrow."

Smiling, I say, "I'm totally there."

When we reach an area devoid of people, he locks his arms around my waist and hauls me against his chest, staring into my eyes. I stare into his mesmerizing blue ones, getting lost in them.

"I know I keep telling you this," he whispers. "But you're the best thing that could have happened to me. You changed my life, Kara. I love you so much."

I snake my hands up his hard chest, feeling the muscles underneath, then tangling them in his soft sandy brown hair. "You changed my life, too. For the first time since my mom died, I finally feel happy again. I love you, Brayden."

He moves his face closer to mine and gives me a sweet but passionate kiss. I push myself closer to his body, wishing I could get even closer than I already am. He and I have been on such a long journey, but there's still a long road ahead of us. A road that is full of so many possibilities. I don't want to share it with anyone other than him.

When we break apart from the kiss, he strokes my cheek. "I know you've always felt invisible, but you are the most *visible* person in my life. You always will be. Forever."

I smile and press my cheek to his. "How are you so perfect?"

He laughs. "Me? Perfect?"

I nod as I play with the hair at the nape of his neck. "You're the best boyfriend a girl could ask for. Thank you for being in my life."

"And thank you for being in mine." He nods in the distance. "I have a surprise for you."

I turn to where he's facing and my eyes widen as I take in the orange, red, and purple colors of the sun kissing the horizon. "Sunset," I gasp. "It's beautiful."

"*You're* beautiful, my special, wonderful girlfriend." He

brings his mouth closer to mine. "I want my sun to rise and set with yours. I want to be at your side always."

"I want that, too," I whisper. "More than you can ever imagine."

He closes his mouth over mine and we kiss gently yet fervently, with the sun painting the sky behind us.

Also by Emma Dalton

About the Author

Emma Dalton is a sweet young adult romance writer. When not writing, you can find her devouring heart-melting romance novels. Her titles include the Invisible Girls Club series, the Hotties Next Door series, and Don't Kiss The Brooding Artist. She loves hearing back from her readers. Email her at authoremmadalton@gmail.com or follow her on Facebook.

Made in the USA
Las Vegas, NV
07 October 2023

78725018R00194